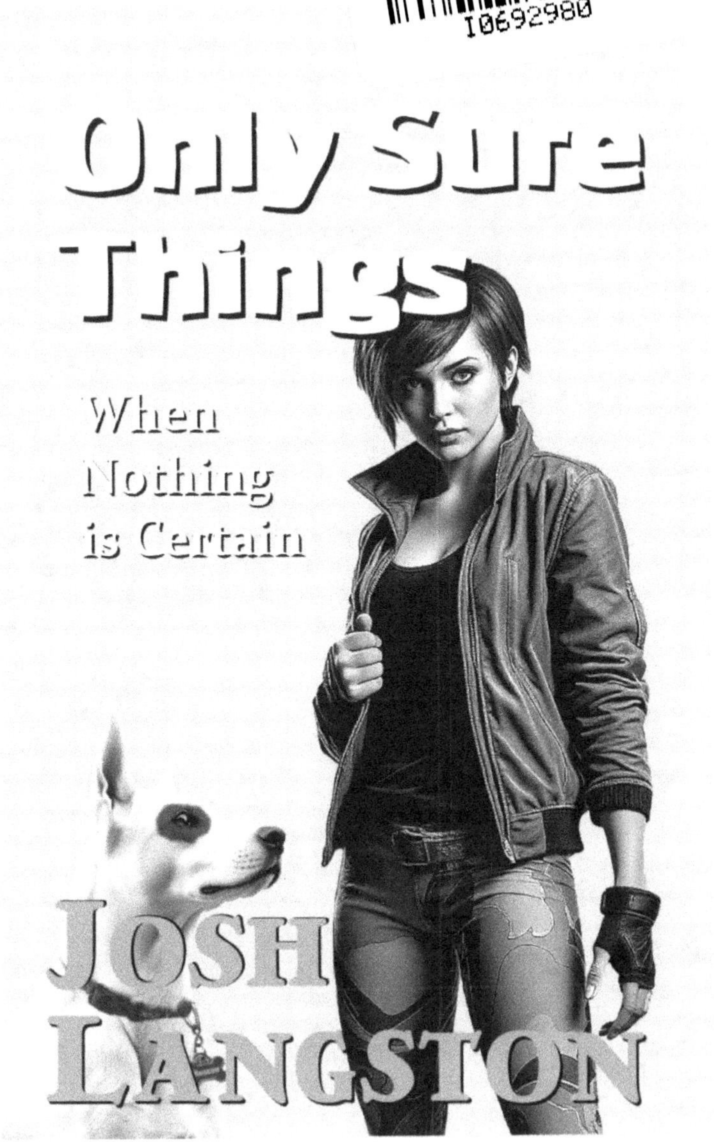

Only Sure Things

When
Nothing
is Certain

JOSH
LANGSTON

More books by Josh Langston

Novels:
Resurrection Blues
A Little Primitive
A Little More Primitive
A Primitive in Paradise
Primitives in Peril
Treason, Treason!
The 12,000-year-old Whisper
Oh, Bits!
Voices
Greeley
Zeus's Cookbook
Garden Clubbed!
A Season Gone to the Dogs
Hyde and Zeke
Veils
Raising Rosie

Novels with Barbara Galler-Smith:
Druids
Captives
Warriors
Under Saint Owain's Rock

Short Fiction Collections:
Mysfits
Christmas Beyond the Box
Dancing Among the Stars
Who Put Scoundrels in Charge?

Textbooks on the Craft of Writing
Write Naked!
The Naked Truth!
The Naked Novelist!
Naked Notes!

Dedication

To all the wonderful people who have taken
my classes and listened to my rants, raves, and
ridiculousness. You laughed at all the
right times. You ignored my gaffs,
and made teaching—for me anyway—a
thing of joy and celebration.
I pray this tale will put a
smile on each of
your faces.

Chapter One

*"Being homeless is like living in a post-apocalyptic world.
You're on the outskirts of society."* — Frank Dillane

Danica sat cross-legged on a thick layer of pine straw just outside her makeshift tent. She stared into her nearly empty pack of smokes and grunted. *Stupid, stupid habit. I gotta quit. I can't afford this shit.* She shook the last cigarette out of the flip-top box, put it in her mouth, and fumbled for her matches. She'd grabbed a couple matchbooks the previous evening from a convenience store where she'd snagged dinner: a pair of two-day-old doughnuts. They were beyond the sale date, but fine for people like her, people who had nothing else, people willing to accept a handout. It beat going hungry, but not by much.

This, she decided as she tore a match from the pack, would be her last cigarette. At least for the day.

1

Maybe longer if she could stand it.

A dog appeared just as she struck the match. Danica smelled the pungent odor of sulfur and blinked at the momentary flash of ignition. The dog ignored both and landed on her like an NFL linebacker.

The match, matchbook, and cigarette flew in different directions, and Danica found herself looking up into the face of a medium-sized dog with extraordinarily bad breath. The animal had a short, mostly white coat interspersed with black spots, one of which covered his right eye. While one of his ears stood upright, the other tipped forward at the end. All things considered, he looked... cute. And reminded her of a pet she'd had as a child. The closest thing she'd ever had to a loving friend.

"Geez!" she whispered, her breath in short supply. "Where the hell did you come from?"

The dog responded by jumping up and down beside her, his leash dancing in the air like a serpent with back spasms. After prancing a few feet away, he returned, bounced briefly on Danica's chest and then moved away again. Though he barked incessantly, he appeared neither playful nor threatening.

"You want me to *follow* you?"

The dog continued to bounce back and forth

as Danica stood and stretched. Her hopes for a drag on the cigarette ended when the dog stepped on it. He took no notice and kept on barking.

"All right, all right. I'm coming."

The dog took off, racing through the thick band of fir trees surrounding her crude campsite. He stopped on the other side, turned toward her, and kept barking.

"Yeah, yeah. I hear ya." Already dressed in her winter clothes, some of which she'd been able to wash in the restroom of the park she called home, Danica left her boots untied and hurried after the dog.

The Georgia sun had been up for a while, but the bite of winter remained in the air and made heavy breathing harsh. It didn't seem to bother the dog, but Danica hadn't done much running since she left the Marines. That had been two years ago. She didn't miss it, much.

Forced to slow down, put her hands on her knees, and breathe, Danica could do little but ignore the dog prancing excitedly at her feet. *God knows what his problem is. Prob'ly lost his chew toy or a tennis ball. Damn dogs always—*

The dog derailed her thoughts by nipping her calf. He hadn't stopped dancing since she first saw him.

"Okay! God-a-mighty. Keep your shirt on."

He didn't have a shirt, but he had a leash, and it brought him up short when the handle snagged on some low brush. His bark became a squeal, and Danica suddenly felt guilty. She prayed the dog was frightened rather than hurt.

When she reached his side and freed the leash, the dog licked her face then went back into bebop and bark mode. With a deep breath, Danica pushed herself forward as the dog angled toward a gravel path, one of several that ran through the park.

Knowing she had no chance of keeping up with him, Danica just tried to keep him in sight and continued her pursuit. The dog would accept no less. As he had already demonstrated, if she fell too far behind, he'd come racing back to her.

She found it annoying as hell.

Eventually, the dog stopped a few feet beyond the edge of the gravel path. He also stopped barking and instead, turned in her direction, looked at her, and whined. He was still whining when she caught up. The dog's leash lay across a body lying face up in tall grass.

Danica inhaled in shock, then dropped to her knees beside the body and felt his neck for a pulse but couldn't detect one. She opened his jacket and put her ear to the chest of the prostrate male, a man she guessed was in his 70s or 80s. His body was still warm, but he had no heartbeat. He looked terrible— pale like a fresh sheet, a sheet with a bright red blood stain from a gash on his head.

Her military field training kicked in hard. The guy still had a chance. Without another thought, Danica began CPR, pushing hard and rhythmically on his chest. She had no phone, and no way to call for help, but she kept on. She soon realized the man she was working on might have a cell phone. Pausing briefly to look for it, she found one in his coat pocket.

She gazed down at the device, ready to call 9-1-1, but her plan was blocked by a login screen. She had no idea what the passcode might be. Praying the man had employed the phone's facial recognition option—something she'd loved on a phone she once owned—Danica held the thing in front of his face until the login screen disappeared. He had a long, thin scar on his cheek, and she wondered if the facial rec thingy took that into account. Shrugging the question aside, she placed the call, put the speaker on, and went back to work.

Danica interrupted the operator when she answered and while continuing with CPR, rattled off her general location and what she was doing for the downed man.

"Are there any visible wounds?" the operator asked, her voice partially blocked by the dog's whines.

Danica bent sideways for a better look at the gash in the man's head. "I think somebody hit him just above his ear. There's a nasty cut and a good deal of blood."

"We have an ambulance on the way."

"Cops, too?" Danica asked.

"That's right, but they're a little busy. We've got a huge wreck on I-75."

"Gotcha." Danica was less than excited about dealing with police.

"Just keep doing what you're doing," the operator said. "The EMTs should be there in a few minutes."

Danica nodded, too tired to waste her breath on words. The dog made a space for himself and curled up between the two humans. When he raised his sad, brown eyes at her, it seemed to give her a jolt of extra energy, enough to keep her motivated and the man alive. *He's got my dog's eyes—Foster's eyes.*

The gravel path wasn't meant for cars, but apparently no one bothered to tell whoever drove the ambulance. She heard the siren before she saw the vehicle and was pleased when it came bouncing toward her, its wheels straddling the gravel trail.

A man and a woman exited the ambulance, both wearing dark uniforms. Neither appeared as anxious as Danica felt. But then again, neither had been sweating their ass off under winter clothing while working hard to keep a downed man alive.

"Okay, we'll take it from here," said the woman as her partner pushed both Danica and the dog out of the way.

"Do you know what happened?" the female EMT asked.

"Based on all the blood pouring outta his head, I'm guessing somebody whacked him pretty damned good." Danica reached for the dog and pulled him into her lap.

"What's his name?"

Danica felt her eyebrows drift down into a deep V. "Who? The dog or the dude?"

The EMT didn't appear amused. "The man's name, of course."

"I dunno. Gimme a sec." Danica reached for the dog's collar and rotated it around his neck in hopes of finding an identifying tag, maybe one with a name and phone number. She remembered providing Foster with a similar ID. Surely a grown man would do the same.

"The dog's name is Roscoe," she said after squinting at a round tag with a footprint on one side and an inscription on the other. "The owner didn't bother putting his own name on it."

The EMT pursed her lips. "How 'bout a phone number?"

Danica read the number under the dog's name on the tag while the EMT made a note on a pocket-sized pad.

"I'll put in a call to Animal Control," the EMT said. "They'll take—"

Danica cut her off in mid-sentence. "The hell you will. Fos— I mean, Roscoe, stays with me."

"It's not your dog. Why do you care?"

Danica tried to dial back her temper, something she'd never been particularly good at. "If that guy lives, it's because his dog came looking for me. You think I'm going to let somebody stick him in a cage? No way. I'll take care of him. I'll keep calling the phone number on his collar until I find the owner or his family."

The EMT looked at her with suspicion. "You've got a phone?"

"Of course," Danica lied. She'd lost it when her car was stolen, along with most of everything else she owned.

"I'm gonna need your name and address," said the EMT.

"Hurry it up," said her partner. "We've gotta get this guy to the ER."

"You want me to come with you?" Danica asked.

"Not if you intend to bring the dog."

"C'mon, Sue," the male EMT groused. "We're outta time. This guy needs more help than we can give him."

"Coming!" EMT Sue blinked at Danica. "Name and number? C'mon. Hurry!"

Though tempted to bark out her name, rank, and serial number, Danica felt no need to reveal anything about herself. She settled for naming a girl she disliked in high school. "Myra O'Meara." Then she added a number she completely made up.

"Great," said the EMT as she stuffed her notepad in a pocket and helped her partner load their patient into the ambulance. "If necessary, we'll be in touch. The police are on their way, so you need to stick around and talk to them. Let 'em know what happened. We've gotta go."

Danica watched the ambulance rumble away. Once out of sight, she headed back to her campsite with Roscoe at her side. "I don't know about you, buddy, but I'm hungry. And I need to find a phone. I don't think you'd like livin' with me. Not right now anyway. My tent's thin and pretty small."

Roscoe responded with the big, brown-eyed stare he'd used on her earlier.

"Don't look at me like that. Someone's already taking care of the old guy who brought you out here. But I'll do my best to look after you, at least until I can figure out where you live."

The weather remained cold. She needed food, and she needed a phone. What she didn't need was a dog. *What the hell is the matter with me? Why am I always willing to take care of strays? It's what bankrupted me and left me living in a friggin' tent in the middle of winter!*

She and Roscoe continued back toward her secluded spot within the clump of fir trees. Roscoe stayed so close she could feel the heat of his body on her leg. His close presence gave her a sense of security she hadn't known for far too long.

Unfortunately, that feeling disappeared the instant she pushed through the evergreen boughs that camouflaged her campsite.

Chapter Two

*"The problem of social organization is how to set up an
arrangement under which greed will do the least harm.
Capitalism is that kind of a system."* — Milton Friedman

Braden Daley found it hard not to be jealous. Going on his fifth year with the brokerage firm of Greystone, Ellis and McComb, Braden had been introduced to wealth beyond anything he'd ever imagined. He'd always thought being a millionaire would be the epitome of cool.

But then he began working for *multimillionaires*, a few of whom would likely become billionaires. Braden did not have the connections, the insider links, or the kind of investment chops the ultra-rich demanded of those handling their portfolios. His role was to keep them happily up to date about their holdings.

In bullish markets his job was easy, but when the bears nibbled on the profit margins, it became difficult. And when the market hit a severe downturn, it seemed like he caught hell from every client who lost money. For reasons he would never understand, most of them blamed him.

Yes, he occasionally recommended various stocks, but only when asked, and his picks were based on all the traditional measures. But even the best stocks have an occasional bad day. It was Braden's job to quiet the anxiety of investors, especially those few who had followed his advice. They never seemed to thank him when cashing in, however. It was hard to take.

When not engaged in the never-ending need to analyze investment opportunities, old and new, Braden spent his time probing the accounts of those who enjoyed the greatest amount of success. There were several who met his personal ideals, investors who regularly beat the averages. He ignored those where the margins were just a few lousy percentage points. Instead, he focused on the ones who crushed the averages.

But there was only one who crushed everything, all the time. In fact, as far as Braden could tell, the guy never lost a dime on anything he'd invested in—stocks or options. Most remarkably, when a high-priced stock took a beating, this one man *always* unloaded his shares before the crunch.

Braden was determined to find out how he did it. And he didn't care what it would take to learn the man's secret.

I'm coming after you, Wynn Albright. One way or another, you'll tell me what I want to know.

When Danica stopped, so did Roscoe. He leaned against her as if offering support. A man wearing the brown uniform of a park ranger frowned as he looked first at her and then down at the dog. He appeared to be at least ten years her senior. Tall, thin, and slightly stooped, he looked more like Dicken's Cratchit than an outdoorsman.

"What do you want?" she asked.

The man pursed his lips and exhaled through his nose. "I want you out of here."

"Why?"

"Because this isn't a campground. You can't just throw a tarp over some dead branches, start a fire, and move in." He pushed his ranger hat toward the back of his head and rubbed the bridge of his nose.

"Why not?" Danica asked. "It's public

property, isn't it?"

"It's *national park* property."

"Bought with taxpayer money, right?"

"So what?"

"So, some of that was my money. I own a piece of this park."

The ranger uttered a snort of humorless laughter. "Just pack up your stuff and get out of here."

Danica swallowed before admitting an embarrassing truth. "I— Look. I've got nowhere else to go, and this has been a crazy, traumatic morning. Can't I just stay here for a while longer, another night maybe, or at least until I get myself together?"

"I dunno," the ranger said as he kicked apart the stones Danica had carefully arranged for her campfire. A pitiful wisp of ash drifted in the wind from the remains of the previous night's blaze.

"Please?"

He appeared indecisive, but then resumed his official role. "Okay, but no fire. You hear me?"

"But it's cold!"

"Then put on more clothes."

"I don't *have* any more clothes! Geez. I've got a blanket; that's it. And now I've got a dog. You want him to freeze, too?"

The ranger stepped closer and knelt down to get a better look at Roscoe. He took a quick peek at the dog's collar and tags, then muttered something she couldn't quite make out. When he stood back up, he squinted at her. She didn't like being the object of his suspicion. "What is it?"

"I know this dog. I've seen him often enough. But this is the first time I've ever seen you." He put his hands on his narrow hips. "What're you doing with him, and what happened to his owner?"

"The old man?" Danica replied. "He was taken to the hospital. I—"

"What happened?"

"He had an accident. Or maybe he got attacked. I'm not sure. Anyway, his dog came and got me. I followed him to where his owner was—stretched out on the ground, face up. He had a nasty head wound, too. At first I thought he was dead."

"You were the one who called for an ambulance?"

"Yeah. I gave the guy CPR, too. His heart must've stopped right before I reached him."

"But you didn't stick around after the ambulance arrived?"

"I stayed right there and talked to the EMTs," she said. "They were in a hurry to get him to a doctor. And when they left, so did I." Danica focused on the ranger's name badge: Johanson. "Do you pronounce it 'Joe-hanson' or 'Yo-hanson'?"

"Joe-hanson," he replied. "Richard Johanson. Rick."

Great. I'm dealing with Ranger Rick. In the flesh.

"And your name?" he asked.

"Danica," she said before mentally kicking herself. She'd told the EMTs she was Myra O'Meara. "Danica Winters. Do you need to see my ID?" *Which I no longer have.*

"Nah. I'm a ranger, not a cop." He looked up toward a bright spot in the cloud cover. "Not much sun today, I'm afraid. And it's supposed to dip below freezing tonight. Why don't you let me take the two of you to a shelter? At least for the night."

"I dunno." She looked at Roscoe. "I'm worried about the dog."

"I'm worried about his *owner*," Rick said.

"Well, yeah. Of course. But he's already got somebody taking care of him. I just want to tell him Roscoe is okay. I'd really like to take the dog back to wherever he lives. I like dogs, but I'm not exactly in a position to adopt one." *No matter how much he looks like my poor Foster.*

Rick appeared to ponder that for a moment, then changed the subject. "I'm curious about the guy you found. Was he wearing a coat with a Georgia Tech logo on it?"

Danica huffed. "I didn't pay any attention to his outfit. That wasn't exactly part of my training."

"Sure, I get it. But you must have noticed something about him."

"He's old. Has grey hair. No, wait. He doesn't have much hair at all."

"Anything else?"

Danica thought for a moment. "A scar. On his jaw. From his ear to his chin, I think. I didn't make anything of it at the time." She shrugged. "I was kinda preoccupied."

Rick bobbed his head up and down as if he'd just solved a puzzle. "He's the guy I've been thinking of. His name's Albert or Albright. Something like that. He's a professor at Tech or used to be. I can't remember. But he's always comin' out here to walk that dog. I've seen him any number of times. I've spoken to him several times, too."

"Do you know where he lives?"

"No, but he said he walks here from his house,

so it can't be very far away."

Danica shivered. Much as she wanted to, she couldn't hide it.

"C'mon," Rick said. "It's already getting colder. I know of a shelter where you can stay. The dog, too, I think. And if that's against the rules, he can stay with me for a while. We can swing by the hospital on the way and check on Roscoe's dad."

"His *dad?*"

"You know what I mean."

"It just sounded funny."

He shook his head. "Lemme help you with your stuff. It's a bit of a hike to my car."

Though she hadn't known him long enough to trust him, he didn't look like a hood or a rapist. No tats, no swagger, and he hadn't tried any funny stuff. Besides, she doubted he weighed much more than she did. She opted to take the risk; it was too damned cold not to. "Thanks," she said. "That'd be... great."

When he turned to clear a path, Danica reached into the depths of her bedroll and grabbed the batteries she'd taped together. They weren't as heavy as a roll of quarters, but they'd still add some heft if she needed to punch him and run away.

She really missed the roll of quarters she'd

once had. But at least they'd covered the cost of food which, at the time, she'd needed more.

Jeffrey Albright pretended not to hear his wife. Over the years he'd become adept at tuning her out. Beatrix, his chubby, never-satisfied wife of nineteen years, eight months, and many interminably long days, went on as if he actually was listening. Not that it mattered; in her mind, his opinion counted for precisely nothing.

"Did you hear what I said?" Beatrix enquired, her voice as flat as a placemat.

"Yes, dear."

"Well? What d'you think?"

"About what?"

She shuffled from the hallway into the living room and stopped in front of the television set, blocking his view. Jeffrey looked up at her. "I can't see."

"You can't hear either, Jeffy, and I'm getting tired of it."

"Okay. Sorry. I—"

"I have some very specific thoughts about how we'll redecorate this place."

"*This* place?" he asked, looking around his father's living room. "Or our own?"

"This place, of course," she said. "As soon as we get your father moved out, we'll be able to sell that pile of junk we've been living in and move here. It's winter, in case you hadn't noticed. Your Dad's furnace doesn't constantly crap out like ours does. Still, there's a lot we'll need to do before we can move in."

"Dad has no plans to move out," he said. "We've talked about this."

Beatrix frowned, her expression even more negative than usual. "We both know it's time he went into a retirement home. We need the space here, and he doesn't. Just look around! I'll bet he hasn't added a fresh drop of paint anywhere in this house for the last thirty years."

"That wasn't really his thing."

"What? Painting?"

"Decorating. He left that up to Mom."

"And she's been dead for how long?"

"I dunno. I was in high school. So... Thirty years or so?"

"And he never remarried."

"Nope."

Beatrix huffed. "Can't say I'm surprised." She looked around the living room with utter disdain but never moved from her spot between her husband and the TV. "Do you know where he is?"

"Out walking the dog. Don't you remember? He came out the front door just as we drove in with the doughnuts from Iggy's. You said if he didn't come back in a half hour, you'd eat his share."

She licked her lips. "Sucks for him."

Jeffrey looked at his watch, mildly concerned. "Come to think of it, he's been gone an awfully long time. We got here around nine, and it's nearly lunchtime."

"Speaking of which," Beatrix said, "is there anything here we can eat? There's no point in going back to our place until the furnace is repaired. I would kill for a Snickers bar."

"Screw that. Snickers have some kinda nuts in 'em. You know I can't tolerate that shit."

"I wasn't talking about a Snickers bar for you."

"Good. You know better. Dad's food? I dunno. Look in the fridge." He glanced toward the front window. "But maybe we be out looking for him."

"Why?"

"In case he got hurt or something."

"Or lost. I don't think he's as sharp as he used to be. That's another reason we need to put him in a retirement home somewhere."

Jeffrey tried to think of another way to say what he'd already explained a million times—his father would have to be forced from his home; he would never willingly leave, no matter how nice the retirement accommodations might be. Jeffrey's cell phone rang before he came up with anything.

"H'lo?"

"I'm calling from County General Hospital. Is this Jeffrey Albright?"

He tensed up instantly. "Yes."

"Your name is listed as an emergency contact in your father's phone."

"*Dad?* Oh my God! Is he okay?"

"He's much better and conscious for now, but the doctors say they want to keep him here under observation for another 24 hours."

"But— But what happened? Why is he in the hospital? What are—"

"I really don't have any details, Mr. Albright. You'd best come down here and talk to him yourself. Just know that our visiting hours end at eight PM."

Chapter Three

*"A bone to the dog is not charity. Charity is the bone
shared with the dog, when you are just as hungry as
the dog."* —Jack London

Danica sat in the front seat of Ranger Rick's
car, a dark green, late model Jeep and far nicer than
the car she'd lost. Roscoe occupied the back seat
along with the bulk of Danica's gear, not that it took
up much space. The dog seemed to enjoy sprawling
on top of her bedroll.

"I had no idea Buford House didn't have any
vacancies," Rick said. "They put you on the waiting
list, but honestly, your name isn't anywhere near the
top."

Danica continued to stare out the window as
they drove to the hospital. "Good thing I didn't get my
hopes up."

"I'll figure something out," Rick said.

Danica turned and stared straight at him. "It's not your problem. Hell, *I'm* not your problem. My situation is my fault, my consequences. Don't worry about it. I'm a grown-up; I can take care of myself."

They rode in silence for a while until he asked, "How'd you end up like this?"

"Like what?"

"Homeless. No job. No... I dunno, anything. Family?"

"I have a sister, or used to. Caitlyn."

I doubt I'll ever know if I'm the one she hated, or if it was Foster. Either way, I'll never forgive her.

"Caitlyn... Anyway, we had a falling out. My situation isn't her fault. I've made a few bad decisions, one or two of 'em really bad. I should've stayed in the service. I had friends there, a life, a purpose. I should've stayed in."

"Which branch?"

"Marines."

He glanced briefly in her direction. "Why didn't you stay in?"

"I got in trouble with a junior officer named Mundt. He uh... He did something I didn't like."

"So?"

"So, they said I damn near killed him. I had no idea Mundt was such a wuss. One solid shot to the nose, and he was done." She shook her head. "And so was I. I broke his beak and got a lot of blood on his pretty uniform, but it wasn't really all that bad. Guys in my unit got a lot worse in the sandbox."

"Sandbox?"

"Yeah. Afghanistan. Anyway, Mundt had connections. It's sad but disgustingly true: who you know means more than what you did. I was a damned good Marine. Proud. Happy. Most of the time, anyway. Until that jackass showed up."

"What'd he do?"

"Other than get me dishonorably discharged?" Danica pondered a moment before continuing. "He thought he was entitled to privileges that don't come with rank, his or anyone else's."

"In other words, he's an idiot."

"A horny idiot. With a funny-looking nose."

They both chuckled at that, and Danica relaxed.

"I've got a spare bedroom," Rick said. "If you'd be okay with that, I—"

She aimed a thumb at the dog. "And what

about Fos— er, Fido?"

"He can stay with you. I imagine he's housebroken, and if he's not, I can provide cleaning supplies. Besides, we'll be returning him to his owner soon."

Danica glanced at his hand and spotted a wedding band. That didn't mean anything conclusive; he could still be a serial killer or a rapist, though she seriously doubted he was either. Besides, if he tried anything, she knew she could take care of him the way she'd taken care of Mundt. "Your wife won't object? Shouldn't you check with her first?"

His lips drew together in a tight line before he spoke. "She won't mind. I promise."

"Then, yes. Thank you. I definitely need a place to stay." Danica sighed. "It's just— I can't seem to get ahead with anything. I want to work, but I can't get a job unless I can get cleaned up. I can't get a bank account without an address and some seed money. I can't go on welfare 'cause I'm able-bodied and don't have any dependents. I don't know what comes first!"

"Survival," Rick said. He wrapped the word in a smile. "Starting with food. Have you had anything to eat today?"

"No."

"Then that's job one."

"Speaking of jobs," she said, "what about yours?"

"I'm pretty much my own boss. All the other park employees work in the visitor center, and I outrank all of them. I can take some personal time; I've earned it. Now, let's get you something to eat. My treat. What're you in the mood for?"

She couldn't help but wonder what he was up to. *Does he think he can use food as a way to get in my pants?* "You're serious?"

"As a train wreck."

"Then I'd dearly love to have some prime rib, a big ol' baked potato, and oh… hell, I don't know, maybe a case of beer."

"How 'bout a burger, fries, and a shake?"

"Or that," she said. She rubbed her stomach at a distant memory of a thick, juicy, medium-rare ribeye.

"Great. We can drop the dog off at my place on the way and head back toward the hospital after we eat."

She'd almost forgotten about the hospital. "Yeah, right. County General."

He lowered an eyebrow at her. "Don't you want to tell Roscoe's owner that he's safe?"

She nodded, taken aback by Rick's generosity and feeling guilty about asking for a rich meal. Rather than let him see her tear up, she went back to staring out the window. "I don't know how to thank you. I mean... I don't have—"

"You're a good person who's down on her luck," Rick said. "You saved a man's life today, to say nothing of taking care of his dog."

"How do you know what I've told you is true?"

He shrugged. "You've got an honest face. At least, I think it's honest. You know, under all the dirt and stuff."

She turned to face him, fully prepared to respond to his insult, then saw his smile and realized he was teasing. She gave his shoulder a gentle punch. "Is my face really all that dirty? Be honest."

"Nah. You look fine. Prob'ly need a shower. I imagine I do, too."

She expected him to suggest they shower together, but he didn't. Instead, he parked the car in front of a fast-food restaurant, said, "C'mon" and motioned for her to follow him.

"What about the dog?"

"We won't be here that long," he said. "He'll be fine."

Danica hurried after him, utterly unsure how she'd hit the jackpot. More than likely a small jackpot, but one that promised to keep her alive for another day.

~*~

Finding Wynn Albright's home address required no detective skills. Braden Daley simply dug back into the man's brokerage account. Instead of looking at his portfolio, he checked the personal information and was mildly surprised to see that he lived in Woodstock, a town just north of Atlanta, Georgia.

Braden couldn't imagine actually calling Albright and suggesting a chat or requesting a bit of investing advice. The man would most likely raise hell and get him fired. It's what his regular clients would do, and this one wasn't anywhere near Braden's list of regulars. Albright was top-top drawer, the kind his firm referred to as GEM quality. Only the most senior people at Greystone, Ellis and McComb could deal with him and did so as if he were royalty.

Braden needed something else, some reason to get in touch, some reason to dig into the man's investing secrets. A trip to Woodstock, even if he never saw Albright, might prove helpful. If nothing else, Braden could observe how the man lived. It might provide a hint about how he spent his fortune.

His boss and a secretary who left most of the male staff at GE&M drooling, wandered into view. Conrad Simkins, a mid-level manager who'd do anything to climb another rung on the corporate ladder was regaling the short-skirted young woman with his prowess at chatting up the company's biggest clients.

Braden briefly listened to the one-way conversation, then shook his head. There was no way in hell he'd have the authority to wine and dine a high-roller.

"You got a problem, Daley?" Simkins scowled down at him over the wall of Braden's cubicle. "I saw the look on your face."

"A problem? No, no. 'Course not. I was just thinking how much I'd like to have an expense account so I could entertain clients."

"Don't get your hopes up," Simkins said. "You need a GEM-studded client list first, and you've got a helluva lot of work to do before that happens."

He watched the older man saunter away with his arm around the secretary's shoulder, chatting as if he were sharing state secrets. She didn't seem to mind. Maybe she wanted to climb the corporate ladder, too. When Simkins reached his office, he guided the young woman inside with a hand on her back. His hand slid lower and lower as the door closed.

She's no GEM quality client, Simkins, you lecherous shithead. And as it happens, I only need one such client, provided I can choke the bastard's methods out of him.

~*~

Jeffrey let Beatrix out at the hospital's front entrance while he parked the car. It made sense. She hated walking anywhere except at estate sales or shopping malls, and he needed a break from her incessant chatter.

He caught up with her in the lobby.

"I've got his room number," she said. "Fifth floor. They said to follow the orange stripe on the floor." She shook her head. "They wouldn't tell me what happened to him."

"That's why we're here, isn't it? We can ask him."

They followed the marking on the floor to an elevator, went up, and from there entered a long hallway. Room numbers were clearly marked, and in moments they entered his father's room. It held a single bed and was nicely decorated if not luxurious.

Jeffrey surveyed the room, and when Beatrix

elbowed him, gave out a plaintive, "Dad? It's me and Bea."

"Come in; come in," Wynn said.

Jeffrey slowly approached the bed where his father lay face up, staring at the ceiling. A bandage encircled his bald head. "Geez, Dad. What happened?"

"I tripped and fell. Hit my head on a rock. Where's Roscoe?"

"The dog? You're worried about the damn dog?"

His father stared at him as if he'd just peed in the church punch bowl. "Yes. I'm worried about my dog. He's the best friend I have."

Jeffrey shrugged. "I've no idea where he is. The hospital called and told us to come talk to you."

"Well, I'd rather you spent your time looking for Roscoe."

"Are you going to be all right?" Beatrix asked.

"As far as I know, yes." He glared at her. "I hope you're not too disappointed."

"C'mon, Dad. That wasn't nice. You know Bea and I worry about you. We just want you to be safe."

"Locked away in a prison for old farts, right? Try to be useful for once, Son. Go find Roscoe."

Jeffrey ignored the jibe. "The woman who called us said the doctors want you to stay overnight for observation."

"That'll give you plenty of time to find my dog. I'd start with the local pound. They said some EMTs brought me to the ER. I didn't have a chance to thank 'em, much less ask about Roscoe. I was out cold. Anyway, I had him chipped when he was a pup. Any vet can check that, ditto for the pound. So, if you don't get any calls from anyone, you'd best hoof it out to the park and start looking for him there. Maybe do that first, come to think of it. He could be anywhere, poor guy."

"Are you serious? It's going down below freezing tonight," Beatrix said.

"Then you'd better bundle up and get moving. I don't want to see my best friend frozen."

"We'll do our best," Jeffrey said.

His father didn't look confident. "Bring me some clean clothes when you come back tomorrow."

"Will do," Beatrix said as she dragged Jeffrey out of the room. Once in the hallway, she frowned at him, a look he'd seen all too often. "If you think I'm going to traipse around in the woods looking for a stupid dog, you're crazy."

"Well, I'm sure as hell not going out there

alone."

"Wanna bet?" She crossed her arms, daring him to argue.

Jeffrey stared back at her. "I'll call animal control first."

"You do that," she said.

"What's your problem?"

"Your *father* is my problem! He's old and cranky, and he hates me. I try to be nice, but—"

"But he knows you're full of it."

"Are you on *his* side? If so, remember: you're married to me, and I'll be around a helluva lot longer than he will."

Jeffrey opted not to answer as her words prompted him to give more serious thought to some ideas he'd been mulling over for quite some time. Chief among them were visions of Caribbean beaches, pretty young women in bikinis, and no Beatrix. He could easily sell his father's house to cover the cost of two burials *and* an extended vacation somewhere in the islands.

Chapter Four

"Dogs and philosophers do the greatest good and get the fewest rewards." —Diogenes

For reasons she didn't quite understand, Danica felt nervous entering the hospital. The meal she'd had with Ranger Rick sat heavy in her stomach. She'd gotten used to eating far less. Her clothing, what little she had left, hung on her frame. She had no idea how much weight she had lost since leaving the Marines, but it had to have been a lot. She'd run out of holes to tighten her belt and had nothing with which to poke new ones.

"Okay," said Rick. "Let's do this." He walked directly to the information desk in the lobby with Danica in tow. A stern-looking woman with deep scowl lines glanced up at his approach, her expression neutral.

"We're here to see a man who was brought into the ER late this morning," Rick said. "His last name is Albert or Albright. I'm not exactly sure which."

"So, you obviously aren't relatives."

"True."

"And you don't even know his name?"

"Not exactly, no."

"Then why on Earth would you think I'd tell you who or where he is? That information is privileged. Visitation is for family and friends. You're neither. Forget it." She made a shooing motion as if they were insects bothering her tea party.

Rick pointed to the badge on his chest. "I don't need to know the exact spelling of his name."

The woman squinted at his badge. "Is that a buffalo on there?"

"Yes," he replied.

"You're not a cop!"

"Say that again when you need help in a national park."

"Go on now," she said. "Leave."

"You don't understand." Rick pointed at Danica. "This young lady saved the man's life. She found him unconscious in the park and performed CPR on him until help arrived."

The woman at the desk looked suspicious of them. "Oh, I get it. I've heard it all before. She's here hoping for some kinda reward, right?"

Rick's face registered disbelief and diminishing patience. "Don't be ridiculous. She saved the man's dog, too. Took it under her wing when his owner ended up here. All she wants to do is assure the man that his pet is okay and arrange to get it back to him. That's all. Listen, I know dog lovers, and this guy thinks the world of his. He walks him in the park nearly every day. I'll bet he's just as concerned about Roscoe as he is about himself."

"*Roscoe?*"

"His dog," Danica said.

The woman's lips twisted as she looked Danica up and down. "I don't know...."

Rick chimed in. "Are visiting hours over?"

"Well, no. But—"

"Then let us in. We've got every right to see Mr. uhm... Albright. What room is he in?"

"Albright." She exhaled in a huff and examined her paperwork. "His family's in there with him now. You'll have to wait."

Rick and Danica took seats in the lobby to wait and watched visitors stream in and out. Some stopped at the desk for information and some cruised right by. "Busy day," Rick said.

Danica nodded. "You think Roscoe's okay all alone? He's not used to your house. We left him there all by himself. What'll your wife say when she comes home and finds him?"

"My wife..." Rick paused, swallowed hard, then went on. "I lost Cindy two years ago. She died in a car wreck on her way home from work."

Danica put her hand to her mouth, instantly regretting having said something that upset him. "I'm so sorry. I didn't know. I didn't mean to—"

"It's okay," he said. "I've had some time to get used to being alone."

Danica patted his arm. "Me, too."

"It sucks."

"No shit."

They sat in silence until a middle-aged couple wandered by. The woman was clearly unhappy; the man didn't appear to care.

"You and daddy Albright are exactly alike," she said, her voice rising as if gathering strength with each word. "You're both cold, selfish, and rude."

"Wait here," he grumbled. "I'll bring the car around."

"Be quick about it," she said as he scurried away. "I don't like hospitals. Never have."

"Yeah, yeah," he said without looking back.

When the man exited the building, Rick stood up. Danica put a hand on his arm. "What are you doing?"

He nodded at the woman waiting near the entrance. "I was going to tell her we have Mr. Albright's dog."

"Not a chance," Danica said. "Did you see the look on her face? That woman's mean. I don't trust her, and I sure wouldn't let her have Roscoe, no matter who she is."

Rick responded with a snort of laughter. "Suit yourself. But we definitely need to let Professor Albright know. He urged her to stand, and they both walked back to the information desk. "Looks like Albright's family is leaving," he told the frowning clerk behind the desk. "Can we see him now?"

"If he's awake, they'll be serving his dinner before long," she said. "He may not want any company."

"That's his decision, isn't it?" Rick tapped the desktop with his index finger. "C'mon."

"Please," said Danica. "We've been patient and played by the rules. Just give us his room number. We won't stay long. I promise."

"You'll probably get me fired," the woman said with a sigh. "He's in 5041."

"Fifth floor, right?" Rick inquired.

"Yeah. Just follow the orange stripe on the floor."

Braden left the office early complaining of a migraine headache. He'd never actually had one, but he knew people who did. Since a headache didn't require that he bleed, cough, or run a fever, visible evidence of illness wasn't needed. Besides, migraines were common among his coworkers.

Though eager to at least drive by Albright's house, Braden was also keenly aware of the insanely bad traffic during rush hour. Atlanta commuters numbered in the gazillions, and they all hit the road at the exact same time, or so it seemed to him.

The drive north didn't take too long, and he followed the instructions from a GPS app on his cell phone. It got him to his destination in a reasonable amount of time. What didn't seem reasonable was the house that bore Albright's address. Embedded in a decidedly middle-class neighborhood, Albright's home appeared to be a study in all things average, or slightly below that rank.

Braden had envisioned a mansion or a chateau—something artsy or manorial, something worthy of a man of multimillion dollar means. This house, by comparison, was a dump.

He double-checked his notes to be sure he'd written down the correct address. He'd made no mistakes. He checked to make sure he'd entered it properly in the GPS but found no errors there either.

It made absolutely no sense.

Puzzled, he sat in his car, unsure of what to do or where to go next. As he mulled the improbability of an impoverished Albright, a car with a damaged bumper pulled into the driveway and parked near a sidewalk to the front door. The vehicle's arrival perked him up.

Braden watched as a woman roughly his mother's age, and twice her size, lumbered out of the car. A nondescript man of a similar age and bearing emerged from behind the wheel. She spoke briefly to him then turned and marched toward the entrance. The man stayed behind, his lips twisted in irritation. He soon shook his head, smoothed back his hair, and started up the walk as the woman entered the building.

Braden couldn't stand it; he had to find out what had befallen his textbook-perfect high-roller. Without another thought, he got out of his car and jogged toward the man. He smiled and waved, hoping to put Albright at ease.

"Mr. Albright? Hi there," he said when he reached the man's side. "I'm Avery Collins, from Greystone, Ellis, and McComb." Avery Collins was a new hire at GE&M, the perfect fall guy if Albright complained.

The man appeared totally disinterested. "If you're selling something—"

"Gosh no," Braden said, putting on the biggest smile he could muster. "I just wanted to take the opportunity to say hello and maybe chat with you for a minute. I hope you can spare me a bit of your time."

"Actually," Albright began "I only dropped by for a second. I have to—"

"I promise I won't hold you up long," Braden said. "It's just... Well, to be honest, I'd like to nominate you for Client of the Year."

Albright looked puzzled.

"It's something new the marketing people dreamed up. We pick a few of our clients who have been profoundly successful in their investing and interview them for TV. Marketing thinks they can do a series of commercials featuring them. The final winner would get a cash prize."

"When it comes to the stock market," Albright began, "I'm afraid I'm not much of a player."

Braden laughed. "You've taken modesty to a new level. I mean, seriously, your picks have consistently outperformed those of our top analysts." He lowered his voice to a conspiratorial level. "I'd dearly love to know your secret. I'll keep it to myself if you wish."

Albright cleared his throat. "My secret?" He chuckled and lowered his voice to match Braden's. "Okay, here it is: buy low and sell high."

"Of course, of course," Braden said. "But knowing when to do that... I mean, you're something of a magician." He brightened. "Or maybe a clairvoyant."

Albright shrugged. "Some of us have it, some don't. If I told you my secret, it wouldn't be a secret anymore, would it?"

"Well, perhaps if—"

Albright checked his watch and began to walk away. "I've really got to get going. I wish I could help you, but you know how it is. Duty calls."

"Right, right. Thank you for your time."

He watched as Albright ambled up the walk and into the house.

What an asshole!

~*~

Jeffrey Albright entered the house and cruised straight into Beatrix. She stared directly at him with her flabby arms crossed upon her chest.

"What took you so long?" she asked. "And who were you talking to?"

Jeffrey shook his head. "He said his name was Avery or Emory; I forget which. Anyway, he works for an investment firm that wants to feature me in a commercial."

"What on Earth for?"

"According to him, I'm one of their most successful investors."

Beatrix burst into laughter but eventually got herself under control. "He's nuts! You're probably the world's *worst* investor. This has got to be some kind of joke."

Jeffrey's pride took the hit even though her comment wasn't far off the mark. He'd lost some money in the market, but he'd never invested in a big way.

"He must've been talking about your father,"

Beatrix said. After a moment of reflection her usual frown appeared. "Did you know Wynn was a big investor?"

"I seriously doubt it." Jeffrey rubbed his jaw. "He's a retired college prof. If he made a ton of money in the market, wouldn't he have done something to fix this place up?"

"No," said Beatrix. "He's a damned miser, and you know it."

"Whatever. I've gotta go look for his stupid dog. I wish he cared for me as much he does for that mutt."

Jeffrey buttoned up, threw a scarf around his neck, and headed for their car. *Bea will park herself in front of the wide-screen television; that and a toaster are the only new things in Dad's house.*

While walking to the car he mentally replayed his discussion with the investment guy. *Could Dad really be a super-savvy investor? If so, what's he done with all his money?*

His father had never discussed finances with Jeffrey. Wynn gave him and Beatrix generous gift cards for Christmas and birthdays, and he took them out for dinner on occasion. Other than that, he hadn't helped them out financially since paying off Jeffrey's college loans.

Maybe he's punishing me for not finding a job for someone with a journalism degree. Newspaper jobs pay shit wages, and nobody wants me as a TV news dude; I'm not hunky enough.

But what if he is loaded, like that investment guy said? If Dad hasn't spent his money, then he still has it. And I'm his only heir. The thought brought a huge smile to his face as he pulled into an empty space in the national park's lot.

I can't believe Dad walks all the way here. It's a good half mile. He was probably exhausted keeping up with that stupid dog. That's why he took a header on the trail. What a dumbass. He's an old man; he shouldn't be doing that, and by God, I'm going to tell him so!

While walking slowly up the main trail, Jeffrey called for Roscoe but got no response. After a half-hearted search of thirty minutes, he called it quits.

Damn dog's probably holed up somewhere with a tree-hugger. Or maybe he's dead. If so, good riddance.

His thoughts drifted back to his father's money. *I need to call the investment firm. What did that guy call it? Jim something? No. Gem something. Whatever. I'll figure it out and give them a buzz. What could it hurt? What if the old man really is loaded?*

If Jeffrey inherited it, his life would change

dramatically. *I could travel and see parts of the world I've only dreamed of. And Bea....*

He suddenly stopped moving. *Bea? She'd insist that I take her along. Everywhere! Geez. But what if she were no longer around, no longer an anchor on my ass?*

Whistling for the first time in a long time, Jeffrey got back in his car and drove away.

Chapter Five

"True courage is being afraid, and going ahead and doing your job anyhow; that's what courage is." —Norman Schwarzkopf

Danica paused just outside the door to Wynn Albright's room and put her hand on Rick's arm to slow the ranger down.

He turned to face her. "What?" he asked in a gentle voice.

"You should go in first. He knows you."

"Sure, but you're coming in right behind me, okay?"

She nodded, feeling meek and wondering if she should have showered and washed her hair when they dropped Roscoe off. But then, she didn't have anything clean to wear, so what difference would it make?

And why do I give a damn? I don't even know this guy.

"Mr. Albright?" Rick inquired.

"That's me," he said, his voice gravelly. "C'mon in. The water's fine."

Water? Danica frowned. *What the hell?*

Rick laughed and walked toward the bed with his hand outstretched. Albright put his glasses on and smiled when he recognized the first of his visitors. "Well, I'll be damned. It's Ranger Rick."

Rather than take it as an insult, Rick merely laughed and shook his head. "It's good to see you Doctor Albright. I'm glad you're still with the living."

Albright chuckled in response, then turned his attention to Danica and appraised her from head to toe. "And who's this fine young lady? Your girlfriend?"

"I wish," said Rick. "Allow me to introduce you to Danica..." He paused and looked at her in embarrassment. "I've forgotten your last name. Please forgive me."

"No worries," she said. "It's Winters. Danica Winters." She held her hand out to the man in the bed.

"I thought you'd like to meet the woman who

saved your life in the park," Rick said.

Albright's face broke out in a huge smile. He sat upright, grabbed her hand in both of his, and squeezed gently. "Oh, my dear! How can I ever thank you?"

"And that's not all," Rick added. "She also saved your dog."

"Roscoe?" Albright fell back into his bed. "I can't believe it. I've been worried sick about him. You really have him?"

She read his response as genuine joy, and she couldn't help but return his smile with one of her own. "He's a sweetheart. I couldn't stand the thought of him being caged somewhere. He's such a free spirit. And, I hope you won't mind, but he seems to like me."

Albright glanced at Rick. "She's not only an angel, she's a dog lover! My God, Rick, wherever did you find her?"

"I uh... We bumped into each other in the park," he said.

Albright turned toward Danica. "I don't suppose.... Uhm, would you mind if I asked you a question or two? Nothing personal, I promise."

Danica shrugged. "Sure."

"First off, where do you work?"

She swallowed. "Actually, I'm sorta between jobs."

"Sorta?"

"Okay. I'm currently unemployed."

Albright smiled. "Might you be interested in working for me?"

"Doing what, exactly?" she asked, instantly suspicious.

"I need a companion, basically. Especially after my... accident. Someone to help me with my work, help me take care of Roscoe, drive me places. That sort of thing." He paused, then asked, "You can drive, can't you?"

"Sure, though I haven't since my car got stolen. But I did a lot of driving in the Marines. I'm pretty good at handling armored vehicles."

"The Marines?" He appeared pleasantly surprised. "So, you've some knowledge of self-defense?"

Finally, someone had asked her about something she was proud of. "I was an MCMAP instructor," she said, unable to resist a smile.

Rick nodded. "That makes sense. Did Mundt know that about you?"

"Not 'til later." Her smile faded.

"I've no idea what you two are talking about," said Albright. "Can you break down the acronym for me? It sounded like something I ordered at a burger joint."

His question restored Danica's mood. "It stands for Marine Corps Martial Arts Program. I did a few rotations as an instructor before I got shipped out."

Albright laughed. "My dear, you are astonishing. You'd be perfect."

"For what?" she asked. "You need someone who can drive *and* knock heads?"

"Yes! Plus the other things I mentioned. Lately I've realized I need someone with the kind of skills you have—to look out for me. I'm old and unfit." He gestured at the room they were in. "I'm here because I fell down while walking my dog, for cryin' out loud! I don't even want to think about what I'd do if someone attacked me."

"So, you want me to be your *bodyguard, too?*"

"Yes, I do."

"I dunno," Danica said, still suspicious.

Rick chimed in. "Sounds like something I might be interested in. I did some wrestling in college."

His comment caused her to turn sharply in his direction. "Hey!"

"Just kidding. About the wrestling I mean; that was a long time ago." Rick then turned to Albright and added, "What would this job pay?"

The bandage around Albright's head had slipped a bit, and he adjusted it while responding. "Good question. I was thinking a thousand dollars a week, plus expenses."

Danica felt her eyes widen, but before she could accept the offer, Rick motioned for her to stand by.

"That doesn't sound like nearly enough to me," he said. "You want a chauffeur, a companion, a clerk, *and* a bodyguard. Do you expect her to cook and do laundry, too?"

"No, of course not."

"Still, I think you need to offer more."

Danica stared hard at Rick, certain he'd screwed up the sweetest deal she'd ever been offered.

"You're right. It's not nearly enough." Albright smiled at Danica. "How does *two thousand* a week sound? Plus housing."

"And expenses?" Rick asked.

Albright kept his eyes on Danica. "Certainly.

And if what you're wearing is typical of your wardrobe, Ms. Winters, you'll need some new clothes. I'll cover those, too."

Momentarily speechless, Danica tugged Rick's sleeve. "What d'ya think?"

He grinned. "I think if you don't take it, I will."

"You mentioned housing," Danica said. "Where would that be?"

"In my house, of course. Or, better yet, I'll have a guest cottage built. I have a fairly extensive lot."

"Go for it, kid," Rick said.

"Oh, there's one thing I failed to mention," Albright said. "Travel."

Danica frowned. "Like around town?"

"Actually, no. I'm talking about around the country."

~*~

Braden's frustration with Albright's snarky dismissal eventually morphed into anger. His envy turned into jealousy, and what little patience he had disappeared. Albright had obviously played him, though he doubted the man saw through his effort to pawn himself off as a minor player at GE&M.

Everything about Albright rankled him. The

man was the middle-class version of a hermit. His demeanor matched his decidedly dumpy dwelling; his clothing looked sad and wrinkled, and his wife... well, she looked worse than the building they lived in.

The more he dwelled on the deficiencies he observed in the couple, their car, and their home, the more determined he became. He'd get the man's secret if he had to beat it out of him. Although, he reflected, it might be easier to beat the wife until hubby spilled his guts. That thought appealed to him even more.

Wynn Albright lay back in his hospital bed, more contentedly amused than at any time in the past few years. He'd given up long ago on his hope that Jeffrey might exhibit signs of maturity and kindness. Instead, his son jumped into a marriage with a shrew who only pushed him further away from the goals Wynn espoused.

But now there was Danica. Not only a fresh young face, but a woman with backbone, survival skills, and a love for dogs. She seemed to have the strength of character he'd hoped to find in his son. Though she had obviously fallen on hard times, she impressed him. And, best of all, she had accepted his tentative job offer.

He pondered the best course of action for

providing her with private living quarters. He had used his spare bedroom for storage, primarily because he'd gotten too shaky to climb the fold-down stairs to the attic. Jeffrey had flatly refused to help and declared the stairs unsafe. Beatrix might have had trouble fitting through the opening in the ceiling, assuming she ever volunteered to try. She never had.

If Danica was agreeable, he'd spend whatever was necessary to update the bedroom for her use until he could have a guest house built. Jeffrey and Beatrix would raise hell about it, but he didn't care. Over the years they had plenty of chances to prove themselves worthy of his generosity, but they fumbled every opportunity. Worse still, they lacked the ability to see themselves as anything but victims.

There was no way he would tell them the secret to his wealth. And quite soon, they'd discover that when it came to the things Wynn truly wanted, prices didn't matter.

Jeffrey inherited a good deal of Wynn's intellect but none of his drive. Though pushed to succeed, he'd been content to just get by. That lack of motivation continued well into his adulthood and had driven Wynn to hide the discoveries that made his wealth possible. They were secrets he never intended to share; they would die with him when the time came.

Despite his fall, the cause of which he knew all too well, he had noticed no decline in his emotional control or mental capacity. Wynn hoped for at least a year or more of decent health. He'd given millions to charities and programs he deemed worthy, and he had no plans to slow down such donations. He felt sure Danica would help him.

~*~

During the return drive to Wynn's house to pick up Beatrix, Jeffrey got a call from his father. "Dad! I'm glad it's you, but I'm afraid I have some bad news."

"Really?" Wynn replied.

"It's about your dog."

"What about him?"

Jeffrey had anticipated disappointment in Wynn's voice but was surprised by its absence. "I searched the park all afternoon and couldn't find him."

"All afternoon?"

"Yes."

"Must've been cold out."

"No shit. I thought I'd freeze to death!"

"Well," Wynn said. "You can relax. Roscoe's safe. And I appreciate your efforts to find him."

"Thanks." *For wasting my time. You probably knew the dog was okay from the start.*

"Where are you now?" Wynn asked.

"I just pulled into your driveway. I've gotta pick up Bea. You're staying in the hospital tonight, right?"

"Yes. But I'm glad the two of you are at the house. I need your help with something."

Instantly suspicious, Jeffrey responded with a cautious, "Oh?"

"I've decided to redo the spare bedroom. I'm having everything in it stored elsewhere, given away, or thrown out, including the furniture. If you're interested in any of it, take it home with you tonight. If you want the bed or dresser, I can have it hauled to your place."

"Wow. What brought this on?"

"I'm going to hire an associate, someone to help me with some ongoing ventures."

"Ventures?" Jeffrey paused. His father often made trips out of town, but he never discussed them. *Could this be about his investments?* "You've never said much about what you do since you retired from teaching. I thought you were taking it easy."

Wynn chuckled. "Teaching wasn't the only

thing occupying my time. I've been engaged in other projects, too."

"Like what?"

"For one thing, I've made some progress in a very narrow and highly speculative field. I enjoy conferring with associates who've helped me. The same goes for some of the people I've helped. I seriously doubt you'd be interested in any of it. Not unless you've suddenly become a fan of theoretical physics."

"Nope. That's not gonna happen. So, the spare bedroom? That'll be this guy's office?"

"It's going to be a young woman, and the bedroom will become her temporary quarters. Later on, it will just be her office."

"A young woman? How young?"

"Mid-twenties, I'd guess."

"You don't know?"

"I don't care."

Jeffrey needed a moment to process the news. *A woman will be moving into my Dad's house? She's young, but he doesn't care how young?* "Have you thought this through? It sounds kind of rash."

"I need someone to work with me, and take me places, and provide some other things."

"Like what?" He couldn't imagine his staid old man setting himself up with a mistress.

His father took a moment before responding. "Not that it's any of your business, but due to recent circumstances, I've decided I need someone to provide security services, someone who can look after my personal safety."

"Like a bodyguard?" *A bodyguard for cryin' out loud? What the—* "Why? Why on Earth would you need something like that? What the hell have you done?"

The elder Albright exhaled as if exhausted, then said, "Don't worry about it. I'm probably just being foolish. Miss Winters is perfectly capable of looking out for me."

"Miss Winters?"

"Danica."

"You're going to have a female bodyguard?"

"That's right."

"No, it's not. It's crazy!"

"I guess we'll see, won't we?"

Chapter Six

"I was once fired as opening act for Seals and Croft because I got loaded and introduced them as Arts and Crafts." —George Miller

Braden ignored the email waiting for him the following day when he returned to his cubicle at the headquarters of Greystone, Ellis, and McComb. Instead, he stared once again at the portfolio of Wynn Albright. Tiring of that, he pulled up Albright's trade history, marveling at the profits accumulated by the mousey little jerk.

How could he have possibly managed it?

When his phone rang, Braden noted the inter-office call light and immediately answered it.

"Daley?"

"Yes, Mr. Simkins?" There was no mistaking

his boss's voice.

"In my office, now."

Crap! Braden walked straight to Conrad Simkins' office and entered without knocking.

"Sit down," his boss said. "I just got off the phone with our IT department. Did you know they record just about everything we do?"

Braden shook his head. "Really? You mean... like, with hidden cameras?"

"I mean keystrokes."

Shit.

"They can use keystroke recordings to figure out everything any of us do on our computers."

"Yeah, okay. So?"

Simkins frowned at him. "Apparently, you're a fan of one of our Gem-level clients."

"I've checked the records of several, sir," Braden admitted. "I thought it might be... you know, educational."

"They weren't your clients though, and they never will be."

"I don't—"

"We got a call from Mr. Albright. He wanted to know about some sort of contest we're supposedly staging. He said he heard about it from an employee here, but he couldn't remember the man's name."

That's a relief. Braden swallowed, though he knew it might make him look guilty.

"Our IT people tell me you're the only one of late who's consistently accessed Mr. Albright's account."

"Well, like I said, I—"

"What the hell were you thinking? Some stupid award supposedly put on by our advertising department? We don't even *have* an advertising department!" Simkins appeared ready to levitate. "And as for Mr. Albright's account, that data is confidential—all of it. What part of that didn't you understand?"

"I just... It's not what you think."

"You have no idea what I'm thinking. And it's probably better that you don't." Simkins eased back in his chair and took a breath. "Grab your hat and coat and report to Human Resources."

"But—"

"Do not remove anything else from your workspace. That includes any personal items you may have in there. Understood?"

"Of course, but—"

"Goodbye, Mr. Daley, and good luck getting another investment job with the kind of endorsement I'll write."

"If you'd just—"

"Go! Now. We're done here. HR will have your things mailed to you." He nodded toward his office door. "Don't come back."

~*~

When Rick ushered Danica into his home, her mind still reeled from the rapid-fire changes in her life. A homeless nobody who took the time to respond to a frantic dog and help a stranger had been given a meal. She'd been offered a place to stay, two in fact, plus the friendship of a man who seemed too good to be true, and a potential job that could drastically change her life.

Assuming, of course, all of it was legit. Danica hadn't known much of that in her life. A target of mean girls from the time she started school until she escaped via graduation, she had few friends, and none who would stick up for her. She learned to be self-reliant at a time when self-reliance held no value among her peers. It didn't dawn on her until she joined the Marines that all the young people she left behind were simply "cool girl" mob members, followers, social media addicts. They didn't like her because she didn't need them, and told them so.

That might have been a mistake. It gave her very few connections. Though assured by her parents and her dog-hating sister, Caitlyn, that she was attractive, she never believed them. If she were pretty, she contended, guys would have asked her out on dates. Few did.

Her attitude became a massive chip on her shoulder that ultimately drove her to join the Marines. She didn't need the stupid parties; she didn't need cutesy dresses, fancy underwear, or sexy swimsuits. She needed people in her life who would respect her for her ability and not her looks, her bra size, or her social media contacts.

Roscoe definitely lightened her mood. With his tail wagging furiously, as soon as they walked in the door, he bounced between the pair allowing each only the briefest opportunity to pet him. Eventually, he grew calm and lay on the floor with his chin resting on his front paws. When they left the room, he followed them like a servant.

After showing her around the house, Rick swept his arm toward a bedroom at the back of the first floor. "There's your room. I'll be back in a minute with fresh towels and stuff. Then I thought I'd hit the grocery store and find something for dinner. Got anything in mind?"

Danica responded with a smile. "I would

dearly love a shower and a nap. I'll leave dinner up to you."

"No problem. How does pizza sound?"

"Wonderful."

"Okay then, I'll grab the towels and be back in a jiffy." He turned to leave, then paused and nodded toward the bedroom she'd be staying in. "A while back I put my wife's things in the closet and dresser. I've been meaning to take them to Goodwill or the Salvation Army. I just..." His sigh was audible. "I guess I just wasn't ready. Anyway, if there's anything of hers in there that you like, help yourself. You're about the same size."

Danica felt her eyebrows draw together. "Are you sure? I mean, I'd hate to stir up memories by wearing her things."

He shook his head. "No, it's fine. I want you to have them. Take anything that fits you. I... I need to move on."

"I know the feeling," she said. "I lost my parents shortly after I joined the service."

Rick's lips pressed tightly together. "I'm sorry for your loss. They must've been fairly young."

She nodded, trying hard not to get sentimental and teary. "You have been so... kind to me. But I honestly don't know why."

He reached down to pet Roscoe who had finally taken a seat. "I've said this before. I think you're a good person dealing with tough times."

Danica winced.

"Okay. *Shitty* times. Whatever. I just wanted to give you a little boost back up." His face lit with a smile. "And based on your connection with Professor Albright, it looks like it might have worked."

"But, I don't—"

"Hush. I'll bring you a towel. While you take a bath or a shower, I'll zip over to the pizza place and grab a pie. What d'you want on it?"

"Meat."

"Chicken and pineapple?"

She tried not to squint, but failed. "You can put whatever you want on your half, but I'd like meat. You know, like cow, or maybe hog. Something that walked on four legs."

Rick was laughing. "Got it. Worry not. I've also got to stop at the drugstore and pick up a prescription. Need anything?"

"I'd kill for a new toothbrush."

"Your wish is my command."

"Rick?"

"Yeah?"

Though unsure how he'd react, she had to know. "How do you expect me to... uhm... You know. Pay you back?"

"I dunno. Take me out to dinner with your first paycheck?"

"I mean, you're not looking for any special sorts of... favor?"

He grinned at her. "You mean sex?"

She slumped her shoulders. "Well...."

"No," he said. "I'm not that kind of guy, and I hope like hell I never will be. Now, quit messin' around and get yourself cleaned up."

"Thank you," she said, somewhat relieved if not completely. As Rick walked away and out of earshot, Danica looked down at the dog. "You'll protect me, won't ya?" She prayed she wouldn't have to find out.

~*~

With his hat and coat in hand, Braden took the walk of shame down the center aisle of the cubicle farm where the herd of GE&M low-level investment advisors grazed for clients. Since it was nearing the end of the work day, he hoped his colleagues would think he'd just knocked off early. *Colleagues.* He chuckled to himself at the thought; on a good day he might be able to name three of them.

He took the elevator down two floors to the accounting and human resources area and made his way to the office of the HR manager. He walked in without waiting.

"Braden Daley?" asked a slender woman with gray hair. She had an open file folder on her desk and seemed engrossed by its contents.

Braden guessed her to be somewhere in her late fifties. "Yes. Mr. Simkins told me to—"

"Have a seat. I'll be with you in a moment."

He settled himself in a wooden armchair wedged between two massive, gray file cabinets. Aside from a small photo frame on the woman's desk and a wall plaque in recognition of something innocuous, the room held nothing decorative or personal. She could have been a temp or an imposter. He smiled at his own foolishness; this woman was the 21st century equivalent of an executioner. He was merely waiting for her to hand him his head.

As she set the folder aside and drew a sheaf of blank forms from a desk drawer, her phone rang. She held out her hand, palm up, for Braden to sit quietly while she answered it. "Human Resources, Helen Bancroft speaking."

Braden watched half-heartedly until the woman frowned after listening to the voice on the phone.

"Yes, he's here, now. And I was about—"

Though he could hear a voice on the other end of the phone, the words were faint, unintelligible.

"Of course, sir," she responded, "but—"

Cut off again, the woman frowned and nervously tapped her fingernails on the paperwork in front of her. "I will, yes. Right away."

She lowered the phone and carefully returned it to the cradle on her desk. After restoring the pile of blank forms to their home in a desk drawer, she folded the personnel file she'd been looking at and handed it to Braden.

"What's going on?" he asked.

"You need to take this file upstairs and have a chat with Mr. McComb."

"*McComb?* Now? I thought—"

"I'm very busy, Mr. Daley. Just take the file and go. Mr. McComb's office is on the twenty-ninth floor." She pointed toward her door. "That way."

Though he'd met the only surviving partner of the firm at a Christmas party, he'd never actually had anything to do with the man. As far as Braden could tell, he kept himself surrounded by suck-ups like Simkins. He couldn't imagine why the rich old fart wanted to see him.

~*~

Wynn pushed away the tray that supposedly contained his evening meal. Though far from being a foodie, he considered the stuff they'd given him an assortment of stable droppings. The green beans looked gray and felt squishy; the meat might have come from a squirrel, and the mashed potatoes smelled like something that should've been thrown out a week ago.

His thoughts were tossed into disarray when a tall, thin, dark-visaged man entered his room, closing the door behind himself. Wynn had seen him before and hoped he'd never see him again.

"Mr. Albright! I heard you was in here, so I thought I'd drop by and see ya."

"Do I know you?" Wynn asked, hoping the man would just go away.

"C'mon now. You know me; I'm CeeJay. Ah'm a friend, right?"

"More like a friend of a friend."

The visitor smiled wide. His teeth appeared to have been spray-painted with the brightest shade of white imaginable. "My man Hank tol' me all about you."

"I'll bet." *And if I survive this visit, Hank can damn well start mowing the lawn for somebody else. I told him to keep his mouth shut, but—"*

"Lissen. I jus' dropped by to see what you thinkin' about the big game comin' up."

Wynn played dumb. "Big game?"

The man laughed. "The Superbowl, of course! You bein' a wise ass?"

"No, no. I just don't follow sports much. That's all."

"You don't follow sports, and yet you tol' Hank what the final score in the Iron Bowl was gonna be before the game even started. How's that work?"

"Lucky guess," Wynn said.

"Bullshit." The man's smile dissolved into a grimace. "Hank says you always know. You always git it right. You can't be fixin' all them games, so how you do it?"

The door to Wynn's room opened at that point, and his doctor entered. She was accompanied by two others, a male nurse in blue scrubs, and a second woman wearing a white lab coat like the doctor.

"Please excuse us," the trio's leader said as

they advanced on Wynn's bed. She looked his visitor in the eye. "You'll have to step out. We need to examine Mr. Albright now."

"Ah'll be back," CeeJay said. He lifted his hand, pretended he was aiming a gun at Wynn, and pulled the imaginary trigger.

Wynn didn't respond. Instead, he cast a grateful smile at his physician.

Chapter Seven

"The chief problem with the individual investor: He or she typically buys when the market is high and thinks it's going to go up, and sells when the market is low and thinks it's going to go down." —Harry Markowitz

The following morning, Jeffrey arrived at the hospital to take his father home. Wynn was eager to leave and hurriedly spread out the clothes Jeffery brought him.

"What's the big rush, Dad?"

"I need to get the hell outta here," Wynn said. "Someone's always barging into the room at odd hours day and night; the hallway usually sounds like there's a freight train going by, and the food isn't fit to eat." He let his hospital gown hit the floor.

"Speaking of food," he continued, "we're stopping at that butcher shop I like on the way home.

I could eat a whole rib roast by myself."

Jeffrey could never be sure if his old man was exaggerating. "It's on Bentley, right?"

"Yeah. By the florist shop." He bobbed his head at a thought. "I probably ought to get some flowers for Danica when she starts work." Then he shook his head. "Nah. That'll have to wait."

"Who's Danica?"

Wynn gave him a sidelong look as he pulled up his pants and zipped them. "I told you about her."

"Oh, yeah. Right. The twenty-something who's gonna change your life."

Wynn looked at him in disgust. "Get your mind out of the gutter. If everything works out, she'll be helping me, not marrying me."

Jeffrey smirked. "She's not after your money?"

Wynn stopped buttoning his shirt and peered at him. "What're you talking about?"

"Some guy from your investment firm came by. Said he wanted to nominate you for Client of the Year or something."

Wynn merely stared at him.

"He said it was only for their most successful investors. He said you were top-notch."

"Remember his name?"

Jeffrey shook his head. "Sorry. He's young. Maybe in his late twenties, early thirties. Outgoing. One might say friendly, except I thought he was full of shit. I mean, if it were on the level, they'd have contacted you by phone or mail. But this—"

"Is complete crap," Wynn said. "This yahoo said he was from Greystone, Ellis, and McComb?"

"I think so. Why?"

"Scams come in all flavors and sizes. I'm sure that's what this is."

"So, you're saying you're *not* a big-time investor? You don't gamble in the market?"

Wynn laughed and patted him on the shoulder. "I never gamble, son. Never."

~*~

Danica looked back on the previous evening and smiled. The shower had felt better than any she remembered, and she actually left some of her amazing pizza dinner uneaten. She'd stayed up late watching TV with Rick who made no advances or suggestions other than which shows to watch. And at bedtime, after taking Roscoe outside for a few minutes, she locked the bedroom door and crawled between clean sheets under a warm blanket.

The nap she'd taken earlier didn't keep her from being sleepy, and when Roscoe curled up beside her, she felt safer and warmer than she had for months. He so reminded her of Foster. For once in a long, long while she felt *alive!*

Well after the morning sun had slipped through the blinds, Roscoe decided she needed to get up. Tail wagging furiously, he crawled on top of her, worked his way toward the headboard, and nosed his head under her pillow. It made her giggle, and she gave the dog a gentle rubdown.

Afterward, she stretched, yawned, and smiled. Roscoe burrowed into her again as if his sole purpose in life was to shove her out of the bed. Still smiling, she donned a bathrobe she found in the closet and fell back into a late morning routine she'd lost along with her apartment.

Rick and his car were both gone when she stepped into the kitchen, but he'd left a selection of breakfast items for her. He also left a handwritten note that featured a good morning greeting, his phone number in case she needed to reach him, and a reminder that they were scheduled to meet with Professor Albright at one that afternoon.

My God—what an angel Rick is!

After a leisurely breakfast which she shared with Roscoe, she figured it was time to take him for a walk. Rick's home was nowhere near the national park where he'd found her illegal campsite. Instead, he lived two blocks from the town's main square. That became her destination, and Roscoe appeared eager to get going.

She found jeans and a sweatshirt in the closet. While the top was a bit baggy, the jeans were a tight fit. *Rick's wife must've been petite.*

Bundled up against the cold thanks to a coat, hat, and gloves she also found in the closet, Danica feared Roscoe might need something, too. Unfortunately, the clothing she found was only meant for people.

"We'll keep the walk short," she told him. "If you start shivering, we'll come straight back here, okay?"

Roscoe was too busy wagging his tail to offer any other sort of response.

"All righty then, let's boogey!"

As they hustled out the back door, Danica worried about not locking the house since she had no key and wouldn't be able to get back in. She almost went back inside to call Rick and ask him about it, then decided they wouldn't be gone long; it was too cold to go far.

They reached the outskirts of the town square

in minutes. A brisk pace had them both exhaling steamy puffs of breath. Few other people were out in the cold weather, but Danica spotted three teens arguing in the space between a pair of old, brick buildings. Curious, she paused to watch them.

Of the three, two appeared older and taller than the one in the middle, and they were giving him a rough time. Danica had no use for bullies, and her sympathies went immediately toward the boy being picked on.

"Hey!" she called to them as she approached. "What's going on?"

"Nuthin'," came the reply from a teen wearing a red, woolen ski cap with an NBA logo. "Mind yer own business."

"They're cheating me!" cried the boy in the middle. Ski Cap silenced him with a quick jab to the stomach.

Danica noted with interest that the apparent leader of the two-person assault team had one hand on the front of his pants to keep them from falling off. Showing the back of one's underwear seemed to be a fashion statement for a certain class of creep.

"Leave him be," she said in a command voice.

"Fuck you!" Ski Cap grumbled. "Now git!"

The kid in the middle, who looked younger

than he had at a distance, held a small cardboard container labeled "X-BOX" in large, poorly shaped letters. Tears streaked down his face as he silently begged her for help.

Seeing a knife in the second teen's hand sealed the deal. Ready to drop Roscoe's leash if necessary, Danica entered the narrow space between the buildings. The dark corridor blocked the wind.

"Let him go," Danica said, this time in a more conversational voice.

Ski Cap glanced at his pal. "You believe this bitch?"

His response came quickly, "She crazy, man. Want me to cut her?"

"Maybe. I dunno." Ski Cap smiled. "Maybe later. She looks pretty hot. We might have to do something else to her first."

Danica snorted. "Oh, please. If you try something—*anything*—you'll regret it." With her hand hidden behind her, she let go of Roscoe's leash.

Both of the thugs laughed.

"C'mere, bitch," Ski Cap said as he grabbed for her. To his dismay, he didn't connect.

Instead, Danica gripped his arm with both hands and gave it a savage twist for which the limb was not designed. Ski Cap's cry rattled off the walls. She continued to twist the arm until he had turned completely away from her, still shrieking in pain.

While the other thuggish teen stared at them with his mouth open, Danica yanked Ski Cap's jeans down with one hand and grabbed his scrotum. With her other hand she continued to grip the injured limb.

With Ski Cap immobilized, she addressed him calmly. "Tell your pal to back off, or I'll turn you into a one-armed soprano."

"Don't!" he cried.

"Don't *what?*" she asked calmly while applying additional pressure to both places.

"Don't hurt me!" he squealed.

"What's your friend's name?" she asked.

"Dontae."

"Tell him to drop the knife. Now."

"Do it," Ski Cap said, his voice reduced to something between a whine and a whisper.

Dontae let go of the blade and stepped back.

Danica smiled at the boy with the box. "Did they take anything from you?"

"Not yet," he said. "They said they were selling an Xbox. I thought it would be a real one." The boy tossed the empty box on the ground. "Can I go?"

"Of course," she said and watched him run to the main sidewalk, turn right, and disappear from sight.

After shoving Ski Cap face-first to the ground, she picked up the knife and folded the blade back into the handle. "I'll just hang on to this, Dontae. You know; in case I see either of you bothering someone else."

Ski Cap rolled over and struggled to pull up his pants. He succeeded only after standing up. The glare on his face reflected both rage and humiliation.

"There's a reason why people wear belts," she said. "Now, unless you want me to kick your ass again, you'd best get outta here."

Roscoe had been waiting patiently for the event to end and growled at the two teens as they shuffled away, turning left when they reached the sidewalk.

Danica picked up Roscoe's leash and patted him on the head. "That's enough excitement for one day, don't you think?"

From her spot between the buildings, she was unable to determine how far any of the three had gone. With a sigh of resignation, she unfolded the knife blade before following the teens out of the dark space.

~*~

Totally baffled, Braden headed straight for the top floor where McComb and the rest of the big dogs had offices. Braden had never been up there, but he'd heard plenty of scuttlebutt concerning how lavish the accommodations were and how intimately some of the support staff treated the occupants.

Only one of the building's four elevators reached that floor, and access to it meant clearing one's entry with security first. The guard monitoring the elevator checked Braden's ID badge, looked at a text message on his cell phone, and waved him in. When he reached the top floor, he found himself facing a desk occupied by another sour-faced rent-a-cop.

The big wigs must think this is where the Federal Reserve stores their cash.

The guard at the desk also checked Braden's ID badge then pointed to the last of three over-sized doors in a high-ceilinged wall. Braden felt sure the wall faced a park on that side of the building.

He walked to the massive door and knocked. It opened silently, and he stepped in. He paused to take in the view through a wall of glass. An attractive brunette smiled at him from behind a nearly empty desk in front of the window.

"Mr. McComb is waiting for you," she said. At the touch of a button somewhere out of Braden's sight, the senior partner's door quietly opened. "Go right on in."

McComb sat behind a desk significantly larger than that of the young woman who opened the door for Braden. Unlike the floor-to-ceiling windows in the outer office, McComb's were tinted, greatly reducing the light level. The heavy-set senior executive leaned forward, showing the top of his head, which was covered in thick, white curls. Braden couldn't see his eyes as the man's attention was focused on the contents of an open folder in front of him.

McComb cleared his throat before he spoke but didn't look up. "Bailey?"

"It's Daley, sir," Braden said.

"What? Oh, yes. Right."

When the old man finally looked up, Braden was surprised to see he had a dark mustache. The contrast with his hair felt disturbing.

"I'll keep this brief," McComb said. "I understand you've been doing a bit of amateur sleuthing."

Braden tried not to fidget. "Well, uhm—"

"Wynn Albright is our most unusual client."

"I know," Braden said. "That's why—"

The look on McComb's face was sufficient to shut Braden up. "He is *distinctly* different from our other GEM-level investors. Do you know why?"

"Because he's never lost money in the market?"

McComb took a sip of coffee before responding. "That, plus he always withdraws his profits from a sale. The vast majority of investors plow their funds back into the market. They're usually intent on increasing the size of their holdings."

Braden shrugged.

"I've chatted with the heads of a number of our competitors—unofficially, of course—many of them also have Mr. Albright as a valued client."

"And does he reinvest with them?" Braden asked.

"No. Not a one."

This revelation struck Braden as even more puzzling than the sorry little house Albright lived in. "I don't get it."

"Tell me, Daley," McComb said. "Are you still interested in the mysterious Mr. Albright?"

"Yes, sir," Braden said. "I definitely am."

"Then I have a proposal for you."

(clearing)

Chapter Eight

"Gambling has brought our family together. We had to move to a smaller house." —Tommy Cooper

Wynn Albright gazed at himself in the mirror. The bandage once wrapped around his head lay in a heap on the bathroom counter. Rather than replace it, he left the wound and the stitches holding it together exposed. "It'll heal faster that way," he told himself. He tilted his head up for a quick look at the scar on his jaw, the result of a traffic accident that occurred long before seat belts became mandatory.

After showering and donning clean clothes, he headed for his office, formerly the second of three bedrooms in the original floorplan. That room, and the one destined to become temporary living quarters for Danica Winters, were about the same size. He toyed briefly with the idea of renting a small apartment for her, but that wouldn't work because he needed her nearby for protection, which he wanted around the clock.

Any money saved by that decision would go towards a firearm—that or whatever other weapon Danica might prefer. What she chose didn't matter. What *did* matter, was having someone who could shield him from CeeJay, the only gangbanger Wynn had ever met. And possibly more just like him.

Thanks Hank, you idiot! Why couldn't you have told me your bookie was connected to the Bloods, or the Crips, or whatever stupid gang he worked for? That's what I get for feeling sorry for someone and for trying to help. You sure won't be doing any more yard work for me!

It was the only such mistake he'd made since he began his life's most important work: philanthropy. For that, he had one person who truly deserved his thanks, Dr. Annabelle Knox. He missed her. He missed her brilliant mind and her undaunted spirit. He did not miss her guilt. That, he felt sure, was the reason she did nothing to spare her own life.

He shook off thoughts of his mentor and dearest friend. The past could not be changed. He chose to focus on the present instead, beginning with CeeJay.

However, CeeJay was not his only worry. He'd

been besieged by requests from "representatives" of a dozen different investment firms, all wanting to know how he knew which stocks to buy and the optimum time to sell them. At some point, he presumed, one or two of them would try a more sinister means of gaining the information. Then, too, there were a couple of characters he'd encountered during his frequent casino trips. Winners, it seemed, always attracted attention.

Having Danica at his side would give him a measure of safety, assuming she still had the sort of skills she taught in the Marines. The thought triggered a smile. *Won't CeeJay be surprised!*

A second thought erased his mirth. What if she merely made up the kung fu shit she'd talked about?

That led to additional thoughts, each more depressing than the last. What if everything he thought he knew about her was pure fiction?

The Ranger assured me that she saved my life, but then how well do I really know that guy? He could just be playing along with her! And what if they were driven by one of the investment firms, or a gambler, or even CeeJay himself?

He forced himself to relax. There was no future in tormenting himself over things about which he could only speculate. He knew better. *I'm an educated man, for cryin' out loud. I must be rational and stay in control.*

If Danica—assuming that was her real name—returned his beloved Roscoe, it would lend some credence to her story. It wouldn't prove anything definitively, however. That would only come with time and a thorough background investigation that would address his concerns.

In the meantime, Wynn vowed to remain vigilant. With that, he pulled a small taser from a dresser drawer and put it in his pocket. It might not kill anyone, but it would sure as hell slow them down if he had to make a hasty retreat.

He checked his watch. It was nearly one, the appointed hour for the rendezvous Ranger Rick suggested.

Danica returned to Rick's house and entered through the door she'd been unable to lock when she left. After letting Roscoe off his leash, she took a quick look around for evidence of an intruder. Fortunately, everything looked just as it had when she left. That much, at least, she could relax about.

The adrenaline rush she'd had when dealing with the young thugs in town diminished when she realized the two who had been picking on the younger kid hadn't hung around. She'd folded the knife she'd taken from them and put it in her pocket. Though not a big fan of knives, they certainly had their place when it came to self-defense.

Maybe I should give it to Rick as a thank you. But then, what if this Albright character turns out to be something other than a gentleman? A knife in my hand would give him a good reason to leave me the hell alone.

She reread the note Rick left then checked the clock on his stove. He would be home soon, and she'd have to give Roscoe back to his owner. The thought depressed her. If given the option, she'd love to adopt Roscoe as her own. The idea hardly seemed realistic though, considering her current status.

Unable to foretell what her new job would entail, assuming she got it, or how it would work out, she was left with two options: either she gave Albright's offer a try, or she could return to living on the street.

Roscoe sat beside her, looking up expectantly. She grinned at him, feeling complete, even though they would soon be separated.

I could leave now. Take Roscoe with me. Go back to what I'd sort of become used to. But how long could that last? I barely have the resources to feed myself, much less a dog, too.

Her thoughts turned to Roscoe's efforts to rouse her from bed that morning. A more welcome and gentle alarm she'd never known. *Not even Foster had done that.*

If I get the job, I'll at least have a chance to see Roscoe. And he'll receive far better care than I can afford. The thought process resolved some of her doubts. The rest would be up to Albright. If he was the decent sort of person Rick thought he was, she might finally have a chance at a meaningful life. And though she had no desire to return to the streets, that option would always remain open.

A short beep of a car horn ended her reverie. She glanced out the window and watched Rick pile out of his Jeep. It was time to mount-up for the trip, but she felt ready.

McComb's office hadn't seemed quite as cold when Braden first walked in. Now it had a distinct chill which suited him more. McComb sat behind his massive desk, his expression bland as he waited for Braden to react.

"What sort of proposition?" Braden asked, beginning to feel comfortable for the first time in the presence of one of GE&M's senior execs.

"I want you to work exclusively for me,"

McComb said, "and I want your primary focus to be on Wynn Albright."

"So, I'd no longer be an investment advisor?"

"You may retain that title if you wish or sign on as my administrative assistant. I don't care which label you choose. What's important to me is your assignment."

Braden squirmed a bit before responding. "May I ask why?"

McComb's face registered annoyance but soon settled into a look of neutrality. "There are three large offices on this floor. Do you know how many are occupied?"

"All of them?"

"Wrong. My two partners have retired, content to spend what little of their lives remain near the beaches in Florida and California. They're no longer involved in running this company."

"I'd heard rumors," Braden said, "but I didn't—"

"It's true, and it's mainly because I'm younger and a bit more..." He paused, searching for a word. "Let's say 'hardline.' I get things done, and I usually get them done quickly."

Curious, Braden asked, "What exactly do you

expect me to accomplish?"

"I want Albright's secret. Once I have it, I can turn this firm into an industry giant. I can buy up the competition. I could create an investment empire like no other."

"And how do you expect me to get that information?"

McComb didn't react at first, then leaned toward him. "I don't care how you get it as long as I'm not implicated in any way. Understand? Not in any goddam way."

"I'm not sure how—"

"You'll need to find out everything you can about Albright. And I mean every damn thing. Eventually you'll find a way to crack him." He drummed his fingers on his desk for a moment. "Touch base with my secretary on your way out. She may have a helpful idea."

Braden tried to remain calm and appear professional despite McComb's suggestion that he strongarm Albright. "Two questions," he said.

McComb's eyebrows dipped in suspicion. "Go on."

"Would I be the only one doing this... investigation?"

McComb nodded. "For now, anyway."

"And what's in it for me? Why wouldn't I just keep the secret and use it myself?"

McComb chuckled. "Because you're a pauper. What's your portfolio worth?"

"About thirty thousand, maybe a little more. I started with almost nothing."

McComb glanced at his computer screen, tapped a key, then turned to look at Braden. "It currently sits at twenty thousand, eight hundred and change. Not exactly a fortune."

"It's a start!" Braden felt his face flush.

"You currently hold shares in..." McComb looked once again at his computer screen. "Nothing worth owning. You sold your winners, but left the money in cash. You won't get rich that way."

"I buy and sell the same stocks as Albright," Braden said. "And usually on the same days. The cash is ready for the next buy."

McComb chuckled. "I never said you were stupid. And when it comes to Albright, I do something similar. It took me a while to catch on to him, but once I did..." He paused and cleared his throat. "But even copying Albright, it'll still take you a good long while to pile up a few million. And without access to our file on him, you'd be screwed."

When Braden didn't respond, McComb continued. "You asked what's in it for you. How would you like an office like mine?"

"One of the two empty ones on this floor?"

"Yes."

"And a secretary like yours, too?"

"Certainly."

"And a raise commensurate with the office?"

"Of course. You might even want to change your title to something like... Oh, I don't know. VP perhaps?"

Braden's pulse ticked up with each of McComb's answers. "When would all this happen? When could I move in?"

McComb's expression turned deadly serious. "The day after you turn Albright's secret over to me. He's getting inside information from somewhere; I just can't figure out where. That's now your job."

~*~

Wynn Albright stood on his front porch waiting when Ranger Rick's car pulled into the driveway. Danica slipped out of the passenger side door and let Roscoe out of the back. He appeared slightly confused until Wynn called his name. At that he perked up, raced around the car, flew along the sidewalk, and hurtled up the steps. He was so eager to snuggle with Wynn that he nearly knocked the man down.

Rick and Danica joined the reunion between frantically wiggling dog and laughing professor.

"I'm glad to see how happy Roscoe is," Danica said.

"Why's that? Was he not a good dog for you?"

She laughed. "He was amazingly good to me, and for me. He's an absolute love."

"That he is," Wynn said. He then motioned for them to join him inside.

Once they were settled on comfortable chairs in his living room, Wynn asked if they'd like something to drink.

"No thanks," Rick said.

"I'm good, too," added Danica.

When one of them stopped petting Roscoe, the dog made a beeline to someone else. After both Wynn and Danica crossed their arms and refused to continue the adoration, Roscoe abandoned them and hurried over to Rick.

"I'm not playin' your little game," Rick said.

Roscoe looked from one face to another, then

lay down, put his head on his paws, and tried to go to sleep.

"Do I need to walk him?" Danica asked. "He hasn't been out in a while."

"There's no need," Wynn said. "There's a pet entrance in one of the bedrooms. He can go out whenever he likes. That side of the yard is fenced."

Rick chuckled. "He's got his own private doggie door?"

"Just his size," Wynn added.

They chatted amicably and Wynn showed Danica the room where he wanted her to stay until the guest house was built. "That is, of course, if you still want the job."

"I definitely do," she said. "And I can't tell you how much I appreciate the chance you're willing to take with me."

Wynn shrugged. "I would have had to make these changes anyway. If things don't work out for you, I'll need to find someone else to take up the load."

Her eyebrows scrunched down. "What, exactly, will that load consist of?"

"Mainly two things," he said. "Security is my primary concern, both here and when I'm traveling.

Beyond that, when not being my shadow, I'd like you to focus on some charities I'm interested in."

"How would I do that?"

He smiled. "By computer. I'll have one installed for your personal use. The task will primarily involve reading reviews and matching them with whatever claims the organizations make. If there's anything sketchy going on, I need to know about it before I consider any sort of donation."

"And that's it?" she asked.

"That's all I can discuss right now," he said. "There's a good deal more we still need to talk about before we finalize anything."

Chapter Nine

"It's not really gambling when you never lose."
—Jennifer Aniston

Jeffrey Albright frowned when he pulled into the driveway of his father's house. It had been two days since the elder Albright returned from the hospital. He should have been alone. Someone had parked a dark green Jeep next to the walkway. *The redhead owns a Jeep?* An aging white Toyota took up the second spot and barely left enough room for him to park his own vehicle.

The extra distance didn't amount to much, but Jeffrey wasn't in the mood for any changes in his routine. The vehicles also meant his father had company, most likely visiting physicists. He'd had other visitors in the past, too, but Wynn never introduced them or explained their presence.

"It doesn't concern you," was the only enlightenment he ever received on the subject.

As he walked by the white car, he realized it belonged to his father's housekeeper who dropped in weekly and kept the place presentable. The Jeep, however, he'd never seen.

He wandered past the cars, continued up the front stairs, and entered the house without knocking. Of the four people he saw standing in the living room, he recognized two: his father and Maria Valdez, the housekeeper. A thin park ranger probably in his thirties and a striking redhead in a sweatshirt and tight jeans completed the quartet.

All four stopped talking when he entered the room.

"It's just me," he said, waving his hand in greeting. "Bea's busy watching her soaps." *And thinking up new ways to piss me off.*

"I didn't know you were coming over," Wynn said.

His father wore a look of concern that Jeffrey had only rarely seen. "What's going on?"

His father exhaled in resignation. "Maria got here earlier and found something deeply disturbing. We were discussing it."

Jeffrey glanced down at the framed photo of

his mother in his father's hand. It had been taken on their wedding day, and it was badly damaged.

"Mom's photo?"

"Yes. And a bullet shell."

"It's a shell *casing*," said the twenty-something redhead. "It's a standard-issue, nine-millimeter NATO round."

Jeffrey's attention was torn between the damage to the photo and the young woman.

"I found it there," Maria said, pointing to the wooden mantle over the fireplace. "There's a word written on the wall where the frame was."

Stepping closer to the mantle, Jeffrey read the letters scrawled with a dark marker next to a bullet hole in the wall:

Score?

"What's that supposed to mean?" he asked.

"I've got an idea about that," said his father. He turned toward the couple Jeffrey didn't recognize. "Uhm, sorry. This is Danica Winters. She may soon be working for me. And that's her friend, Rick... Uhm...."

"Johanson," said the ranger.

Jeffrey nodded at them. "Nice to meet you." *And this hot redhead will be working for you, Dad?*

Doing what, exactly?

"Ammo like that is available all over," Danica said, returning to the subject at hand. "It's nothing special."

"Maybe so," said Rick, "but the fact someone fired a gun in this house and left an oddball message... Well, it's obviously a threat."

Wynn agreed. "It must've happened when I was in the hospital. I haven't spent much time outside my office or my bedroom since coming home."

"It wasn't there last week," said Maria.

When the others all looked at him, Jeffrey felt obliged to respond. "I'd never shoot at a photo of Mom. Besides, we don't own a gun, any kinda gun."

"*We?*" asked Danica.

"My wife and I." He huffed. "There's no way Beatrix would allow a gun in our house."

Wynn's voice grew even more serious. "Maybe it's time to rethink that."

"A gun is a tool," Danica said. "If you don't know how to use one, you're better off not having one."

"A jackhammer's a tool," observed Rick.

Danica nudged his arm. "Do you know how to

use one?"

"No. But I could probably figure it out."

"Before or after you destroyed something you didn't mean to?"

Jeffrey's father showed no interest in his potential employee's banter. He was too busy scowling at the bullet casing in the maid's hand.

~*~

CeeJay sat alone in a booth at the back of Hudgen's, a popular tavern. It was dark but still afforded a good view of several televisions scattered about just below the ceiling. Talking heads filled nearly all the screens, but none of them said anything CeeJay wanted to hear. The NFL playoffs were over, and his favorite teams had done well, but neither made the finals.

He had smoked a cigarette before entering the bar. He would have preferred weed, but the place was too crowded inside and out; someone would likely rat on him. The local cops had crazy ideas about people who smoked shit. They liked to arrest 'em. Besides, he assured himself, he could smoke whatever he wanted when he got home. His old lady didn't like it, but he didn't give a damn. He'd gotten tired of her cranky ass anyway.

After a long swig of his beer, CeeJay smiled.

The old man he'd approached in the hospital had surely found his little message by now. How the old fart knew football scores before the games were played was a mystery.

He's gotta have connections. I'll bet the damn games are fixed. Nothing else makes sense. And, if he knows the outcomes, he prob'ly knows who got 'em fixed.

That kind of knowledge was valuable. Extremely so. And not just for the obvious advantage one would have when placing bets. It could be used as a form of insurance. If he were arrested for something—say breaking and entering with an unregistered firearm—well, the outcome would ordinarily be grim. But if he could trade information for freedom, everyone would win.

"But first things first," he said aloud. "I gotta git the score. The game's on in three days."

Danica's positive thoughts about providing security for Wynn Albright took a hit when she saw the bullet-damaged photo of Albright's late wife. He offered no theories or explanations until after his son had left, and the housekeeper stepped away to clean up the kitchen.

"So, what's the deal?" Danica asked him.

Albright turned toward Rick. "If Miss Winters intends to help me, she'll need to know what's behind all this." He gestured toward the damaged photo. "But before I say another word about it, she will need to sign a non-disclosure agreement. You, on the other hand, won't be working for me, and I simply can't allow anyone else to know the details of my efforts."

Rick pursed his lips before responding. "And that includes your own son?"

"Sadly, yes." Albright didn't look happy about the admission.

"Fair enough," Rick said. "I'll wait outside." Then he smiled at Danica. "Take your time. Don't rush into anything until you've given it serious thought. Okay?"

"Listen, Rick," Albright said, "this may take a while. I'll be happy to arrange a ride for Miss Winters and have her dropped off wherever she needs to go when our interview is over. There are some things we need to work out before I can finalize any employment details. We both need to agree on some important issues; it'll take time to work them out."

Rick nodded. "No problem. I'm in no hurry to go anywhere, and I have a book in the car I've been meaning to read. So, unless either of you object, I'll just sit in my Jeep and read. It's warmed up outside a little, and I could use the peace and quiet."

Danica smiled her thanks, and Albright said, "Suit yourself."

When Rick closed the door behind him, Albright ushered Danica into his office that, despite the availability of a housecleaner, appeared never to have been tidied.

Albright beckoned her toward a loveseat in front of a window that looked out over a wooded backyard while he closed the door and settled into a chair behind his cluttered desk. She recalled seeing a photo of Albert Einstein's desk supposedly taken shortly after his death. Albright's was remarkably similar in its disarray.

"There are some things we need to work out before this arrangement goes any further," he said. "And that begins with the need for you to be perfectly honest with me. I obviously know little about you, your past, or where you come from. It would be extremely foolish of me to share anything I hold dear that you might mention elsewhere. I need to know that I can trust you, completely and absolutely."

"You make it sound like you've got state secrets," Danica said. "Look, I've never held a top-secret clearance in my life. Never wanted one. I was a grunt in the United States Marines. I can't—*won't*—claim a higher status. What I can tell you, is that I've never violated a trust, unlike some people I've run into. If you tell me something in confidence, I won't share it with another soul."

Albright puckered his lips and then relaxed. "I expected no less. All the same, I'm going to have to run a background check on you before I do anything else. So, if there's something in your past that you might want to explain before I read about it in a report...."

"I'm no angel," Danica said. "I've made mistakes in my life. A couple big ones, in fact. Starting with a dishonorable discharge I got for punching an officer."

Her comment took him by surprise. "Why would you do something like that?"

"Because he wanted to have sex with me, and I told him to go screw himself. He wouldn't stop, so I... I stopped him."

"You *killed* him?"

"Nah. I just took him down. Hard."

Albright clenched his jaws and frowned. "And for that, *you* were punished?"

"Yessir. Can't say I'm proud of it, but I refused to apologize then or later, and that pretty much sealed the deal."

"That's terrible."

She nodded.

"You mentioned *two* big things," Albright said after a moment's reflection. "What's the other?"

"Once I was out, I got a little apartment, but I couldn't find a job. My skills weren't exactly in demand, and my discharge wasn't something I could brag about. When my money ran out, I had to give up my little furnished apartment." She took a deep breath and then exhaled.

"Go on," he said.

"I lived in my car for a long time, and then one night I met a guy in a bar who offered to buy me dinner. I was starved, and I had way too much to drink. He fed me some bullshit story about being in a country western band. Said his car broke down, and he had to get it repaired before he could tow the band's gear to their next gig. I not only believed him, I let him talk me into spending the night with him."

"Oh Lord," muttered Albright.

"Yeah. Well, we ended up in a hotel. I could barely walk by the time we got there. I fell into bed and passed out. When I woke up the next morning, Prince Charming was gone, along with my purse, my phone, and my car keys. He was kind enough to toss some of my stuff out in the parking lot before he left, the bastard."

"Were you able to track him down?"

"No. The cops found my car abandoned in a ditch. Totaled. My insurance had lapsed because I couldn't afford the payments." She felt the tears in her eyes as she looked at him. "I swear to you, I'm not a rotten person. I'm really not. I just need—" She took another deep breath. "I just need a break."

Albright appeared to mull over her remarks. "You haven't told me anything I have doubts about. At least, not yet. Have you ever been arrested?"

"No. Well, except for the incident I told you about."

"Okay. How about drugs? Are you addicted to anything?"

"Do cigarettes count?" she asked. "I quit a couple days ago." She didn't mention that she could no longer afford the damned things.

He continued with a series of other questions, none of which she was embarrassed to answer. Eventually, he eased back in his chair and smiled. "I think we're done. I feel you've been honest with me, and I sincerely appreciate that."

"Does that mean I get the job?"

He drew his lips into a straight line. "Probably, so I think you can relax. But I can't absolutely promise anything until I get your background check back.

Although, to be completely honest, I doubt there'll be much in it."

"Thanks for giving me the chance," she said. "Oh, and by the way, I noticed a latch on a window in your living room that looks funny. Sorta twisted. Could be whoever put a bullet in that photo forced his way in through there."

Albright's face spread into a big smile. "I'll have that background check hurried up. I think our arrangement is going to work out just fine."

Chapter Ten

"Show me where Stalin is buried, and I'll show you a communist plot." —Edgar Bergen

Braden left McComb's office juggling a pair of emotions: sudden power and growing skepticism. The man had given him free rein to do things to Wynn Albright that Braden had previously thought about but knew he'd never try. Now, however, he'd been told such things would be rewarded, and not just handsomely, but profoundly. He suddenly wondered whether McComb would pay for his defense if something went wrong, and the cops nailed him.

As the door to McComb's lair whispered shut, Braden again looked at the brunette beauty sitting behind the desk in the outer office. She raised one hand, extended her sleeveless right arm, and beckoned him with her index finger.

Braden stepped forward, his previous thoughts dispelled by the notion that if he managed to pull off McComb's project, a gorgeous, accommodating, young secretary like this one would be his.

He stopped inches from her desk. "Mr. Mc—"

She silenced him by moving her index finger to her lips. Then she used her left hand to slide a slip of paper toward him across her shiny desktop. Braden focused briefly on the woman's sharp, silver-tipped nails.

Shaking off thoughts of how those nails would feel when tickling his spine, he picked up the paper scrap and glanced at the neat handwriting on it. In addition to a phone number, it presented a name: Shaughnessy.

Puzzled, he looked directly at her. "Your boss—"

Once again, she silenced him with a finger on her lips.

"Listen, I—"

"Thank you for coming by," she said, then added, "Have a nice day" as she reopened McComb's office door, stood up, and walked through it. The door closed behind her with its customary whisper.

He looked once more at the note in his hand.

Shaughnessy?

~*~

As soon as Danica left with the park ranger, Wynn got on the phone and arranged for housing the young woman. He doubted her background check would turn up anything he couldn't overlook. He had no time to waste. It would cost much more to have her future room emptied, painted, and refurnished virtually overnight, but CeeJay had made it clear Wynn had few other options. He needed security, and he needed it in a hurry.

He could leave, of course, but CeeJay had already broken into the house while Wynn was in the hospital. The hood could do it again, and there was no telling what sort of nastiness he would leave behind. He might even uncover Wynn's hidden equipment, not that he'd know what to do with it.

Fortunately, Wynn had Roscoe back, and the dog would likely bark a warning if the thug returned. The problem, of course, was that CeeJay not only had a gun, he had no qualms about using it.

A glance at a calendar on the wall reminded Wynn of the need for a visit to Las Vegas. He opened the drawer in the center of his desk and pulled out a notepad on which he'd jotted down a few essential details concerning the upcoming Super Bowl. They would be easy to remember, so he removed the relevant page, crumpled it, and set it on fire in a metal tray he often used for the purpose. He dumped the ashes in a wastebasket.

Betting on various sports had generated a great deal of cash for him. There were popular sporting events somewhere in the world at virtually any time of the year. Using the facilities of legitimate, well-run casinos to place his bets, Wynn knew he could stay on the right side of the mob and the law, but most importantly, on that of the Internal Revenue Service. The casinos made sure the feds always got their share. Accordingly, Wynn bet big, and there was always enough left in his share to finance whatever investment he had in mind. In this case, he could use the funds to cover the immediate and future lodging for Danica, or whomever else he might have to employ. He sincerely hoped she would prove to be the perfect choice.

Since little time remained before the big game, Wynn knew he had to give Danica a heads-up about the impending trip. Suspecting she might be wary of going somewhere with someone she hardly knew, he planned to book adjoining rooms rather than asking her to share a suite with him. Casinos usually comped his accommodations. The size of his bets, even though he won them all, generated some nice benefits.

Once he'd squared away the details of the

bedroom renovation, he put in a call to Danica at Rick's house. He prayed his plans would meet with approval rather than dismay.

~*~

Jeffrey couldn't get his father's hot, redheaded security babe out of his mind. Her tight jeans, red hair, and fair complexion created an indelible image in his brain. The more he thought about her, however, the angrier he grew over his father's unwillingness to confide in him.

Jeffrey would return home soon, and Beatrix would likely be in one of her typically pissy moods. He hadn't taken out the trash quickly enough, or he hadn't cleaned up the kitchen appropriately, or he didn't bring home enough money from his job as a customer service representative for an online retailer. Nothing he ever did was good enough for her. As he recalled, she had even complained about their honeymoon. It wasn't lavish enough; he didn't perform well enough in the sack, and their budget for meals out, in her words, was "meager." With apologies to Steinbeck, their marriage had become her winter of discontent.

Earlier in the day, while sitting at his desk waiting to deal with another of the endless stream of customer complaints, he'd logged on to a social media site. There he found a note proclaiming that a zoo in

Texas had offered to let people name a cockroach after an ex-lover or former spouse. The insect would then be fed to a zoo animal. The idea of naming a cockroach after Beatrix enchanted him, almost enough to make him feel better about being shut out by his father.

He wondered how much such a bug-naming would cost, if he'd be allowed to witness the feeding, and if they had any roaches big enough to warrant her name. He'd heard there were some the size of an avocado. That thought was enough to put him off of guacamole forever.

Juggling mental images of a Beatrix roach with that of Danica Winter's butt-hugging blue jeans made him a bit lightheaded. He shook it off as he considered an entirely new possibility. What if Danica offered him the same sort of erotic services he imagined she was providing his dad? That thought drove the Bea bug completely from his gray matter.

Sex with Danica Winters?

A quick look in his rearview mirror featured the rapidly diminishing sight of the stop sign he'd just run through.

Get it together, for cryin' out loud!

But the thought remained.

He just could not shake it.

~*~

"Hello?" The voice on the phone sounded bored, but it definitely belonged to Wynn Albright, the crooked professor and possible mob associate.

CeeJay smiled. "You get my message?"

"Who is this?" Albright demanded.

"You know who it is," CeeJay said. "You ready to give me the damn score now?"

"Oh, *you*. Geez. Like I said before. I have no idea what—"

"Don't bullshit me!" CeeJay yelled into the phone. "You want me to come git it in person?"

Albright didn't respond.

"Well? Do I need to drop by? Maybe me and the hot bitch in that picture, what's left of it, can git it on. You dig? I might just take your old lady for a ride."

"Good luck with that," Albright growled. "I never pegged you for a necrophiliac, but I'm not surprised."

A necro... Negro-feel... Whatever. "You think you funny, asshole?"

"No, just tired. Mostly of you. So, stop bothering me. And don't even think about coming back here. I've got a guard dog now."

"You mean that lazy, white mutt your handyman told me 'bout?"

"No," said Albright. "I've got a new one."

CeeJay cut the connection. He hated dogs ever since one bit him as a kid. That dog belonged to one of his mother's boyfriends; they were both big and butt ugly. CeeJay got his revenge, though. He let the dog out during rush hour and threw some food scraps in the road for him. Whoever ran over him didn't bother to stop, and CeeJay was long gone before his mama's squeeze found the well-flattened body.

"I ain't scared of you or your damn dogs," he said out loud. "All I need is a quiet, easy way to git in yo house. You'll be happy to tell me everything I wanna know then."

Braden phoned the mysterious Shaughnessy, a man who sounded more like a Pakistani than an Irishman. The call lasted long enough for Braden to agree to meet him at a fast-food restaurant in Buckhead, a swanky area on Atlanta's north side.

"How'll I know who you are?" he asked.

"I'll be wearing a sweatshirt with the name of my favorite hockey team on it."

"Dude," Braden said, "I don't know jack about hockey. What team is it?"

Shaughnessy sighed. "The Macon Whoopies."

"You're kidding me."

"You wanna meet up or not?"

"Yes, yes. Sorry. It's just— You kinda took me by surprise with that hockey shit."

"You called me, by name: Shaughnessy. So, I already know who you work for and what you want."

"Great," said Braden, not at all sure how the man was supposed to help.

"But it's gonna cost you."

Of course. "How much?"

"I charge five K for a hack and cough, unless it involves the government or a big corporation. I get half up front and the rest when I'm done. I only take cash."

"A *hack and cough?* What the hell is that?"

"I'll explain when we meet. Half up front, remember?"

"Right, right. I'll—"

<Click>

Braden looked down at the dead phone in his hand. *Where the hell am I supposed to find twenty-five hundred bucks?*

~*~

Danica smiled at Rick, then drew her shoulders up toward her ears. "I just don't know how to thank you. I mean, what you've done for me is... It's amazing. Kind. Generous. More than I—"

"Deserve?" Rick shook his head. "Nonsense. You spent a couple nights here, that's all."

"You got me a job—a real job. That's beyond incredible, it's—"

"Karma." Rick held out his arms, and Danica stepped into them. The hug made her feel even more grateful.

"Y'know," Rick said as he released her, "just 'cause you're moving to a new address doesn't mean we can't still see each other."

"You make it sound like we've been... you know... dating."

"We're friends, Dani." He grew a bit serious. "Can I call you that? I mean, is it okay?"

"Sure. Some of the guys in the Corps called me that." She felt wistful just thinking of them. "I don't know if I'll ever see any of them again. A couple are... gone."

Rick nodded. "Once you're settled in your new job, and you've got some time and money to play

Josh Langston

with, you could look 'em up."

"I don't know. They might not want to hear from me after the whole thing with Mundt. The trial. Me getting kicked out."

"Nonsense. That's more than likely a reason they *would* want to hear from you. I know I would."

"You're just saying that."

He laughed. "Actually, no. I'm not just saying that. I mean it. If it was me, I'd damn sure feel that way."

"Oh, right. 'Cause you've known me for what, forty-eight hours?"

"A bit longer than that but, yeah. So?"

"And you think you *really* know me, understand me?"

Rick's lips moved, but no words came out.

"What? What is it?" she asked.

"It's just— Well, no. You're right. I haven't known you long enough to completely understand you. And that's okay, I guess."

"C'mon, Rick. What are you trying to say?"

"Based on what I know about you now, and what I've seen and learned over the past couple of days... Well, damn it, I'd like to learn a helluva lot more."

She stared at him. "You're blushing!"

"No, I'm not!"

She touched his cheek. "I think it's cute."

"Criminy! I feel like a junior high school kid asking a girl out for the first time in my life. It's kinda weird. I'm not used to it."

"Is that what you're doing? Asking me to go out with you?"

He shrugged. And smiled. And shrugged again. "Yeah."

"You know I'm supposed to go to Las Vegas with Wynn, right?"

"You said he called you out of the blue."

"Yeah. So, maybe when I get back, we can talk about it."

"The trip?"

"No! About maybe going out."

"Oh. Okay."

She patted his hand. "Wynn's call took me by surprise."

Rick looked suspicious. "What d'you suppose he's got in mind?"

"I'm not sure. He said we'd only spend a little time in the casino wherever we're staying, and then he wants me to go with him to see a show."

"A Vegas show. Damn. Which one?"

"He wasn't sure. Said he'd arrange something when we got there." She twisted her lips. "Am I crazy to go with him?"

"I can't say. And I've never been to Vegas. Have you?"

"Nope. And what am I supposed to wear? I know you said I could help myself to your wife's clothing, but she must've been petite. Not much of her wardrobe fits me."

"Did you mention that to Wynn?"

"I did."

"And what did he say?"

She still couldn't believe it. "He told me we'd go shopping when we got there. He seemed pretty eager to get going, too. I just wish I knew why."

Chapter Eleven

"I take the invasion of my personal space very seriously." —Kid Rock

The more Wynn thought about the possibility of CeeJay invading his home, the more he worried about it. Based on the suggestions of Annabelle Knox, his late mentor, Wynn had spent a great deal of time and effort hiding the equipment she invented. CeeJay wouldn't find it. Though far from perfect, her gear made possible everything Wynn needed to do. Every single donation he'd made was done as a credit to her memory, even if they had to be done anonymously.

A more troubling issue kept nagging him. He finally admitted to himself that Annabelle's efforts to keep him safe when using her devices had been ineffective. The fall he had blamed on a rock in the path at the park was pure hogwash. He fell because he ignored the symptoms she had warned him about. He simply fainted. The only rock he encountered was the one on which he smacked his head and knocked himself out.

The cold weather and his lousy heart would have killed him if not for Roscoe and Danica. He owed

Josh Langston

it to the young woman to explain what had really happened.

But there's still time, and I have so much left to do. Explaining my health concerns will have to wait for now.

He knew he had to tell Jeffrey about his condition, too. But Jeffrey would tell Beatrix, and that would only push her harder to have him stashed away in a retirement home. Envisioning himself playing bingo with a room full of dementia patients terrified him. There wasn't anything wrong with *his* mind, though his store of patience had grown thin.

Danica could make it possible for him to keep going and continue doing what meant so much to him. But before he could share any of his secrets with her, he had to know beyond any doubt that he could trust her. The hurried background check he'd received contained nothing she hadn't already mentioned. A more detailed account of her service record was forthcoming, but he doubted it would change anything.

Only time and their relationship would provide the answers he sought. He prayed the time he had left would prove him right to trust her.

~*~

CeeJay figured waiting another day wouldn't

cut it. He needed the game score quick if he had any chance of placing a bet. Though sports betting wasn't legal in Georgia, he knew a couple of local bookies who would take his bet. This time, however, he intended to bet everything he had, and he didn't trust the locals to pay up. Instead, he'd have to make the two-plus hour drive to Murphy, North Carolina, and visit the Cherokee casino there.

It was time to move, time to get the information he needed, time to put a gun to old man Albright's head and scare it out of him.

CeeJay took his time driving to Albright's house, hoping the so-called professor would be in bed when he arrived. He knew exactly how he'd get in, and it had nothing to do with the window he'd jimmied before. By leaving it damaged and easy to find, he hoped Albright would focus on the windows in his house and ignore the doggie door.

CeeJay had purchased a makeshift silencer for his gun. Made from PVC tubing and other odds and ends, he'd been assured it would work "pretty good." It would have been nice if he'd been able to test it, but the guy who sold it to him said it would only be good for one round.

That would be enough to take care of Albright's dog if he caused any trouble. As an added bonus, the dead dog would provide proof that CeeJay wasn't screwing around. Either Albright spilled his guts, or CeeJay would spill them for him.

He parked several doors away from the old man's house, just as he'd done the night he broke in and shot the framed picture of the man's bride. A quick search of the house had turned up no evidence that a woman actually lived there. That was fine with him. If Albright's old lady still lived there, she'd likely be his age. Not exactly the tender sort of tail CeeJay liked.

Moving as quietly as possible, CeeJay crept toward a side of the house and climbed over the chain-link fence. Once inside, he had to step cautiously to avoid dog crap. He could have used the light built into his cell phone, but he didn't want to take a chance on alerting his target. Advancing in the dark didn't make avoiding the dog shit easy. *That's another reason not to own one of those fucking animals.*

Eventually he located the section of wall he'd seen the first time he broke in. As he suspected, Albright had lowered a slide inside the house which supposedly sealed the doggie door. During his first visit however, CeeJay damaged the plastic guides in which the barrier slid.

Flat on the cold ground in front of the canine passageway, he pushed through a flexible flap which served to keep bugs out. With his silenced gun in one hand, he pressed hard on the slide meant to keep unwanted critters out, but the damned thing didn't give; the guides held.

CeeJay set the gun down and pushed with both hands until the heavy plastic door finally popped free and clattered on the hardwood floor inside the house.

He whispered a curse when he heard a dog bark. There was no time to lose. Thankful he hadn't gained much weight since his teens, CeeJay rolled on his side and began to worm his way through the tight opening. He kept the gun in front of himself as he went, confident that if the dog showed up, he'd be close enough to shoot without having to aim.

Additional noise from inside the house caused him to freeze with one shoulder partially through to the other side.

According to the brunette babe behind the desk outside of McComb's office, the CEO was out of town and not taking calls. Braden didn't believe her but couldn't do anything about it. And, since he no longer had a desk anywhere in the building, he went home. There he accessed his GE&M account on a laptop, issued a sell order for one of his better-performing stocks, and had the funds sent electronically to his checking account.

On his way to meet Shaughnessy, Braden withdrew twenty-five hundred dollars from a branch of his bank then moved on. He soon arrived at a small, franchise restaurant still crowded with customers gobbling down late breakfasts. The place sported more guests than seats. The smell of waffles, eggs, and grits permeated the air and reminded him he hadn't eaten yet.

I'll get something later.

Braden scanned those already seated and spied a slight, male figure with olive skin and straight, jet-black hair sitting at a corner table. When he leaned back, Braden saw a peculiar logo on the man's sweatshirt: an angry, cartoon whooping crane brandishing a hockey stick.

That's gotta be him.

Trying to appear casual, Braden meandered through the tables toward the occupant in the corner. "Shaughnessy?"

"Yeah." The man pointed to a chair opposite his own. "Sit," he said. "Bring my money?"

"Of course. But it stays in my pocket 'til you tell me why I should give you a dime."

"I told you what I get for a hack and cough."

Braden frowned at him. "That makes about as much sense as you calling yourself Shaughnessy."

"My real name's Raj."

"Patel, right? Or Singh. Or no. Wait. It's—"

"Gupta."

That figures. "So, you're not Irish."

"Do I look fucking Irish?"

Braden closed his eyes and shook his head.

"Okay," Gupta said. "Here's the deal: the hack and cough." He reached into his pocket, pulled out a small metal device, and held it above the table.

"What's that?" Braden asked.

"It's a tracker. You need to attach it to whatever vehicle your subject drives."

Braden stared at the matchbook-sized mechanism. "Attach it how?"

"It's magnetic, dumbass. Stick it inside a wheel well, or crawl under the car and stick it to something down there. It doesn't matter. Just put it somewhere the driver won't see it."

"Okay, then what?"

"I track the vehicle, figure out where your target lives—"

Braden waved him to silence. "I already know his address. It's—"

"Lemme finish."

"Okay."

"The tracker lets me know where he is *and* whether he's home or not. That makes it easier to know when to break in, hack his computer, and install a listening device."

It was beginning to make sense. "That's the hack part, right?"

"You're a fucking genius," Gupta muttered. "Can I go on now?"

"Yeah, sure. Sorry."

"I'll monitor everything he does online for a couple days, and I'll record any conversations he has. Then we'll meet up again, and I'll give you a thumb drive with everything on it—recordings, emails, all the websites he uses, passwords, whatever."

Braden couldn't help but smile. "So, the thumb drive is the cough."

Gupta exhaled what sounded like a very weary, "Yeah."

When Braden reached for the tracker, Gupta pulled it away. "Half up front, remember?"

"Right. Sorry." Braden pulled the bank withdrawal envelope from his pocket and handed it over.

Gupta counted the cash before giving him the tracker.

"Where and when do we meet next time?" Braden asked.

"Here. In three or four days," Gupta said, "unless something goes wrong."

"Like what?"

"I dunno! Like maybe he goes on vacation or gets run over by a fucking dump truck. I don't have a crystal ball. I'll call you when I'm ready. Then we can meet back here. Okay?"

"Right. I get it," Braden said. "No pro-blay-mo."

"I'm Pakastani, you moron. The only Spanish words I know are taco and tequila."

Braden dearly wanted the last word, but Gupta/Shaughnessy was already headed toward the door. He didn't appear interested in looking back.

Danica was already awake when Roscoe barked. Flat on her back, she'd been staring at the dark ceiling and worrying about the upcoming trip to Las Vegas, but Roscoe's alarm drove her quickly from the bed. The dog rarely barked at Rick's house.

With her eyes adjusted to the dark, she moved toward the barking dog, wondering how long Wynn would take to join her. She paused only a moment at the thought she wore nothing but panties and a thin T-shirt. *Can't worry about that now.* Roscoe's noisy efforts to scratch his way into Wynn's next-door office took priority.

If Wynn hasn't already seen a half-dressed woman in seventy-something years, he's about to.

She pushed the door open and bent low as Roscoe raced, snarling into the room.

Someone inside, on the floor, cursed, and she heard a muffled gunshot. Praying Roscoe hadn't been hurt, Danica darted into the dim room, dodged around Wynn's paper-strewn desk and spotted the intruder attempting to crawl through Roscoe's pet door. It was a tight squeeze, but the trespasser had progressed and was nearly halfway through.

Roscoe appeared unhurt and continued to bark which kept the intruder's attention. The man's back was to the dog, and he struggled to turn within the narrow opening, presumably to take another shot.

Danica climbed up on Wynn's desk, trying not to make a sound or send any of his stupid papers flying. She took a single balanced step, then jumped and hit the floor with one bare foot; the other landed squarely on the intruder's wrist.

He yelled, and his gun went off again; this time it sounded much louder.

Wynn finally arrived and flipped on the overhead light. Danica ignored him and kicked the man on the floor in the head. He appeared stunned.

"Crap!" Wynn exclaimed. "It's CeeJay."

"We've got to get his gun," Danica said, her voice stern. Wynn moved way too slowly to suit her, so she kicked the intruder's head a second time.

Damn, that hurts! She wanted to rub her sore foot but knew she couldn't take it off the man on the floor even as he began to move once again.

Finally, Wynn moved in and stomped on CeeJay's gun hand. He released the weapon, then screamed when Roscoe bit him.

"Stop! Stop! I give!" he cried. "Let me up, damn it."

Danica wasn't having it. "Get me a frypan," she yelled over CeeJay's ongoing protests.

Wynn looked puzzled. "What for?"

"I'll bash his head with it until he quits moving!"

"But that's—"

"Forget it," she groused and reached for a

stout coffee mug on the desk. She waved it in CeeJay's face. "You move one goddam inch after I get off your hand, and I'll beat you to death. Understand?"

"Yeah, yeah, whatever. Just call off the damn dog."

Wynn grabbed Roscoe's collar and dragged him a few feet away. The dog continued to snarl and lunge.

"Lemme up, will ya? I won't do nuthin'," CeeJay whined.

"Not a chance, asshole." Danica rubbed her sore foot with her free hand. She smiled at Wynn and the dog. "He's something, isn't he?"

"Oh, indeed he is," Wynn said. "Keep an eye on that jerk while I call the police."

"Got it," Danica replied, threatening CeeJay once again with the mug. "Don't move, or it's me, the mug, and the dog."

CeeJay stared straight up at her and gave her a smarmy smile. "Nice outfit," he muttered. "Is that a thong?"

Danica kicked him again but used her heel. "Hey, Wynn!" she called. "How 'bout bringing me a bathrobe or a beach towel when you get off the phone?"

Chapter Twelve

"Dignity does not consist in possessing honors, but in deserving them." —Aristotle

Jeffrey Albright sat at the computer in his half of the couple's second bedroom and stared at the screen in dismay. An email from the CEO of the company he worked for had announced a "change of direction" in their efforts to improve customer service. The solution, according to an unnamed but "highly respected research firm" they hired, was to improve response time by using customer service call centers overseas. According to the CEO, the move would significantly reduce overhead and generate more goodwill with their clients.

In other words, Jeffrey—who was mere months away from qualifying for the company's promised retirement program—would shortly be unemployed. Unless, of course, he wanted to transfer to the Black Hole of Calcutta, at his own expense, and resume the drudgery he had suffered for nearly ten years.

He checked the time. Two hours remained before he had to show up for his mid-day shift. That gave him a substantial chunk of the morning free so long as Beatrix hadn't planned something stupid to occupy his time. Just the thought of having to tell her he'd soon be out of a job put a tremor in his spine.

Maybe Dad can bail me out this time. He's rich, after all. And if he needs an employee, why not me? Why that damned redhead? I'm family, for cryin' out loud! Family should come first, shouldn't it?

He sat back in his chair and switched off the computer.

It's high time Dad and I had a chat. I can't charge his motor or warm his sheets the way little Miss Winter Sunshine can, but damn it; he owes me. He needs me, and I need him.

Jeffrey took care not to make any noise as he gathered his wallet and car keys from the kitchen counter before tiptoeing outside. Once behind the wheel, he drove straight to Wynn's house, fully prepared to make his demands.

~*~

Braden had but one mission that morning: find Wynn Albright's car and attach the tracker to it he'd gotten from Gupta, the phony Irishman. That would be fairly easy, he thought, and since Albright was retired, Braden decided he could wait until after rush hour to drive to the man's house.

Rather than stay at home, he treated himself to breakfast out. Georgia winters were notoriously fickle, freezing one day and pleasant the next. Braden needed his hat, coat, and gloves that morning, but by lunchtime he could wear a sweater and go golfing, a luxury he rarely indulged in despite being a modestly good player.

Once I've claimed my throne in the GE&M empire, I can play the finest courses in town. A sudden golf-oriented thought made him pause. *I could join Augusta National! Hell, all you need is a butt load of money, and I'll definitely have that.*

Then he remembered hearing that membership was by invitation only.

Damn socialites!

He soon brightened. *I could get Gupta to do a hack and cough on a current member, find some dirt, and use it to blackmail him into giving me an invitation. Why the hell not? I oughta get* some *benefits from joining the dark side.*

Feeling better about his future prospects, Braden finished eating and drove by Wynn Albright's suburban home. There he saw the same vehicle he'd seen the day he tried to con him with his phony Client of the Year scheme. The damage to the car's bumper remained unrepaired.

Shaking his head, Braden drove a short distance away, parked, and crept back to Albright's house. Ducking low, he got close to the car, reached past the front right tire, and held the tracker next to the wheel well. With a barely audible click, a magnet on the device pulled it from his fingers and held it firmly in place.

Braden kept low and left the property behind. He smiled, knowing Gupta's hack would soon be underway. All he needed to do at that point was wait for the temperature to rise and break out his golf clubs.

Wynn mentally reviewed events of the pre-dawn hours. The police had arrived quickly enough after Wynn called, but they insisted on discussing the break-in even after they'd loaded CeeJay into a police cruiser and taken him away. It was just as well; he and Danica remained too keyed up to return to their beds. Instead, Wynn brewed coffee which they shared with a cop, a detective, and someone they'd brought along with a camera.

Wynn explained that CeeJay was a friend of a former worker, but he said nothing about sports betting. CeeJay had raised hell about the issue, but Wynn pled ignorance.

Eventually all the questions had been answered; all the statements had been recorded, and all the photos had been taken. The authorities then left. The coffee was gone, too, and Danica went back into her room and closed the door.

Wynn managed a few hours of fitful sleep, but gave up when the sun rose. He'd been waiting for Danica ever since. He planned to make her a nice thank-you breakfast, but the hours passed, and a lunch seemed more likely.

As Wynn laid out cold cuts, bakery bread, and assorted condiments for the meal, Roscoe announced a visitor, and Jeffrey entered the house. He walked through the living room, marched into the kitchen, sat down at the table, and announced, "We need to talk."

Wynn stared at his son and tried not to look as disappointed as he felt. What he had to say to Danica was far more important. "Oh?" he managed.

"I got some crappy news this morning. My job's been eliminated."

"Is that your way of saying you got fired?"

Jeffrey looked genuinely offended. "No, 'course not. The company's moving my department, customer service, to Bangladesh or Bombay or some other godforsaken place where they can get people to work for slave wages."

"I'm sorry to hear it."

"That's it? You're sorry to hear it?"

"Well, yes. Would you rather see me bare my chest and wail? Throw myself on the floor, roll around, and scream at the unfairness of it all? Come on. Stuff like this happens all the time."

"Not to me, it doesn't," Jeffrey said, looking distinctly pouty.

"Have you told Beatrix yet?"

"Are you kidding? Hell no."

"It might be a good idea to line something else up before you do."

"Like what? I'm fifty-four years old! Who's gonna hire me at my age?"

Wynn took a moment before saying anything. "I'm sure there are plenty of jobs going begging right now. You've got skills, and you're in good health."

"Here's what I think," Jeffrey said. "Instead of

hiring some redheaded bimbo off the street, you oughta give that job to me. Family comes first, doesn't it?" His face slipped into a smirk. "Or maybe she provides services you'd rather not talk about? How is she in bed?"

Before Wynn could respond, verbally or with a slap to his son's face, Danica entered the kitchen. "What's going on? I could hear you two a mile away."

"My son just informed me that he's been surplussed." Wynn turned away from her and scowled his resentment at Jeffrey.

Danica appeared not to understand.

"My job's been cancelled," Jeffrey said. "The company found people who'd work longer hours for less money. So, basically, I'm screwed."

"What're you going to do?" she asked.

"Dad and I were just discussing that."

"And," said Wynn, "we'll have to finish that up later. Right now, Danica and I have matters to discuss."

"Like what?" he asked. "Like why she gets to sleep late after her first day on the job?"

"That's enough," growled Wynn.

Danica looked surprised. "You didn't tell him?"

Jeffrey rolled his head back and stared at the ceiling. "Oh, for the love of God! Please tell me you two didn't get married."

Wynn burst out laughing.

"What have you been smoking?" Danica asked with a smile. "Whatever it is, I could probably use some."

"We had a break-in last night," Wynn said as he wiped mirthful tears from his eyes. "Some idiot tried to crawl through the doggie door. Danica kicked the crap out of him. Quite literally."

"Did he get anything?"

"A headache," Wynn said, chuckling.

"And Roscoe left a few toothmarks in him," added Danica.

As Jeffrey was about to say something, Wynn waved him to silence. "Like I said, Danica and I have some important things to talk about. You and I can get together later and discuss your future. You're bound to get a severance package which should keep you solvent until you find a new position somewhere. And besides, you know I won't let you and Bea starve."

Though he looked ready to protest, Jeffrey slumped his shoulders as if defeated. "Yeah, sure. Fine. We'll talk later. It's just... Aw screw it." He turned and left without another word.

While Danica helped herself to a cup of coffee, Wynn sorted his thoughts. Jeffrey's insinuation had rattled him, but he shoved those feelings aside. As he'd promised, they would talk about it later. For now, he had to focus on Danica.

When she sat down across the table from him, he began. "I've got good news and bad."

"Start with the bad," she said with a hint of suspicion. "That way I can look forward to the good part."

"The bad is simply this: you don't have a valid driver's license, a passport, or any other ID with your photo on it. Correct?"

She nodded her agreement, and he continued. "Until we get your license reissued, you aren't going to be able to board an airplane."

"And that," she said, looking relieved, "means I won't be going with you to Las Vegas."

"I'm afraid so. I promised to take you to one of those big, fancy stage shows, but that'll have to go on the back burner. At least until the state of Georgia replaces your license and you can once again travel by air. There's no way I'd want to drive there."

"I'm actually kinda glad," she said. "I haven't got anything nice to wear, and I just started my job. I haven't earned anything."

He laughed. "Seriously? You say that after what you did last night?"

She shook her head as if it was nothing.

"The job is yours. You definitely earned it last night," he assured her. "As for your wardrobe, we'll get that sorted starting tomorrow. And I definitely want to get you up to speed on your business duties, too. So, touch up your coffee and have a bite to eat. When you're finished, come see me in my office."

"Aren't you going to join me?" she asked.

"My son's unexpected arrival..." His voice trailed off, and he exhaled in frustration. "Please forgive me. My appetite seems to have disappeared. Take your time and join me when you can."

He walked down the short hallway to his office. The room sat in even greater disarray than usual. That was hardly surprising in light of the upheaval the previous night. After straightening up the bigger messes and putting furniture and scattered paperwork back where it all belonged, he approached the wall behind which he'd hidden Annabelle Knox's creation.

The space had formerly served as a closet, but Wynn had turned it into a small, concealed room. A shallow bookcase served as the door that could only be unlocked using a paddle switch located behind a painting on the opposite wall.

After feeling behind that artwork and pressing the switch, Wynn recrossed the room as the bookcase slid aside. He looked down at the machine hidden in the tiny room. A small light on top of the boxy apparatus normally blinked red, but it had gone off.

He put his hand on the device, expecting to feel a bit of vibration, something he'd done a thousand times. This time he felt nothing at all.

The machine felt cold and dead.

And Wynn began to feel the same way.

Chapter Thirteen

"It seems to be a law of nature, inflexible and inexorable, that those who will not risk cannot win." —John Paul Jones

Danica inspected herself in a mirror in the guest bathroom of Wynn's house and pronounced herself "okay." Never one to obsess about her looks, Danica had scant knowledge of, or interest in, fashion trends. They simply didn't mean anything to her.

Out of respect for Rick, however, she wanted to look nice since he was taking her out for dinner. Wynn's generosity had made her attractive appearance a reality. They'd spent some time clothes shopping, and Wynn insisted she consult the shop's salesperson, a girl who appeared to be in her teens.

Danica tried on several outfits while the girl made pointed comments for and against each selection. Wynn smiled at Danica's reluctance to try things on, especially those suggested by the girl. By the end of the day, however, Danica had become the proud owner of a half dozen new outfits, one of which she'd actually put together herself.

Surprisingly, she had agreed with the clerk on one particular item of apparel. Danica liked the look and feel of leggings and yoga pants. She even ware a pair back to the house.

The following morning Wynn insisted that she do a "Spa Day," something she'd never done before. When she protested, he said it was merely a thank you for the way she'd handled their doggie door intruder. He departed before she returned but left a note explaining he'd taken an earlier flight to Florida to place a bet on the Super Bowl.

Now, minutes away from her date with Rick, Danica felt uncomfortable. Her skirt suddenly seemed too short; her trendy leggings looked way too flashy, and her blouse didn't button nearly high enough. She shook her head at her image in the mirror. "I should've just worn my stupid fatigues."

Rick's so nice, he probably wouldn't say a word if I did wear the damned things, even as nasty as they are now. Living in 'em probably wasn't very smart.

"But all that's in the past," she told Roscoe, who sat at her feet. "No more bad choices. No more being stupid. I know better now, and thank God,

Wynn Albright's given me a chance to make something of myself. I just wish I had a better idea what that's going to be."

Roscoe looked up at her with soulful eyes, just like her beloved Foster's. "I won't stay out late," she said, gently stroking his chin. "Your daddy's in Florida somewhere, trying to win a bet on a football game. He'll be back in a day or so. It all depends on the flights. But don't worry, my handsome boy, I'll be here to keep you company. Okay?"

Rather than reply, Roscoe turned and trotted out of the room.

Danica stressed about Wynn traveling to a casino just so he could make a big wager. Gambling had never been a part of her life, and she couldn't understand Wynn's desire to risk money. His desire eclipsed his expressed need for a bodyguard. He hadn't shared any details of his plan with her, and she prayed whatever he was up to was legitimate.

The guy who tried to sneak into the house through the doggie door made it very clear what he thought about it. He had shouted as the cops dragged him away that Wynn was the "real crook," and that he'd somehow managed to fix the Super Bowl.

She figured the last blow to his head must have scrambled his brains, assuming he had any. *Wynn fix a professional football game? The biggest one of the year? Preposterous.*

A knock on the front door helped her clear the questions from her mind. She put on a happy smile, tugged at the hem of her skirt, walked to the door, and opened it.

Rick Johanson greeted her with flowers and a grin that seemed electric. Dressed in khaki slacks and a navy blazer, his white shirt looked good against his tanned skin. He'd even worn a tie.

"For you, m'lady," he said, bowing as he proffered a corsage. When he straightened up he added, "You look absolutely stunning."

"Aw," she said, "thank you," feeling a blush in her cheeks.

He held up the tiny bouquet. "May I pin it on?"

She blushed even harder as he attached the arrangement to her blouse. "This is a first for me. I've never worn a corsage before. I feel like this is prom night!"

"I get it," he said. "I kinda feel the same way." He stepped back as if to get a better look at her and shook his head. "The flowers don't do you justice."

His flattery left her momentarily speechless, then he asked, "Are you hungry?"

"Nope. Starved," she said.

~*~

For two full days, Braden Daley had done his best to avoid stressing out over the silence from Gupta. Even though the dark little man had told him it would take some time to do the "hack and cough" Braden had purchased, he remained impatient.

Braden's review of Wynn Albright's GE&M account had revealed only one transaction, but it was hefty. He'd withdrawn an even million dollars from his investment account and had it transferred electronically to his checking account. Such transactions were not all that rare among high rollers, but it seemed odd for Albright, who usually only withdrew large amounts after selling price-bloated shares of common stock. This time, there had been no such exchange.

He finally gave in and dialed Gupta's number, then sat through a lengthy delay waiting for him to answer. Rather than go to voice mail, the phone just kept ringing.

"What d'you want?" Gupta said when he finally answered.

"I want to know what you've learned about Albright!"

"You don't wanna wait for the thumb drive? I'm still recording stuff from inside the house. Some of it's interesting."

"Like what?" Braden asked.

Gupta laughed. "Can't say. Job's not done."

"I can't wait any longer," Braden said. "I need something to go on. Now!"

"Fine. No problem. Just pay me the rest of my fee. I don't do discounts."

"Good. Can I meet you where we met before? In Buckhead?" Braden glanced at his watch. "Gimme half an hour."

"You want me to drop what I'm doing and drive across town right now?"

"Yeah."

"The thumb drive isn't ready."

Braden ground his teeth. "Can you tell me just one thing?"

"Maybe," Gupta said. "It depends."

"Did Albright do anything with any of his brokerage accounts?"

The phony Irishman remained silent for a moment. "How 'bout I tell you that when we meet? *After* you pay me."

Braden sighed in resignation. "All right. I'll see you in a half hour."

Though midday traffic in Atlanta wasn't quite as bad as rush hour, it still sucked, especially the drive down Peachtree Street from midtown to Buckhead. Lunch hour boosted traffic nearly as much as the proverbial five o'clock whistle.

Gupta was nowhere in sight when Braden arrived at the crowded restaurant, so he claimed the lone, empty table near the entrance and waited. Several customers looking for a place to sit and eat eyed him with disgust when he refused to share his space. Eventually, Gupta strolled in.

Braden waved, and the little man took a seat across from him. He cleared his throat and spoke without a greeting, "Like I said on the phone, the thumb drive isn't ready."

"You also said you heard some interesting stuff. Like what? Anything about investments?"

"Money?"

Braden handed him the remaining cash from his earlier stock sale. "Now spill it."

Gupta rubbed his dark, stubbly chin. "Frankly, I think your man Albright is a loser. When he's at home, and he's not arguing with his wife, he spends his time watching porn and playing solitaire. If he's dealing in stocks and bonds or hobnobbing with the rich and powerful, he sure as hell ain't doing it at home."

"Where else could he have gone to connect with a broker?"

"On his cell phone, maybe. But I don't recall him making any calls. Oh, except one. He ordered a pizza. I remember 'cause his wife got all pissy about it." Gupta raised his voice an octave and mimicked her, "'You never order what I want, Jeffrey. Blah, blah, blah.'"

Braden stared at him. "She called him *Jeffrey?*"

"Yeah. So?"

"That's not his name! You were supposed to do your scratch and sniff, or whatever the hell you called it, on Wynn Albright. *Wynn*, damn it, not Jeffrey!"

"Well, way to go, dumbass." Gupta laughed. "Maybe you shoulda checked to see whose car you put the fucking tracker on."

~*~

Wynn's flight to Las Vegas and his ride to the hotel and casino complex went off without a hitch. The rooms he booked met all his needs and then some. If Danica had been able to travel with him, it would have been perfect. When returning the empty room to the hotel's inventory, he connected with the concierge and secured a car and driver for the casino rounds he would soon make.

Done with the mundane, his thoughts returned to what he discovered when inspecting Annabelle Knox's amazing device. One of the bullets CeeJay fired during his ill-fated attempt to break in had destroyed a delicate component and caused a leak in the containment system. Wynn had serious doubts about his ability to make the repairs.

For two years, the machine faithfully provided a limited amount of data from the near future. Annabelle said there was a distinct correlation between the size of the data transferred and the date from which it came. The more data was transmitted, the closer its origination to the present.

In the beginning, they had focused on the stock market. That met with limited success because they moved too much data, and the time window amounted to roughly three months. That caught the biggest short-term rises and falls, but the profits were less than spectacular. That's when Wynn suggested they delve into sporting events and lottos.

By limiting the stock data to just the biggest winners and losers, they were also able to chart the winners in a host of big-time sporting events around the world.

The demise of Annabelle's machine left Wynn with roughly a month of data. There would be plenty of things to bet on, but the end of the data stream seemed definite. The data from the future that he had was likely all he would ever have.

Unless he could somehow repair the device, he would no longer have a reason to keep it nearby. If the machine were removed, he would get a break from its toxic side effects. He'd still be sick, but he'd likely live a bit longer.

It was an issue he absolutely had to discuss with Danica. At some point, anyway.

The more Jeffrey thought about it, the more his anger grew. His father's disregard for him spelled betrayal in the clearest possible terms. Jeffrey wanted to strike back; he just didn't know how.

And, of course, Beatrix was no help at all. He still hadn't summoned enough courage to tell her about his lost job. Telling her would only generate another round of criticism. He didn't need that. He never had. He never wanted to hear it again.

Why should I have to tell her anything at all? What's she done for me lately other than complain?

And suddenly, he had an inspiration.

There's more than one female standing in the way of my happiness. It's not just Beatrix; there's also Danica—Dad's little sleep-in... What? Helper? That's a laugh. She's a whore, a homeless hooker. There's no doubt about it.

But what if I could get rid of them both? How could I eliminate Beatrix and make it look like Danica did it?

The wheels in his brain began to spin faster than ever.

Chapter Fourteen

"Love is a friendship set to music." —Joseph Campbell

Danica felt a bit more comfortable riding shotgun in Rick's Jeep. Her coat was short but comfortable, and her yoga pants kept her legs warm under her short skirt. Her cheeks had cooled as her blush faded, and she was determined to mask her wardrobe irritation. She fiddled with the corsage Rick gave her while her thoughts wandered.

Stupid sales clerk! I should've realized she was trying to dress me like some horny teenager. I need to have my head examined. I still can't believe the way Rick looked at me when I opened the door. I might as well have been naked. And God knows, I felt that way.

"By the way," Rick said, his voice hesitant, "I knew the day we met that you were... attractive, good-looking. But tonight..." He paused and took a deep breath. "Tonight, you look absolutely stunning."

Danica stared up at the roof of the car. "Aw, c'mon, Rick. That's not—"

"I'm serious! You look amazing."

"You're killin' me, Rick!"

He smiled at her. "It's okay to accept a compliment, y'know."

"I know; I know. It's just... I'm not exactly used to getting them."

"I can fix that!" he said.

"Just drive. Okay? I'm hungry."

"Yessum. Got it. No more compliments, no matter what."

She punched his upper arm ever so lightly. "That's not what I meant!"

He snickered. "Right. It's a timing thing. I'll get it figured out eventually."

They rode in silence for a while, and Danica looked at the dark, wintery scenery. Spring couldn't come soon enough. She occasionally glanced at Rick and rolled the word "friend" around in her head. He *was* a friend, the only new one she had since she left the service.

Could he be more than a friend? He looks

younger than I thought he was at first. 'Course, he's spiffed himself up a bit since that day in the park. Haircut. Shave. Nice clothes. I wonder….

She focused on him directly. "Mind if I ask you a question?"

"Fire away. I have very few secrets."

"How old are you?"

He glanced briefly her way, a sly look creeping across his face. "You want the truth?"

"Of course!"

"How old would you like me to be?"

The question took her by surprise. "I… Uh…."

"Lemme explain," he said. "There's a theory about the age thing."

"Age thing?"

"Yeah. It got started a long time ago, maybe a hundred or a hundred and fifty years back."

Danica shook her head. "I don't…."

"Bear with me. Some guy way back when wrote a book or a pamphlet or something that supposedly spelled out the proper ages for a husband and wife. He had a formula, and some people swore by it. Wanna hear it?"

She squinted at him, unsure of where he was

headed. "I guess so."

He lowered his voice and adopted something like an official tone. "The proper age for a wife, according to this dead guy whose name I probably never heard, is half her husband's age plus seven years."

Danica swallowed hard. "Are you *proposing* to me?"

"No, of course not." Rick chuckled. "At least, not yet. It might depend on the formula."

"Well," said Danica, "I'm twenty-five."

He kept smiling. "Oh ho! That's very interesting."

"How so?"

"I just turned thirty-six."

Danica quickly did the math in her head. *Oh, my God!*

Rick waved his hand as if to dismiss the idea as nonsense. "I can't believe anyone really believes in that sorta stuff anymore."

"It is interesting, though," she said. "I mean, we hear all the time about guys who marry younger women."

"That's true."

Desperately needing to change the subject, Danica said, "Can I ask you another question?"

"Sure. Are you wondering what's the best month to get married?"

"Actually, no. I was wondering if you could find a place to stop so I can use a restroom."

Wynn's driver in Las Vegas was a pleasant, older man named Sanchez who had a heavy Spanish accent. He maintained a steady dialog as he drove down the strip, stopping at each of the casinos Wynn wanted to visit—the ten biggest. Sanchez would wait patiently while Wynn went into each of them and placed his Super Bowl bet.

It had been a while since Wynn had been to the gaming paradise. This time the weather was pleasant; the last time he'd visited in the summer, and the heat nearly wiped him out.

Now, it wasn't the heat that made him miserable. It was the need to keep moving and keep making the same wager over and over. Even knowing that he couldn't lose, that the score had been preordained, didn't make the process any easier.

Some casinos took his bet without quibbling; others took a while longer before ultimately accepting his terms. He made the wager too compelling to refuse. He wasn't just betting that the Chiefs would defeat the 49ers. He bet they would do it in overtime, something that had only happened once in the fifty-two previous matchups.

He got odds of ten-to-one and bet a hundred thousand dollars at each of the ten casinos. He could have approached the other 165 of them, but two things stopped him: he had depleted his limited energy supply, much as he had the last time he'd walked Roscoe in the park. He also ran out of the seed money he'd taken from his GE&M account.

By the time he made his last bet, he could not get out of his seat. A casino security guard had to put him in a wheelchair and trundle him out to Sanchez waiting in his car. When he reached his hotel, Sanchez hurried inside to get assistance.

Somehow, Wynn managed to talk the staff out of sending him to the Emergency Room at nearby Sunrise Hospital and Medical Center. "I need food and rest," he told them. "That's all. It's happened before." He didn't mention that his malady had a distinct cause and no cure. He went to bed as soon as they wheeled him into his room.

He didn't need to watch the game. It was the easiest ten million dollar haul he'd ever made. Though bone weary and knowing he would soon be unable to repeat the challenge on his own, he looked forward to marshalling Danica through it as soon as she could travel. That couldn't come soon enough, and he had already planned a slightly modified procedure for the upcoming NCAA men's and women's basketball tournaments.

Annabelle, my dear, I hope you're proud of me. There's still a lot of good we can do.

~*~

"Jeffrey, I'm disappointed in you."

Beatrix spoke from her perch on the sofa in front of the TV when he entered their living room. He'd planned to go straight to his desk in the second bedroom without having a conversation. That plan died a speedy death.

He stopped in front of her and asked, "What have I done now?"

"It's not what you've done. It's what you *haven't* done."

Having ignored most of what she'd said to him that morning, he wasn't surprised that he'd failed to do something she requested. As usual, he played dumb. "I don't understand."

"It's my birthday in two weeks, and you haven't asked me what I want. I find that a little rude, don't you?"

Jeffrey resisted the temptation to grind his teeth. "It was an oversight, and I'm sorry. Please, oh please, tell me what you want for your birthday." He clasped his hands at his chest as if pleading.

"Now you really are being rude. Birthdays are important, to most people anyway. Why can't you be nice?"

"Once again, I apologize. I've got a lot on my mind." *A job, for one thing, and I still haven't figured out how I'm going to kill you and blame your death on daddy's crimson call girl.*

"Well," she continued, "I don't want to make a big deal out of it, but I wanted to remind you in case you forgot."

"Right. Thanks. Why don't you whip up a list for me? That way I can pick something you like, but you won't know exactly what you're getting."

"Good idea," she said. "I'll start on it right after my soaps this afternoon."

He started walking once again and reached the bedroom door when she called out, "Oh! One more thing."

"What?"

"I need you to zip up to the grocery store and get us something for dinner."

"Like what?" he asked.

"I don't care. You choose; you know what you're allergic to. Whatever. Just get something I like."

"My choice, eh?"

"Yeah. Surprise me."

How 'bout a knife to the heart, or a yummy glass of antifreeze? I've heard it's pretty sweet going down. And you're only miserable for a day before you die.

~*~

"Okay, my dear. We've arrived. Welcome to the Pee and Petrol."

Danica looked at Rick in surprise. "You're kidding, right?"

"Right. I just thought P and P was more à propos than Gas and Go. That's so... General. Too non-specific. Sort of—"

"I'll be back in a jiffy," Danica said, unwilling to wait for Rick to dish up something even more silly. Besides, she was focused on her very immediate needs.

"Excellent," Rick said. "I'll gas up the limo."

A Jeep limo. Right. Go easy, Ricky.

The convenience store, while far from new,

appeared neat and clean. A slender young woman stood behind a wide counter displaying a variety of candies and small household items. Country music played from a hidden speaker; the tune was "Chicken Fried" by the Zac Brown Band, Danica's absolute favorite.

Her needs overwhelmed her desire to listen to the music, and she hurried to the lady's room. There she found two stalls, one of which housed an intolerable stench. She held her breath and used the other one.

When finished, she went to the sink to wash up and heard a loud, male voice from the main area. "Open the fucking cash drawer. Now, bitch!"

A hurried look around revealed nothing useful as a weapon. She settled for a toilet bowl plunger standing just inside stall number two. Moving as quietly as possible, she cracked open the bathroom door and peeked out.

Standing in front of the broad sales counter, a man nervously shifted his weight from one foot to the other while waving what appeared to be a cheap, .25 caliber handgun. Danica could barely see the sales clerk, who had withdrawn as far from the thief as possible.

"Open it now, God damn it!"

"There's almost no money in there," the girl protested.

"I don't give a shit. Open it!"

Danica slipped through the door, dropped low, and crept down an aisle that sheltered her from the gunman's view. She estimated the gap at the end of the aisle to be no more than eight feet, a distance she could cross easily, provided the dirtbag continued to look away. A .25 caliber round might not always be lethal, but it would always hurt like hell.

Sneaking a look past a stack of cereal boxes, Danica watched as the clerk inched toward the man and tentatively stretched one arm toward the sales screen above the register. The poor kid was clearly on the verge of panic. *Take your time, honey. Help's on the way.*

"Hurry, damn it!" the thief growled. "I don't have all fucking night."

The girl touched something on the screen and retreated instantly when the cash drawer dinged open.

Danica waited until the man crawled out on the counter, stretching as he probed the cash drawer with his free hand. "Where's all the goddam money?" he yelled.

"I told you there wasn't much," the girl said,

the tremor in her voice making her words hard to understand. "Most people use credit cards."

When the crook turned once again toward the cash drawer, Danica raced from hiding and jammed the cup end of the plunger over the back of the man's skull. Using both hands, she slammed his head into the counter.

It was enough to make him drop his weapon, but not enough to satisfy her. She rammed his face into the countertop repeatedly until he stopped moving. He continued to breathe, not that she cared.

Danica looked at the clerk standing as still as a statue. Her eyes were open wide, and she cradled herself in a shivery self-embrace.

"You're okay," Danica said, finally noticing that she, too, was trembling. "Now, please pop outside and look for a guy beside a Jeep. Tell him I need him. Then dial 9-1-1 and get the cops. Hurry!"

The clerk complied, and moments later, a frantic Ranger Rick burst into the store with a shotgun. The clerk trundled in behind him. "You okay?" he asked as he quickly surveyed the scene.

"Yeah," Danica said, as the adrenaline in her system slowly subsided.

Rick stepped closer and put his arm around her. It felt better than she could have imagined.

"You're shaking," he said, stating the all-too-obvious.

She nodded in agreement, then let her head drop to his shoulder.

"Looks like I need to get you another corsage," he said.

"Huh?" She looked down at the damaged flowers and frowned. "Guess I kinda smushed it. I'm sorry."

He laughed. "Don't be silly. You're a hero. Or a heroine. Can we still use that word nowadays?"

Before she could answer, the sound of approaching police sirens had them looking toward the door. Rick pressed the barrel of his shotgun against the robber's back. When he groaned and began to move, Rick bore down on the weapon and told him to stay still.

Danica walked to the sales clerk and gave her a hug. The girl's tears flowed freely.

Two police officers soon entered the building. When they ordered Rick to drop his weapon, he complied immediately.

One of the officers handcuffed the robber while the other questioned Danica and Rick. His attention was squarely on the park ranger.

"Tell me what happened," the cop said.

"Don't look at me." Rick nodded at Danica. "She's the one who knocked the creep out."

"With the shotgun?" he asked.

Danica shook her head and pointed at the toilet bowl plunger she'd left on the floor. "With that."

The cop appeared shocked. "You went after him with a plunger?"

She smiled for the first time since she entered the store. "Why not? The guy's obviously a shithead."

Chapter Fifteen
"We are moving rapidly into a world in which the spying machinery is built into every object we encounter." —Howard Rheingold

Braden Daley looked at the all-caps text message on his phone:

UPDATE 10:45 AM TODAY

He didn't recognize the number of the phone which sent it, but he had little doubt who wanted a progress report. Between muttering at the injustice and cursing the always heavy weekday traffic, Braden figured he could make it to the offices of GE&M just in time.

Naturally, the parking lot he normally used was full. He was also running low on fuel, and getting gas before he reported to McComb was not an option.

With the clock ticking, Braden double-parked on a side street and hurried toward the building entrance. About to dash through the front door, he heard McComb call out to him. Braden stopped, backed away from the building and toward McComb's voice.

Wearing a hat and a heavy coat with a thick scarf covering his mouth and throat, McComb gestured for Braden to follow him. The older man didn't wait for an answer and strode purposefully toward the far side of the building, out of sight of the front entrance. Braden trailed along behind.

Away from any observers, McComb turned and faced Braden. Though the scarf slightly muffled his voice, McComb's questions came through clearly. "Have you learned anything?"

Braden tried to present an aura of calm professionalism despite his sphincter tightening like a vise. "I've picked up a few things. But nothing... actionable. Yet."

"What's the holdup?"

"It's not like I can march into Albright's house and demand that he give me the secret of his success," Braden said. "Part of my problem is the cost of surveillance."

"How so?"

"I've had to hire a professional to help me get the information I need."

McComb shrugged. "Again, so?"

"It's expensive! My salary is the same as it was before I took this assignment. I can't afford to pay these additional costs and still keep a roof over my head."

McComb rubbed his chin through his scarf. "Evidently you don't understand *my* position. If I suddenly inflate your salary, it could implicate me in what you're doing."

And maybe that's not such a terrible idea! Braden squirmed. "Doesn't the company at least have a petty cash fund?"

"I'm not operating a fucking candy store! We don't have petty cash, other than your portfolio."

Braden's angst was rapidly transitioning to anger. "Do you want me to succeed in this or not?"

"Of course."

"Then how 'bout giving me enough money to show some results?"

McComb laughed. "You don't get it. Here's how this works: First, you show *me* some results. *Then* you'll get a reward. Got that? *After.* Not before. If you're not invested in success, don't expect me to support your failure."

The older man walked away without waiting for Braden to reply.

Rather than try to catch up and plead his case further, Braden turned and scurried back to his car. He couldn't have been gone more than five minutes, tops. But it was long enough to get a parking citation.

Tucked under a windshield wiper, the ticket fluttered in the winter breeze.

~*~

In his younger days, Wynn Albright would never have imagined himself needing wheelchair assistance at an airport or anywhere else. Now, he couldn't imagine getting much done without it.

He generously tipped the attendant who had wheeled him from his arrival gate, through baggage claim, and out to the arrivals area of Atlanta's massive and ever-crowded airport. The attendant took the wheelchair, and Wynn sat on top of his rolling suitcase, glad that it was sturdy enough to support him. He looked around at the traveler mayhem surrounding him. It seemed as though the facility known as ATL was perpetually under construction. But it was, after all, the world's busiest airport, and Georgians often joked that one couldn't die and go to heaven without changing planes in Atlanta.

Wynn was just glad to be going home. Damned glad.

His trip had been worthwhile but exhausting, despite the two extra days he'd stayed at the hotel recuperating. Now, he faced the unpleasant prospect of dealing with Jeffrey, whom he'd called to come get him. Jeffrey's car, however, didn't show up. Instead, Wynn found himself staring at his own vehicle with Danica driving it. He'd have been only slightly more surprised if he'd seen Roscoe behind the wheel.

She pulled to the curb and hopped out, all smiles. "You'll never guess what I got in the mail."

Wynn shrugged. He'd never been good at playing Twenty Questions.

"My driver's license! I don't know who you talked to, but it arrived way quicker than I expected. I hope you don't mind that I drove your car."

"Not at all," he said. "I'm pleased. I'm also a bit confused. I called Jeffrey and asked him to pick me up."

"And he called me," Danica said. "He said since I work for you, I could figure out how to bring you back from the airport. He also said something about not being able to afford the gas since he's being laid off. Then he complained about his wife's birthday coming up. He didn't sound very happy about it."

"I hope he wasn't rude."

She laughed. "He's a little upset, that's all. Now let's get you back home."

While Wynn settled into the passenger seat, Danica loaded his suitcase in the trunk, maneuvered through the crowded sidewalk, and prepared to drive off. An impatient cop trying to manage traffic blew his whistle and waved at her to get moving. Wynn discovered he was holding his breath as she navigated through lanes choked with cars.

"Traffic was never this bad in Kandahar," she said.

They drove in silence for several minutes before Wynn thanked her for getting him. "I've been meaning to have a chat with you. There are some things I need to share."

"Really? I was going to say the same thing!"

Wynn stared at her, wondering what revelation she was about to unleash. "Okay. You go first."

Without breaking her concentration on the Interstate traffic grinding its way through the downtown Atlanta Connector, Danica said, "I'll probably have to go to court in the next few days or weeks. I hate that 'cause it means I'll have to miss work, but I don't think I have any other choice."

"Court? You're involved in a crime?"

"Sorta. I'm a witness to an attempted robbery."

"You mean at the house? When CeeJay tried to get in?"

"Nope. Completely different shithead. It was just the night before last. Rick and I were going out for dinner—"

"You and Rick are *dating*?"

"Yeah, I guess. Kinda. I mean... I don't know. We're friends. And there's the age thing, and he's a widower, and I'm... Well, I'm a friggin' mess."

A wave of confusion threatened to pummel Wynn. "So, what was this other crime? Rick didn't try anything, did he? Because if so—"

"No! No. God no. Rick's wonderful. A real gentleman. Not only that, but he keeps a shotgun in his car. You know, just in case."

"Whoa! Just... Whoa." Wynn held his head in both hands. "Let's leave the topic of Rick aside for now, okay? What crime did you witness?"

"Like I said, Rick and I went out for dinner and maybe a movie, but that didn't happen because—"

"Of the crime?"

"Right," she said. "We stopped at a convenience store so I could use the restroom. Rick stayed outside, putting gas in his car. When I came out of the ladies room, I saw a guy trying to rob the place. He had a gun and was trying to dig money out of the cash drawer."

"Oh, dear Lord. What did you do? Hide, I hope. Sneak out the back?"

She pursed her lips and gave him a brief look of disdain. "I snuck up on him and smashed his face into the counter. He dropped his weapon, and then Rick came in and held him at bay with his shotgun."

"Why do I get the feeling you may have left out some details?"

"It wasn't a big deal, really. I mean, it wasn't like the place had been attacked by ragheads. Believe me, the Taliban can be seriously nasty."

"So, when is this trial supposed to be held?"

"I don't know. I got a call from a detective the next day, and he said the perp was still in the hospital. I guess maybe I bumped his head a little too hard."

"I'm still confused," Wynn said.

She explained about using the toilet bowl plunger. "It was the only thing handy. But, you know, it worked pretty well. That suction cup thing fit right over his head, and I just plunged him into the counter until he stopped bobbing back up. Come to think of it, I may have gotten blood on some of the displays."

Wynn shook his head in wonder. "How often do you beat up criminals? I didn't think to ask you that during our interviews."

She laughed. "Until I met you, I'd never done anything like that. Well, except for Lieutenant Mundt. But I told you about him."

"I do recall that," Wynn said.

Danica turned serious. "The odd thing is, I found out about something I'd never thought of before. And it's something I definitely want to discuss with you. It's really important to me."

Sitting in "his" corner of the couple's spare bedroom, Jeffrey Albright stared at the list of birthday gifts Beatrix said she wanted. She hadn't bothered to assign any prices to them; that would have made it far too easy. This way, he would first have to figure out where the items were sold and then find their prices.

He liked the way his father handled it. Gift cards were easy to find and could be purchased in various denominations, but of course, Beatrix didn't like gift cards. How many times had he heard her say, "Something thoughtful should go into every gift."

I doubt she'd like the thoughts I'm having right

now!

But, if nothing else, the list gave him an excuse to leave the house. It also meant he'd have to choose between actually doing the shopping, a chore he hated, going to a bar and spending money on booze that he could have consumed at home, or going to a library. While not an ideal option, the library did offer computers and an Internet connection that couldn't be traced back to him.

Though never much of a student, he knew he couldn't research ways to kill someone on his home computer. Husbands were always the first suspects in a murder investigation, and one of the first places they'd check was his crappy laptop. Anyone who watched crime shows on TV knew that.

I'm not that stupid. In the public library, I can look up anything.

So that's where he went. While waiting for someone to leave one of the five, still-working PCs, Jeffrey wandered through a section in the library devoted to mystery novels. More of a movie-watcher than a book-reader, he felt lost amid the massive array of books available. He hated that they were arranged by author rather than topic. Having a shelf full of books that focused on murdering one's spouse would have helped considerably.

Jeffrey had been pondering how to eliminate

Beatrix while simultaneously framing Danica for her death. He had yet to come up with a viable plan. Maybe the library needed a section devoted to framing people for crimes, too. He smiled, pleased by his own devilish wit.

A glance at the bank of PCs showed them all still occupied. "There oughta be a time limit," he groused. "It's not fair."

"What's not fair?"

The voice startled him; he was alone in the aisle.

"Over here," said the voice.

Jeffrey turned in that direction, and he spotted a woman looking at him through a gap in the books on a shelf. She stood in the neighboring aisle.

"Didn't mean to startle you," she said. "Can I help you find something?"

He wanted to ask, "Do you have a copy of **Ten Easy Ways to Kill Your Spouse?** Preferably in paperback?" He doubted she would share his humor. Instead, he said, "No. I'm just bored waiting for a PC to come open."

"Then your best chance is to get here early. They fill up quick, and people stay on them all day. Me? I'd rather curl up around a good book."

"Yeah," said Jeffrey. "Me, too."

Chapter Sixteen

"If you have integrity, nothing else matters. If you don't have integrity, nothing else matters." —Alan K. Simpson

They had just passed through the heart of downtown Atlanta when Wynn asked Danica to tell him what she found so important. "I sincerely hope you aren't going to tell me you want to become a cop or a forest ranger."

She chuckled. "That's not even close."

"Well, go on. You've got a captive audience."

"So, there was this salesclerk in the store that got robbed."

Wynn groaned. "A salesclerk like the one in the clothing shop?"

"Nothing like that one," she said. "This girl, a sweet kid really, was the only employee in the store.

Her boss had gone somewhere and was supposed to be away for just a little while. The robbery attempt really freaked her out." Danica blew an errant red curl from her forehead as if it might dispel any lingering tension.

"I talked to her briefly, got her phone number, and told her I'd keep in touch. After the detective called me, I called her, and we chatted for a while. It turns out she lives with another young women in a shabby, one-bedroom apartment."

"And you found that odd?"

"Not really. But here's the thing: both of them had previously been in foster care; they used to be wards of the state."

"So?" Wynn sensed another wave of confusion headed his way.

"When they aged out of the system, they had nowhere to go. Like the others in that situation, they had no jobs, no family, and in some cases, no hope." She took her eyes off the traffic long enough to give Wynn a very serious look. "I want to help them. And other kids like them. Is that something you'd contribute to?"

"I'd need to know a lot more," Wynn said. "I can't see myself standing on a street corner handing out cash to these people."

"Obviously. But there's still a need."

Wynn smiled. "It's equally obvious that it matters to you. So, sure. Why don't you look into it? I suspect there are already programs available for them. Maybe it's just a case of bad communication. Maybe they just aren't aware of what's out there."

"That could be," Danica admitted. "But if you don't mind, I will definitely dig into it." She paused and smiled. "I could use a little help with the PC look-up gizmo."

"No problem. It's called a search engine. And I'll get you up to speed in no time."

"Thanks." She made a face when someone cut her off as she tried to change lanes.

"There are assholes everywhere these days," observed Wynn.

She nodded. "You said you wanted to talk to me about something, too. But I've gotta say, if it has anything to do with investing, I've got an awful lot to learn. I'm not sure I can handle it."

"You could," Wynn said, "but it's more likely you won't have to." He paused to gather his thoughts. Danica's concern for the girl at the convenience store had come as a revelation. Her own history of homelessness obviously played a part, but there was something more to her, something he hadn't really considered before. Danica had a profound sense of justice; she firmly believed in right and wrong. It may have been amplified by her time in the Marines, but it remained a cornerstone of her character.

She cared. She had saved his life and very likely, saved Roscoe's life, too. She didn't hesitate when CeeJay tried his ridiculous break-in, and in the space of two days, she'd foiled a robbery by an armed man. Even more to the point, she seemed almost embarrassed by it and showed more concern about missing time at work to testify at a trial.

He had intended to tell her about Annabelle Knox's creation and how he'd used it to raise money for charitable causes. Now he had second thoughts—significant second thoughts.

"Would you mind if I posed some hypothetical situations and asked you a question or two? I'm curious to see how you'll react. Your answer won't endanger your job. I'm absolutely certain I want you to continue working with me. So please, be honest."

"Okay," she said, looking less than certain. "I'll do my best."

"Let's start with an easy scenario: Robin Hood."

Danica smiled. "I saw that movie! Seeing those Merry Men in tights was kinda weird though."

"Right," said Wynn, wishing she had seen a serious version. There had to be a dozen different films she could have watched. "According to legend, he robbed from the rich and gave to the poor. Do you think that was just and fair?"

"I guess it depends on how the rich got that way. Didn't they tax the workers, the uhm... serfs? They were like slaves almost, weren't they?"

"I suppose so," Wynn said. "Would that make a difference?"

"Sure! It's like the rich used the law to rob the poor. Robin Hood just returned what was rightfully theirs in the first place."

"So, in your mind, Robin Hood was morally okay."

"Yeah, I guess so," she said.

"Let's try a different setup. Let's say someone rigged a game of some kind—football, baseball, tidily winks, whatever—and then they bet big on the outcome, knowing in advance what that outcome would be. Would that be okay?"

"No way!" Danica gave him a concerned look. "That's what that guy who tried to break in said—that you knew the Super Bowl score before the game had been played. That's cheating!"

"You mean CeeJay? The guy who got stuck in

Roscoe's doggie door?" Wynn couldn't help but laugh. "We both know he's a lunatic, right? Anyway, I agree that it's cheating. But think of it in a slightly different way. And I know of another movie that plays this out. Did you ever see 'The Sting'?"

"I think so," Danica said, "but it's been years. I don't remember much about it."

"I won't bore you with details, but the story was all about crooks. Some con artists who'd suffered at the hands of a gangster made it look like they'd rigged a horse race in order to steal from him. It worked, and they all got away."

"That sounds familiar. It was Robert Redford and... Oh... I forget the other actor's name, but he was really famous."

"Paul Newman."

"Yeah! That's him. I'd love to see that one again. I bet Rick would, too." Danica became all smiles. "If he does, would you like to join us?"

"That sounds like fun," Wynn said, hoping he hadn't lost control of his objective. "So, now, what if they didn't rig anything? What if they just knew the outcome before the race was run? Would that be cheating?"

"I guess, but they'd only be cheating the gangster."

"What if no gangster was involved? What if they just bet on a game for which they already knew the final score? Would that be cheating?"

"Yes!"

"Even if the money they won would be used to help people in need? Really desperate people?"

Danica shook her head and sent a wave of red hair swirling. "I was beginning to like this game. Now you've gone and made it difficult."

"Sorry about that," Wynn said. "Don't worry about answering that last one."

"No," she exclaimed. "I'll answer, not that I like what I'm about to say. It would still be wrong."

And Wynn knew he could never reveal Annabelle Knox's amazing device to Danica.

~*~

The traffic citation Braden got for double parking was icing on the cake. More like icing on a turd, he thought. His brief meeting with McComb had done little to replace the enthusiasm he'd lost in paying Gupta for useless information. Knowing that with a little better planning, he might have gotten something valuable didn't change his mood. If anything, it depressed him even more.

Before he contacted the phony Irishman a

second time, Braden decided he could do some sleuthing on his own. He could easily sit in his car and keep an eye on Albright's house, though he had no specific hopes for what such an endeavor might produce.

But what the hell? I don't have anything else to do. It's too damned cold to play golf!

The drive to Woodstock, including a stop for coffee and a doughnut, was uneventful, and Braden found a place to park that afforded a great view of the front and side of Albright's house. From the look of things, no one was home except for a medium-size, white dog with two prominent black spots—one at each end of him. The yard was fenced.

Braden waited as patiently as he knew how and was about to doze off when a reasonably new Ford SUV pulled into the driveway and stopped. An attractive redhead slipped out from behind the wheel and stepped to the back of the vehicle. An older man exited the front passenger side and walked unsteadily toward the house.

The young woman opened the back of the car, pulled out a suitcase, and rolled it along the sidewalk after the man. The dog, meanwhile, watched their arrival through the fence, greeting them with whines, barks, and leaps of joy.

Assuming the dog would soon be all over the

redhead, Braden felt a twinge of jealousy.

Sitting in her room at Wynn's home after bringing him back from the airport, Danica couldn't decide how, or even if, to tell him the rest of the story she'd heard from April, the convenience store clerk. The issue was more serious than Danica had let on. April said her roommate was in an abusive relationship, and she worried about the girl's safety. Even worse, April feared the guy who kept hurting her friend would try to force her into prostitution.

Danica heard enough to be infuriated, and at first all she could think about was how she might eradicate the "boyfriend." Eventually, she calmed down. She didn't want Wynn to think that a simple conversation about people she didn't know could trigger her blind rage. It wasn't a question of whether or not she could put the creep down; most bullies were chickenshit when it came to fighting anyone who knew what they were doing.

That caused her to spin off into another train of thought—what if the creep April told her about *didn't* morph into a spineless loser? Danica knew how to handle herself in a fight, but it had been a long time since she actually did any training. She had lost muscle and stamina while homeless, but that didn't mean she'd become powerless. She just needed to regain the level of fitness she maintained in the Marines.

"But why?" she asked herself. "Why bother? It's not like I'm going to turn into some sort of vigilante, protector of the weak, and bane of bullies." She paused, then said it louder, "Danica Winters, Bane of Bullies!"

I like it! I could get some costume shop to whip up a latex outfit with a big, fat B/B on the chest. Maybe with a lightning bolt or a fist in the background.

The very thought of wearing a superhero costume cheered her up. And yet, in the back of her mind, a far less ridiculous idea along similar lines had planted itself.

With of a toss of her red hair, Danica set herself to taking advantage of the power inherent in the search engine Wynn told her to use. She focused on finding charitable organizations that helped young people like April.

She hadn't been at it long when Wynn popped into the room. "You doing okay? It's been mighty quiet in here."

"I didn't know you were eavesdropping," Danica replied. She smiled to soften her remark.

"Just thought I'd check on you. Whenever I used to drive back here from the airport, it always took me a while to unwind, y'know?"

"Oh, I get it. I really do. I hadn't driven in quite a while before I picked you up. I was a little tense. I think I told you about my car being stolen."

"You did," he said. "I'm sorry about all that."

Danica shook her head. "My fault. I thought I'd developed good sense. I was wrong. I had a sergeant once who said, 'Life is just one learning experience after another.' There's some truth in that."

"More than most folks can imagine." Wynn's laugh turned into a cough.

"Are you okay?" she asked.

"Yeah. Yeah. It's nothing."

It didn't seem like that to her. "Has your son spoken to you since you got back?"

"Nope."

"I find that odd since he seemed really wound up over his wife's upcoming birthday. He said something about asking you to help him since he'll soon be out of work."

Wynn pursed his lips. "Actually, I have given it some thought. But I may need your help with the arrangements."

Chapter Seventeen

"Fame is a beast that you can't control or be prepared for."
—Tom Holland

Jeffrey Albright sat in the relative obscurity of his corporate work cubicle. He left a customer on hold who had asked him about his (soon-to-be former) employer's product return policy. Rather than deal with the annoyed client, Jeffrey found it more interesting to scroll through his favorite social media platform which often featured attractive women in skimpy swimsuits.

What caught his eye was definitely an attractive woman, but she was nowhere near the beach or a pool. She was the featured player in a security video that had gone viral, and for good reason. Jeffrey watched it multiple times.

In the full-color film clip, a shapely female

wearing a short skirt and racy leggings, snuck up on an armed man in the process of robbing a convenience store. He had stretched himself across a wide countertop to empty the cash register. He never saw the woman who snuck up behind him and smashed his head into the counter with—of all things—a toilet plunger.

In the background, some stupid country song blared. The hottie with the plunger appeared to be keeping time to the music while banging the bad guy's head into the counter.

Jeffrey giggled as he watched the scene over and over.

Eventually, the blinking HOLD light on his phone went out; his caller had given up, finally.

The video had garnered hundreds of comments, many of which Jeffrey read with interest. One of them brought him up short. According to the writer, the location of the convenience store was quite close to his father's home in Woodstock.

Jeffrey brought the video up full screen and squinted at the woman as she whacked away at the crook. The enlarged screen allowed him a better look at her profile, and the recognition gave him a solid jolt.

"Holy shit—it's daddy's play pal!"

I wonder if he's seen this?

The temptation to call his father proved too much to ignore. Much like the customer he'd abandoned, Jeffrey was eager to get an answer. *What the hell was up with the hot little redhead?*

Before he'd finished dialing Wynn's number, another thought crossed his mind. If Danica had the kind of nerve and determination to take out an armed robber twice her size, what chance would *he* have of handling her physically?

The answer came quickly: he'd have no chance, at least, not in a fair fight. That left only the alternative.

Wynn Albright had never been so easily worn out. After laboring over Annabelle Knox's machine in an effort to repair the damage caused by CeeJay's errant gunshot, the retired physics professor couldn't wait to lie down, but that would have to wait. Though he felt underpowered, he had more energy now than he would ever have later.

The radiation given off by the apparatus had worsened his condition. But, he reasoned, if he could just extend the life of the equipment a bit more, he'd be able to assemble enough wealth to continue the good work he'd done in Annabelle's name. That mattered more to him than anything, including the danger of shortening his life.

He'd only managed limited progress. The machine would run, but only for a short time, and it would heat up far more than it ever had before. He deeply appreciated its built-in cooling system and thermal cut-off switch.

While waiting for the contraption to cool down, Wynn focused on the simplified controls that drove it. The top of the machine sported a red on/off switch and four buttons, one for each data type desired. The buttons bore a one-letter label which, when viewed together spelled the word S L O W. Annabelle thought that cute since it had nothing to do with the speed of operation.

At first, the machine offered only two options—one for Stocks and one for Sports data. She used the letter "S" for sports info and "W" to indicate Wall Street data. Later, when she realized that her constant proximity to the radioactive drive component was killing her, she added two more. The first of these produced obituaries, since she needed to know how much time she had left. That one she labeled "O." The last of the two new buttons she labeled "L." It would provide a last-minute source of considerable income but had to be used sparingly. Winning one lottery after another would attract far too much attention.

The only other exterior item of note was a small red light which lit up when the machine was on. The radioactive drive pulled all its data from the future.

Because the now-damaged machine could only operate for a short time, the amount of data he could retrieve was severely limited. He had to make it count. Snagging investment data was out of the question, and sports data would almost certainly be incomplete. All data came from yet-to-be published issues of the *Atlanta Courier*, the city's premier newspaper, and it often featured page after page of obituaries. Again, far too much information. That left just one type of useable data, that provided by the "L" button.

If he could get it, he could rest happily. If nothing else, he'd use it to solve Jeffrey's problems. Beyond that, Wynn already had a plan in mind to ensure that his good works in Annabelle's name would continue after his death.

Once that was accomplished, he resolved to destroy the machine and bury it.

He settled in, ready for another test run when his cell phone rang. A glance at the screen told him it was Jeffrey. He let it go to voice mail. He had no desire to deal with his son's current predicaments or his insulting references to Danica.

When the ringing stopped, he waited to see if Jeffrey had left a voice message. He had. Wynn clicked the PLAY button.

> *"Dad—you won't believe what I just saw on the Internet! It's Danica. Please, call me back ASAP. You've gotta see this. You've just gotta!"*

Braden began yet another day of surveillance on Wynn Albright's home. Thus far, nothing interesting had occurred, and Braden had to force himself to continue despite the utter boredom of it.

By midmorning, however, something did happen. The redhead he'd seen the day before left the house alone, got in a car, and drove out of the neighborhood. Braden wasted no time following her through the middling town of Woodstock until she pulled into a convenience store.

That made little sense to him since the store looked old and shoddy compared to several others they had passed along the way.

There's gotta be a reason.

He parked a few spaces away from her car and followed her inside, barely able to keep from staring at her retreating figure as she walked. Her brightly colored yoga pants contrasted with a loose, dark leather jacket. She wore her hair short, and her movements as she walked provided a mesmerizing view.

She strolled casually to the front counter and called out, "April." A salesgirl busy stocking shelves with cartons of cigarettes turned and waved. Country music played in the background as the girl stepped away from her chores. The redhead mouthed the lyrics and nodded to the beat.

"Danica!" said the salesclerk. "Hold on. Let me turn the music down."

Braden pretended to look over items on display near the front counter and got close enough to eavesdrop on their conversation.

"Don't do it on my account," the redhead said. "I love Zac Brown."

"Me, too." The clerk smiled. "I'm glad to see you. I didn't expect you back so soon."

"I told you I would, didn't I?"

April appeared embarrassed. "I don't know if I owe you an apology or not. I hope you aren't mad at me."

The redhead seemed puzzled. "Why would I be mad at you?"

"'Cause I sorta posted a copy of the store's security video online." She swallowed. "It's gotten... I mean it kinda went crazy. It's been posted and reposted... I dunno, a bunch."

"You posted the security video from the other day?"

"Yeah! The part where you whacked the guy trying to rob the store. It's gone viral!"

Bemused, the redhead merely shrugged.

"You're a celebrity, Danica! For real!"

"Is that good for a free doughnut or something?"

Braden couldn't keep from chuckling, and when he did, both of the women looked at him.

"Sorry," he said. "It's just... I've never been around a celebrity before. Don't know if I should be nervous or not." He looked at the salesclerk. "What did you mean when you said she 'whacked' somebody? And please don't tell me someone got killed."

April vigorously shook her head. "No, nothing like that. She just knocked him out."

"It was no big deal," said the redhead.

"Your name's Danica?" he asked.

"Yeah."

He held out his hand. "I'm Braden, and you're the first celebrity I've ever met."

Danica's smile seemed restrained before she responded with a chuckle. "Stop, please. I'm nothing of the sort. I just happened to be here when April needed me. It was nothing, really."

April appraised Braden. "Wait 'til you see the video. Danica's a regulation badass."

"I'm looking forward to it," he said.

Danica glanced at April. "Guess I need to watch it, too."

"You could watch it at our place," April said. "It'd be a good way to meet Libby, my roommate."

"How is she?" Danica asked. "You said she was dealing with a jerk."

"She is, and I'm worried about her. She came home last night with bruises on her face and arms. Said she doesn't want to spend any more time with Tim, the guy she's been seeing, but she's afraid to tell him to take a hike."

Braden watched the expression on Danica's face change from pleasant to pissed. He kept quiet and waited to see where the conversation went.

"How 'bout I drop by your place tonight?

Maybe I could show y'all a thing or two about self-defense."

"Pardon me for interrupting," said Braden, "but I have to ask. When you say 'self-defense,' are you referring to... you know... Kung Fu?"

She responded with a snort of laughter. "It's not that, but it *is* a martial art. Marine style. That's where I learned, and it's come in handy."

"That is so cool," he said, wishing he could have thought of something more original. "I wonder... Would you be willing to tell me a little more about it? Say, over drinks?"

"Oh, go on," said April as she tugged Danica's arm. Excitement colored her voice. "Why not? He already knows if he gets fresh you can punch his lights out!"

Danica had just returned to Wynn's house, and hung up her jacket when he called out to her from his office. He didn't sound good.

"On my way," she said and hurried down the hallway. If nothing else, she thought, it would take her mind off her stupid decision to go out for a drink with a total stranger. *Will I never learn?*

She stopped worrying about herself the moment she looked at Wynn. He appeared even more pale than usual, worse than at any other time she'd seen him, including their first meeting in the hospital. "My God, boss. You're white as a ghost."

He bobbed his head in a weary acknowledgement. "It's my Nordic heritage."

"Bullshit. I'm worried about you. I think we should get you to the ER."

"No," he said, his voice as weak as he looked. "Won't do any good."

"You looked better yesterday," she said. "What have you been doing? How do you feel? What's going—"

"I need to level with you," Wynn said. "I owe you that much at the very least."

Danica simply stared at him, waiting.

"There's a piece of equipment I've been using to uhm... to help with my investments."

"Okay. So?"

"It was damaged when that idiot, CeeJay, broke in. You recall he fired a couple of shots?"

"I do. But I didn't think he hit anything."

"Did you ever look for the bullet holes?"

"No," she said. "You didn't want me hanging around in your office. Remember?"

"Right, right. Of course. And I still don't want you near it, okay? And it's because of a machine in there. It's hidden behind the bookcase, and one of CeeJay's bullets struck it. The damage to one critical part was considerable." He paused to cough and clear his throat.

"That part is highly radioactive, but it's shielded. Or was, mostly, until the bullet screwed it up. Now, that radiation is leaking out worse than before. I've been trying to contain it and fix the machine."

"And that's why you look like shit?" Danica quickly put a hand to her mouth. "I'm sorry! I shouldn't have—"

"Nonsense! You're exactly right. I look terrible. I'm definitely not well. Haven't been for a while. But that's not the issue now. I need to repair that machine. It acts as a sort of focus which..." He stopped abruptly, cleared his throat and then continued. "What it does is irrelevant. The important thing is, it's no longer working properly. If I can't repair it, I need to discard it, but because of the radiation, I obviously can't just toss it out with the trash."

"So, what're you going to do with it?"

"Maybe bury the damned thing in the backyard? That could work."

"Bury it?"

"Yes. What else *can* I do with it?" He exhaled wearily and wiped his forehead with his shirtsleeve. "But I'm going to need your help."

Danica didn't know whether to laugh, cry, or simply run away. "What," she asked timidly, "is it you want me to do? Dig the hole?"

"Actually, yes," he said. "I do."

"How deep?"

"As deep as you can make it."

"Then," she said, "you'd better find someone pretty damn quick who can teach me how to operate a bulldozer."

Chapter Eighteen

"Suspicion is only another form of cowardice. The man who suspects constantly does so because he is afraid. Whenever you find a man with a free, frank, generous, brave nature, you will find that man without suspicion."
—Robert Green Ingersoll

Beatrix noted a change in her husband's behavior. Not that he was a particularly cheerful person, drunk or sober, but over the past several days he seemed more depressed than usual. When she asked him about it, he claimed it was "nothing to worry about." That seemed reasonable to her. If he spent all his time stewing about whatever the issue was, having her worry about it, too, wouldn't accomplish anything. Besides, she had something else in mind, something she deemed much more important.

It had been a few weeks since Jeffrey told her

about his bizarre encounter with someone from an investment firm. The very idea that Jeffrey had amazing skill when it came to buying and selling stock had been a source of laughter for them ever since. It's not that he lacked the intellect to become savvy at something, he simply had no drive, and no desire to learn. He knew it and willingly admitted it.

When the laughter subsided, however, they both reached the same conclusion: the investment analyst had mistaken Jeffrey for his father. She couldn't imagine how that might have happened and frankly didn't care. What *did* intrigue her was the idea that Wynn had the sort of knowledge needed to do well in the stock market. He had been a college professor, after all; they weren't generally thought to be stupid.

But, as was usual for Jeffrey's tightwad father, the old man never mentioned anything about investing to either of them. She knew he had money, and most likely lots and lots of it. Just because he didn't brag about it meant nothing.

Beatrix couldn't help but wonder where Wynn kept his money. A bank, surely, but as much as he traveled, she assumed he kept a decent stash on hand, hidden somewhere in the house. She hadn't said anything to Jeffrey, but as time went on, she felt a specific desire more and more—the need to locate

Wynn's hoard.

She and Jeffrey had cut back on their visits to Wynn's house ever since he hired his floozy. How pathetic that was, she thought. He had lived a presumably honorable life, and now he spent all his time with the homeless hooker he'd pulled from a dump somewhere. It was enough to make a normal person sick.

It also meant she would have to plan her next visit to Wynn's house with care. Ideally, she'd go when he and the redhead weren't there. Lately, however, he hadn't been traveling, so her chances of visiting when he was out of town were nil. On the other hand, his health had suffered. The few times they'd seen him recently reinforced the belief; he looked worse every time they met.

That triggered a new thought: what if the redhead was deliberately making him sick? What if the very thought of sleeping with the old codger was so disgusting she chose to poison him instead? For a moment, Beatrix sympathized with the younger woman.

Her sympathy didn't last long as yet another possibility presented itself: what about Wynn's estate? Would Jeffrey inherit everything? They had always assumed as much, but the presence of Danica might have changed things. It certainly wouldn't be the first time an old man romanced and married a much younger woman only to disenfranchise his family and reward the gold digger in his will.

Surely Wynn had a will, she thought. And it seemed only logical that he would put it in the same secure location he used to store his money.

That clinched it. She had to search his house.

~*~

Jeffrey waited all afternoon for Wynn to call him back, but the phone never rang. Beatrix fluttered about constantly, as usual, but this time she seemed more animated, perhaps even driven. When he asked her what was on her mind, she responded in a most unusual way. Rather than boring him with endless, unwanted details, she waved his question off with a mere, "It's nothing."

"Okay then. I'm going to Dad's house," he announced.

"Why?"

"To check on him. I asked him to call me back hours ago, but I haven't heard a peep."

Beatrix snorted. "As if *that's* out of the ordinary. What's so important that you have to go see him?"

"It's about the redhead, Danica. There's a

video of her on social media, and it's getting hits like crazy."

"Seriously? Is she dancing in the nude or something?"

"They don't allow that on GabFest."

"What the hell is that?"

"It's an online thing. People post all kinds of stuff. There's a video of Danica knocking the crap outta some idiot who tried to rob a gas station. It's pretty cool, actually. Wanna see it?"

"Good God, no!" Beatrix said. "I have no use for that woman or anything she does. And I sure don't think she's doing your father any favors."

He squinted at her. "What're you talking about?"

Beatrix crossed her flabby arms on her chest. "I'm not saying another word until I have some proof. But for now, just know that I'm suspicious of her. Very suspicious."

"Whatever," he said. "I'm heading over there now."

"What about dinner?"

"We can eat later."

"*You* can eat later," she responded. "I'll put

yours in the fridge."

Jeffrey left without another word, got in their car, and drove to Wynn's Woodstock home. He entered the residence without bothering to knock, not that it was a secret; Roscoe raised hell when anyone arrived. As Wynn's four-legged doorbell/security alarm, Roscoe saw to it that nobody got in unannounced.

Danica made a half-hearted attempt to hold Roscoe at bay when Jeffrey came in. Eventually, the dog got bored and wandered away. After a brief greeting, Jeffrey asked how his father was doing.

"You'd best ask him yourself," she said. "Sometimes he can be a bit ornery."

"No shit."

She followed him into the living room where Wynn lay sprawled on the sofa in front of his oversized TV. He had muted the sound and appeared to be reading news items as they scrolled across the bottom of the screen.

Weak and pale, he barely looked up when they entered the room.

"Hey, Dad," Jeffrey said. "You okay?"

Wynn closed his eyes. "Just peachy."

"I think he needs to see a doctor," Danica said.

"But he won't listen to me."

"She's right, Dad. You don't look well at all. I'm worried about you."

Wynn managed a muffled, "Hmph."

Jeffrey hauled out his cell phone and prepared to dial.

Wynn shifted up on an elbow. "What are you doing?"

"Calling 9-1-1. You're going to the emergency room at County General."

"The hell I am!" Wynn groaned, then dropped back against the cushions.

"I'll drive him," Danica said. "It's really not an emergency. He's been like this for a while."

"I don't like ambulances," Wynn said. "I don't want all the fuss. I just need to rest, damn it; that's all."

"Let me help you get him in the car," Jeffrey said. "I'd like to go with you, but I've got a late shift at work." Both comments were bald lies, but he didn't care. A little free time away from Beatrix made it worthwhile.

Once he and Danica had Wynn safely loaded in the old man's car, Jeffrey waved to them as they drove off. Then he called his wife. "Bea? We're taking Dad to the hospital. He looks really sick. I don't know when I'll be back home."

"How ill is he? Like, *terminal?*"

"I don't know. Are you that eager to inherit the house? Geez, Bea. Lighten up."

He cut the connection and used his phone's internet connection to find the nearest strip club. If he stuck with beer and avoided pricey drinks and lap dances, he figured he could afford to stay for an hour or two at least.

The hospital trip allowed Danica to ignore Wynn's desire to bury his mysterious, nuclear gadget, whatever that might be. Another issue took its place. If Wynn had a fatal illness, her job would die along with him. But job or no job, she had to help him stay alive.

When they parked by the entrance to the ER, Danica hurried inside and asked for a wheelchair to bring him in. A nurse's aide answered the call and ushered Wynn into an exam room, leaving Danica to park the car and then sit in the waiting area. She used the time to call Braden, who'd insisted they swap cell phone numbers. The pitiful list of people she could call consisted of Wynn, Jeffrey, Rick, April, and now Braden.

"I'm afraid I have to cancel our get-together for this evening," she said when Braden answered. "I'm at the hospital with my boss, and I don't know how long I'm going to be here."

"Was he in an accident?" Braden asked.

Danica gave him an abbreviated recap of his condition. "I'm sorry about this, but—"

"Please. It doesn't rate any stress on your part," he said.

She thought she detected sincerity in his voice.

"I understand," he went on, "that heroes, and especially *celebrity* heroes like you, have busy schedules."

"Celebrity? Please. I haven't seen the video April was talking about. Have you?"

"Not yet," he said, "but I'm going to find that sucker as soon as I can."

"You're embarrassing me!"

"I didn't mean to. But why not let me make it up to you with a drink *and* a dinner? What d'ya say?"

"Well... I...."

"Think about it, okay? I'll give you a call tomorrow."

~*~

Beatrix realized the perfect opportunity had come much earlier than expected. She couldn't have asked for more—Jeffrey, Danica, and Wynn would all be at the hospital for hours. Surely, she told herself, she could conduct a thorough search of Wynn's office and bedroom in that amount of time. She put aside any interest in the rest of the house figuring that if Wynn wanted to hide something of value, he'd stash it where he'd usually be near it.

Since Jeffrey had their car, Beatrix called a neighbor who made money on the side by providing rides around town and to the airport. The trip to Wynn's house took little time, and she waltzed right through the front door. All would have been serene if Wynn's stupid dog hadn't raised such a fuss. Fortunately, she had prepared for his assault with two, all-beef wieners in a plastic baggy. She threw them in a bathroom and closed the door once Roscoe raced inside to eat them.

After stopping at the refrigerator to grab a soft drink, she headed straight for Wynn's office. His departure must have been hurried since he left his office door unlocked. Beatrix couldn't help but smile at her phenomenal timing.

She had peeked through that door on many occasions and fully expected the room to be a mess. She wasn't disappointed. With the lights and ceiling fan on, Beatrix crept into the room as if someone else were in the house, then realized she was being foolish. She broke into a breathy whistle as she surveyed the room and its messy contents, trying to decide where to begin.

She stepped carefully between various piles of paperwork, publications, file folders, and seemingly random sheets of printer paper, most of which had lists of odd data.

Her first stop was Wynn's desk, the easiest of targets. Locking valuables in a desk drawer, while painfully obvious, also provided the most rapid means of securing something, at least temporarily. All his drawers, however, were unlocked. She couldn't help but think of the junk drawer she and Jeffrey maintained in their kitchen at home. Two of Wynn's drawers appeared similarly laden with stuff he likely didn't need or rarely, if ever, used.

She got down on her hands and knees, an arduous task, in order to inspect the underside of the desk. It would have been simple and easy to tape a cash-stuffed envelope in such dark recesses.

She found none.

She then removed each of the desk drawers and raised them high enough to inspect the undersides for envelopes, codes, deposit box keys, or clues to his hidden treasure.

Again, nothing.

Using the desk for leverage, she hauled herself upright, then gazed at the walls, and more specifically at the artwork on those walls. Paintings and enlarged photos seemed to be everywhere.

What better way to disguise a wall safe?

Her motivation renewed, Beatrix began working her way around the room, systematically inspecting the wall space behind every bit of framed art on display. When she reached behind a painting set squarely in front of Wynn's desk, she discovered a small, flat wall switch hidden there.

Grinning hard enough to hurt her cheeks, Beatrix stabbed the button with her thumb.

The sound of a bookcase sliding to one side startled her, but she quickly realized what caused it.

"Eureka!" she exclaimed and hurried closer to examine the contents of a tiny room that had been suddenly revealed.

Though expecting to find a lockbox or two, a wall safe, or at the very least a briefcase chock full of money, she found nothing of the kind. What sat in front of her was an odd and completely nondescript machine. It had a single light on top alongside a row of buttons. The light was off.

On one side of the device, she discovered a

paper tray, identical to those that come with home office printers. A handful of papers lay in it, but like those on the floor around which she'd walked, these bore data that made no sense to her.

She reached into the tray and helped herself to a sheet from the bottom of the stack.

Maybe Jeffrey can figure out what it means.

Chapter Nineteen

"I'd rather live in a world where firms don't have these enormous incentives to spy on individuals." —Paul Romer

Braden found it difficult to read the redhead. Danica seemed confident and self-reliant, right up until someone complimented her. Then her personality retreated a step. It didn't disappear; it just seemed suddenly unsure, out of balance.

She was most certainly attractive, an added bonus for arranging a date or two that would inch him closer to his target.

Since Danica had backed out on his original offer to buy her a drink, he opted to use the time to look up the video the girl in the convenience store had talked about. It took less time than he thought it might, and he was surprised to see how many hits it had gotten. Calling it viral was an understatement.

He watched the video several times and saved a copy to his phone to peruse later and possibly share with Danica if she took him up on his dinner offer. She had not seemed eager to go out. That made sense; she didn't know him at all. He told himself he couldn't chance doing anything overly forward or stupid. But he knew that might be hard.

The babe in the video captivated him. He'd never seen a woman so self-assured. She didn't hesitate to spring into action, and it didn't seem to matter that her choice of weapon would only strike terror in a turd. She took out a bad guy and eliminated a dire threat to the salesclerk and anyone else who might have wandered into the place.

Danica was impressive, and not just in terms of bravado. She could've modeled sportswear, swimwear, or formalwear. *Hell, she'd make rags look good!*

But as much as he enjoyed thinking about her, he also had to think about McComb. It may or may not make any difference, but the money man needed to know Albright had a bodyguard, and a damned good one. The rich bastard would want another update anyway, and he'd no doubt expect Braden to deliver it as if he were some sort of secret agent.

Well, screw that! If he wants information, he can damn well accept it like a normal human being.

He's rich. He can probably buy his way out of almost any problem anyway. Lord knows I'm not doing anything so shady that he'd need plausible deniability. Isn't that what the crooked politicians called it? Well, screw them, too.

Braden dialed McComb's office, and the call was immediately answered by a female. He assumed it was the same woman who'd slipped him the name and number for Shaughnessy/Gupta. That bit of subterfuge now seemed pathetic, but he felt like tossing it back at her.

"This is... *Shaughnessy's* contact. Tell your boss I have new information. If he wants it, he can call me. He knows the number."

He hung up before the secretary could give him any grief.

~*~

At breakfast the following morning, Jeffrey hoped Beatrix wouldn't get all pissy because he stayed out a little later than usual. She was fast asleep when he got home, and he managed to get into bed without waking her. If he could have patted himself on the back for that, he would have.

Sadly, before he'd taken his first bite of sweet roll for breakfast the following morning, Bea slipped into Chatty Kathy mode. "You'll never guess what I found in Wynn's house yesterday."

"No, prob'ly not," he said. "Pass the creamer?"

Beatrix pushed a carton of flavored cream in his direction. "Seriously. You've gotta guess."

"I dunno. Panties? A stripper pole?" Visions of the dancers from the previous evening still occupied his mind. He added sugar and the creamer to his coffee and stirred it while forcing himself to focus on food instead of naked broads on a stage.

"Don't be ridiculous," Beatrix said. "Not even someone as crass and uncaring as your father would have stuff like that." She stared at him in a way that suggested he'd sprouted appendages found only on the most macabre demons.

"Okay. I give up. What did you find?"

"I'm not entirely sure, but I think it's some kinda printer."

Jeffrey dropped his pastry in mock surprise. "Whoa! A *printer?* In Dad's house? Good God-a-mighty! Who'd have ever thunk it?"

Beatrix frowned. "Okay, smart ass. I'm pretty sure it's not *just* a printer. It's got some switches on top marked with letters that spell 'SLOW.' Weird, right? And besides, he's got a regular printer right next to his desk. Why would he need two?"

"I have no idea. He's strange, but you know that. So, what's the big deal? Why do you think it's special?"

"'Cause he went to a great deal of trouble to hide it."

Jeffrey stared at her. "I don't understand. Where did he hide it?"

"You know that floor-to-ceiling bookcase behind his desk chair?"

"Yeah."

"Well, it moves. There's a tiny room behind it, and that's where the machine is. Hidden away."

"Not very well, obviously."

Beatrix shook her finger at him. "*Au contraire.* The only way to make the bookcase move is by hitting a hidden switch. Then it slides to one side and reveals the opening behind it."

Jeffrey looked at her in surprise. "How did you know there was a switch, or where it was?"

Her lips came together in a pout. "I was looking for a hidden wall safe."

"Why on Earth would you do that?"

"Because we both know your father is filthy rich. He's a big deal in the stock market. He's probably got millions just sitting around while we nearly starve to death in a crappy little house that's about to fall down around us. Does he even think of us? Does he help us out? Does he give a damn? And don't forget; rather than offer you a job, he hired a homeless whore to keep him company."

"About her," Jeffrey began, "she's more than that actually, way more. She's working as his bodyguard, and I've gotta admit, she's got some skills. When you see her video, you'll understand."

"Oh, Lord. Not the video thing again. You understand, don't you, that most of that stuff is staged, right? It's made up. It's bullshit. The people are actors."

Jeffrey shook his head. "It looked pretty damned real to me. But you're gonna believe what you want no matter what I say."

"That's not true. I do value what you think. Sometimes."

"Oh yeah, right."

"Hold on. I'll show you."

She lumbered to a table near the door where she always left her purse. She grabbed it, reached inside, and pulled out a folded sheet of paper, which she carried back and handed to him with a flourish.

"What's this?" he asked.

"I found it in the paper tray of Wynn's secret printer. There were several sheets in there, but I only took the bottom one. I figured he wouldn't notice it's gone. I looked at it before I left, but other than the date, it didn't make any sense to me. The columns of codes, numbers, and percentages are meaningless. I mean, they aren't even in alphabetical order."

He noted a date printed at the top that was several weeks in the future, then he squinted at the columns of figures. There were four blocks of data, each containing two sets of columns with ten lines each.

"Oh, my God," he breathed when he realized what he was looking at. "I can't believe it!"

Beatrix leaned against him while looking over his shoulder, her breasts squished against his back. "What is it?"

Jeffrey pointed to the columns on the left, which all had positive percentages, then at the columns on the right, which were all negative. "These are the big winners and losers on the New York Stock Exchange for this trading date." He stabbed the heading. "The codes are just shorthand for the names of the stocks. They're grouped together by indexes— you know, the Dow, the S&P 500, Nasdaq."

"But how could he have that kind of information for a date that won't happen until later?"

"That's a damned good question."

~*~

Wynn felt better after spending the night in the hospital, despite the frequent, middle-of-the-night visits by staff checking on him.

His primary care doctor had called in a specialist, and between them they'd come up with a treatment plan. They thought his symptoms were consistent with radiation poisoning. That made little sense since Wynn didn't offer any insight to a source. He planned to swear Danica to secrecy, too. The physicians went with their plan anyway.

He felt more sorry for Danica than he did for himself. He'd made it possible for her to step up and away from homelessness, learn new skills, and make a fresh start. All of that within a very short time. And now *he* was faced with an early death? As a spiritual man, dying didn't scare him. He looked forward to rejoining his late wife and his dearest friend as well. But he couldn't leave Danica with nothing. Or Jeffrey for that matter.

And then there was his philanthropy. He couldn't expect Danica to step into his shoes and keep it going. He had no doubts she could develop the necessary skills, but that wouldn't happen overnight. He had to have a plan. And fast.

Danica had offered to spend the night in the hospital, but he told her to go back to the house and take care of Roscoe. "The good folks here will look after me," he'd said.

Now, however, he definitely needed her with him. He also needed his attorney, a long-time friend who'd been after him to formalize his charity giving. The lawyer, Archibald Carnahan, had not only served as Wynn's accountant, too, but as the Best Man at his wedding.

He put in calls to both and waited impatiently for them to show up. Danica arrived first. She looked neat and chipper, as usual, with a smile on her face.

"You look a little better," she said. "How do you feel?"

"Honestly?"

She grimaced and gave him a tiny nod.

"Not great. Weak. And... well... stupid."

"Stupid?"

"Yeah," he said. "I've been putting off doing some things I've known I have to do. I've put 'em off way too long."

"Like what?"

"We'll go over all that when Archie gets here. He's my tax guy. He's also my lawyer." A sly smile crept onto his pale face. "But he's also something of a lecher, so don't let him get too close."

The look of consternation on Danica's face was his reward. "But please, if he tries to touch you, don't hurt him. After all, he's an old man, like me."

~*~

Danica failed to hide her surprise at Wynn's warning and hoped he was joking. He'd done it before. But she didn't always notice it.

When Wynn's friend showed up, Wynn introduced him as Archie Carnahan. She greeted the lawyer/accountant with a smile and a handshake, then backed away.

"I don't know if you're the reason Wynn has finally come to his senses," Archie said, "but if so, thank you, my dear."

Wynn frowned. "She hasn't gotten me to do anything I hadn't already planned to do. The thing is, circumstances have changed. I need to plan for the future, and I definitely want her involved."

"I don't understand," Danica said.

"You will," replied Wynn. "Bear with me while Archie and I get the process started." He frowned. "And can you raise the head of this bed a little? I need to sit up."

While she adjusted his bed, Wynn told Archie what he had in mind for continuing his charitable giving. "I want to call it the Annabelle Knox Foundation. I imagine it'll need a small group of trustees, which I'll head as long as I can. After that, the board can elect my successor."

Danica grew fearful listening to Wynn's explanation. "I hope you weren't planning to put me in that group. I don't know diddly about running anything, much less a charity."

Wynn shook his head. "I wouldn't do that to you. Not at first, anyway. I have no doubt you'd be capable. You're smart, but more importantly, you've got a good heart."

Archie cleared his throat. "So, what exactly *do* you have in mind for her?"

"I want her to be the organization's chief researcher. Or maybe 'investigator' would be more accurate. Whatever. I want her to look into any and all groups that come to us for a donation. If they don't live up to her standards, they won't get a nickel."

"*My* standards?" Danica felt the blood drain from her head. "I'd be the Chief... What did you call it?"

"Researcher. Or Investigator. Pick one; I don't care. You'll have a decent salary, an expense account, a real office—not some crappy bedroom in an old man's house—and you'll probably need some support staff, too. A secretary at the very least."

"But... I... Wynn, are you sure? There must be tons of people more capable than me."

Archie remained silent and smiling as he watched the back and forth between them.

"You're the one I want for the job," Wynn said. "That's the important thing, provided you're interested. Are you?"

"I uhm... I think I need to know more about what my duties would be."

"I'll explain all that. And you'll have time to do some full investigations. If you aren't comfortable with your duties, we'll figure something else out. Fair enough?"

"Yes!" she said, still not quite believing what was happening. "Will I uhm... you know... be working with Mr. Carnahan?"

"It's Archie," the lawyer said. "And while we get this thing up and running, you'll probably see a good bit of me."

He peered back and forth between Wynn and Danica, noted the looks on their faces, and then started laughing. "Did Wynn tell you I'm a dirty old man?"

Josh Langston

Danica looked at Wynn, hoping for a clue about how to respond. She didn't get one.

"My dear," Archie said, "Wynn's done that more times than I can count. You've nothing to fear from me. You're a lovely, charming young woman, but I'm gay."

She felt a flush of relief, but it was short-lived. Her cell phone rang. She answered it and listened to a panicky plea from April, the convenience store clerk.

"I have to go," she told Wynn. "This is an emergency."

Chapter Twenty

"...throughout much of history and in many cultures, redheads have been viewed with suspicion and fear—and even killed—because of their hair." —Kate Williams

"Daley? Braden Daley?"

Braden glanced at his cell phone; the caller's number wasn't familiar. He normally didn't answer calls from numbers he didn't recognize, but he'd abandoned that policy when he agreed to work for McComb. The man was so paranoid, he might call from a different number each time.

"Who is this?" Braden asked.

"It's me, Shaughnessy."

Gupta. Braden rolled his eyes. "What d'you want?"

"Listen up, asshole. Remember you had me bug some loser's house?"

"Yeah. So?"

"I got some very interesting information off my recordings from there."

"Interesting, how?"

"The woman who lives there snuck into her father-in-law's house looking for a wall safe. Instead, she found a machine. I'm guessing it's a printer of some kind. Anyway, there were some papers in it. They're the really interesting part."

"Why?" asked Braden.

"'Cause there's data printed on them. Data that shouldn't exist."

"I don't understand," Braden said. "What kind of data?"

"Well, see, now we've got a bit of a problem. Since you didn't wanna wait for the results of the hack and cough, what I have now is brand new info. And new info requires a new payment."

"That's bullshit!"

"Actually, no. That's business. You're either interested or not. If you won't pay for it, I know someone who will. And when they find out you didn't want it, I'm guessing they won't need to keep your sorry ass on the payroll."

"McComb."

"Who's that?"

"You know damn well who he is."

"Maybe," said Gupta, "maybe not. So, are you willing to pay for the new stuff or do I contact you-know-who?"

"How much?"

"Well, normally, I'd charge my standard fee, five thousand. But since this stuff is hot, and we're talkin' *seriously* hot, I'll have to double my price."

"*Double it?*"

"Yeah. But I'll give you a full copy of the recording on a thumb drive."

"And you'll delete *your* copy?"

Gupta laughed. "Oh yeah, sure. I've no problem throwing away priceless intel. Don't be stupid. Of course I won't delete it. It's insurance. If you try to screw me, I'll screw you even worse."

Braden mentally rattled off every filthy word he could think of, not that it helped. Gupta had him by the short hairs; he had to pay.

"It's gonna take me some time to get the money."

"I'll give ya 'til this time tomorrow. Bring all ten grand. I'll buy you a burger where we met before.

Got it?"

"Yeah," said Braden just before he cut the connection.

And now—oh joy—I get to sell some more of my fucking stock. Or my car. Maybe both!

~*~

Danica already had the address for April's apartment. She and her roomie lived in a second-floor flat in a building that should have been condemned long ago. Because it sat closer to the hospital than to Wynn's house, Danica made the trip in a matter of minutes. She hurried from Wynn's car, up the steps to the second floor, and down the hall to April's apartment where she knocked on the door.

"Libby? It's Danica, April's friend from the Gas n' Go. She wanted me to check on you."

Danica heard movement on the other side of the door and assumed Libby was looking at her through the peephole. Danica smiled and waved. Apparently, that was enough to encourage the girl inside to let her in.

After a quick introduction, Danica asked Libby to give her more of an explanation since April sounded frantic when she called. She hadn't taken the time to delve into details, but her message was clear: her friend Libby was in trouble.

"His name's Tim, and we dated for a while," Libby explained. "It started out nice, and we got along, did some fun stuff. But then he changed, making demands and ordering me around. I told him if he was gonna be mean, I didn't want to see him anymore. That's when he hit me. It got worse after that. He... He made me do stuff I didn't wanna do."

Danica's attitude quickly downshifted from affable to alarmed. "What has you worried right now?"

"He's coming here! Said on the phone he's bringing a friend, and we'd do something super special. I told him no, and he got real mad, scary mad. Said he'd change my mind for good. I don't believe for a second he meant *anything* good. He's just mean. I don't want him to hurt me again."

Danica appraised the petite young woman. She stood a bit over five feet tall and couldn't have weighed more than 90 pounds. She had short, blonde hair and wore jeans and a sweatshirt. She had bruises on her cheek and neck which she'd tried unsuccessfully to hide with makeup.

"How big is this jerk?" Danica asked.

"Tim's tall, maybe six feet. He's kinda thin, but he's strong. He can pick me up like I don't weigh anything at all."

Danica smiled in hopes of calming her. "I was your size in the fourth grade." She walked back to the door, looked through the peephole to make sure no one was lurking outside, then opened it and inspected the latch. Between the hollow core door and the cheap frame, the entryway was anything but secure. "Any idea when he'll get here?"

"Soon. I was about to leave and go hide somewhere."

With a quick shake of her head, Danica squelched the idea. "We need to end this now, otherwise he'll continue to stalk you. And I'm worried about what he has in mind that might be 'super special.'" She secured the deadbolt and set the lock on the wobbly doorknob.

Libby remained agitated. "But what'll we do when he gets here? And he's bringing someone with him! He could hurt us both. When I said he gets angry, I meant it. He gets really angry."

"I understand. He's a hot-head. Impulsive. Probably doesn't take time to think things through. And he probably believes deep down that he's a badass."

"That's a fact," Libby said, her voice shaky.

"But is he, really? I mean, have you seen him intimidate anyone else?"

The girl took a moment before responding. "He mostly just picks on waitresses, kids, too. He thinks he's being funny, but he's just being an asshole."

"I know the type." Danica looked around the cheaply furnished living room in hopes of spotting something she might use as a weapon, but she found nothing. "Is this Tim character likely to be carrying a knife or a gun?"

"Knife? No. But he does have a gun."

"Do you know what kind?"

Libby shook her head. "I don't know anything about guns. Do you? I always thought it was a guy thing. You know—big gun, little wiener."

Danica couldn't help but chuckle. "Sometimes it does seem that way. But yeah, I know a good bit about weapons. The Marines saw to that."

"*You were a Marine?*"

"Yep. I can say oorah, Semper Fi, and all that crap. Now, why don't we look in the kitchen and see if there's anything there we could use."

"We've got a butcher knife," Libby said. "It's not real sharp, but it's pretty big. It might scare him."

"I'd rather not kill him, and that's all too easy to do with a big knife. I've got something else in mind.

You wouldn't happen to have a bottle of wine, would you?"

"We did have some, but we drank it all. April gets it at work." Libby opened a cabinet near the sink, probed briefly, then stopped. "Is there anything else we could use?"

Danica thought for a moment. "Got anything in a glass bottle that's fairly heavy?"

Libby brightened. "How 'bout ketchup?"

"If it's in a glass bottle, it'll do fine."

"It is." Libby pulled an unopened bottle of Heinz's finest out of the cabinet and offered it to Danica, but she wouldn't take it. "I thought you wanted it."

"Nope. It's for you. In case this Tim character gets past me. If he does, use that on him. Go for his throat or anywhere on his head."

Libby showed no signs of confidence, and Danica struggled to find words of comfort. She gave up on that and cut to the heart of the matter. "Libby, if he gets by me, you have to save yourself. Turn your fear into anger. Remember what he did to you. There's no way you can let him get away with that."

"But—"

"No buts, Libby. You can rely on this—even if

he's got enough left after what I do to him, he's not going to be in great shape. You will definitely be able to take him down."

"You promise?" The girl's voice quivered.

"Damn straight."

Before they returned to the living room, someone knocked on the front door then added, "It's me, Lib. Open up."

"It's Tim!" she breathed. The look of terror on the girl's face stiffened Danica's resolve.

"C'mon, Lib!" he said. "Lemme in. I got someone here I want you to meet. You're gonna love him."

Danica leaned close and whispered in her ear. "Don't tell him about me. I won't open the door. If he wants in, he'll have to break it down."

"But... But..." Libby blubbered.

"Do your best to piss him off."

The girl's eyes went wide. "Are you *crazy?*"

"Damn it Libby," Tim yelled. "Open the fucking door."

"No," she shouted back. "Go away. Leave me alone."

Danica gave her a thumbs up and guided her

back toward the kitchen. "Remember what I said," she whispered. "Chances are he won't get near you, but if he does, you know what to do."

"But he brought someone with him!"

Tim pounded on the door. "Now, Libby. Open up!"

"Trust me, okay?" Danica said, her voice low. "Tell him you're busy or something."

As Danica hurried back to the door, Libby took a deep breath and yelled, "Go to hell, Timmy. I never want to see you again."

Danica managed a quick glance through the peephole and saw two men talking. The smaller of the two was visibly upset; the other looked nervous and possibly ready to leave.

"Okay then, bitch. You've brought this on yourself. You get one last chance to do this nicely. Now open the goddam door!"

"Fuck off, Timmy! Go away or I'll call the cops."

"You wouldn't dare do something that stupid!"

After a brief silence, he kicked the door. The first blow accomplished little, though Danica imagined he damaged the thin outer layer. The second kick landed near the knob and deadbolt. It splintered the cheap frame and sent the door swinging wide.

Tim stomped through; his face set in a deep scowl. His focus was on Libby who stood trembling in the doorway to the kitchen. He stepped past Danica as she hugged the wall beside the door. His eyebrows dipped, and he stopped. He made it halfway through a turn in her direction when she chopped him in the throat with the edge of her hand.

Libby held the ketchup bottle in one hand and a cell phone in the other, but she appeared too shaken to use either.

With one hand on his throat and a look of sheer hatred on his face, Tim shifted to stand squarely in front of Danica. She pulled back her fist as if to deliver a second blow, and Tim raised both arms to block it.

That's when she drove her toe into his groin.

The shock on his face as he folded from the waist, accompanied by a sharp but unsuccessful attempt to draw in air, told Danica he was nearly done.

But she wasn't.

Grabbing his hair in both hands, she rammed his face into her raised knee. That sent him to the floor and left one leg of her yoga pants messy from his suddenly bloody nose. Once down, he didn't move.

Danica checked his pulse then signaled to Libby. "He's done."

"Oh my God! Is he dead?"

"Nah. Just unconscious. He'll wake up soon enough."

Danica stepped over Tim and walked toward his thoroughly shocked companion, who backed away. The man's face had gone pale. Heavyset and wearing an Ohio State sweatshirt a size too small, he looked anything but intimidating—at first. But his features soon hardened.

Unconcerned by his apparent switch from faint of heart to being a tough guy, Danica stepped closer and sneered at him. "You want some of me, too?"

Chapter Twenty-one

"A man should never neglect his family for business." —Walt Disney

Jeffrey Albright desperately wanted to quit his shitty job. In fact, he'd dreamed about telling his boss precisely where he could jam his crappy cubicle and everything that went with it. Unfortunately, he couldn't afford to lose out on the severance package the company had promised him.

That didn't mean, however, that he'd do more than the bare minimum to get by. The hours passed slowly, but eventually he made it through the day and out the door.

He didn't know if his father had come home from the hospital yet, but he figured he'd drive by and find out. If Roscoe was the only one home, he'd go look for the secret room Beatrix told him about.

Pleased to find no vehicles in the driveway or the garage, Jeffrey unlocked the front door and let himself in. As usual, Roscoe raised hell, but he knew Jeffrey and didn't try to hurt him. The dog's goal was to annoy, and he accomplished that with canine zeal.

The door to Wynn's office remained unlocked. He assumed Bea was the last person to go inside. He did as she had told him and felt under the painting on the wall in front of Wynn's desk. He activated the paddle switch and waited while the bookcase behind the desk slid aside.

Roscoe had not followed him; he remained in the living room. Jeffrey's walk toward the formerly secret room ended when Roscoe started barking again.

Crap! Dad's back. I've gotta get outta here.

He tried to push the bookcase back in place, but it wouldn't budge. After practically leaping over the desk to get to the wall switch, Jeffrey got the little room sealed off once again. Moving as quickly and quietly as possible, he left the room and went into the kitchen.

That's where Wynn and his old friend Archie caught up with him.

"What're you doing here?" Wynn asked.

"I got here just before you did. Thought I'd

look in on you." *But now that I can see how thin and pale you are, I don't understand why you aren't still in the hospital.* "I didn't know how long you'd be… you know, laid up in County General."

"A call would've sufficed." Wynn shrugged and gestured toward his friend. "You remember Archie, don't you?"

Jeffrey smiled, hoping he didn't appear guilty of anything, then offered his hand. "Of course, I remember Mr. Carnahan. It's good to see you again."

"Archie insisted on driving me home from the hospital since Danica had something else to do."

"I thought taking care of you was her primary responsibility," Jeffrey said. "She's got some nerve taking time off knowing you were in the hospital and would need someone to bring you home."

"I'm not an invalid, you know," Wynn snapped.

"Not yet, anyway."

Wynn pressed his lips together before adding, "You're still pissed about me hiring Danica instead of you."

"Maybe." Jeffrey shoved his hands in his pockets. "I'll be outta work soon, and Bea's making a big deal about her upcoming birthday. I don't know what I'm gonna do."

"I can help," Wynn said. "But you'll have to decide which of you gets the... uhm... present."

"*Which* of us? I don't understand."

"You will," Wynn said. "Now, let me finish my discussion with Arch, then I need to pop into my office for a minute. I'll be right back."

Jeffrey's curiosity quickly shifted into impatience as he watched his father chit-chat with Archie Carnahan. *How long is he going to stretch out his stupid goodbye?*

After what seemed like hours, the lawyer approached Jeffrey and handed him one of his business cards. "I'll be working even more closely than usual with your dad in the next few weeks. I suspect you and I will need to get in touch at some point. The card has all my contact data. Don't hesitate to call if you need me."

Jeffrey glanced at the card, the back of which listed Carnahan's specialties. It included divorce consultation among other things. *Wouldn't that make for a dandy birthday present!*

Wynn told Jeffrey to stay where he was and added, "I'll be right back." Then he accompanied the lawyer to the front door where they shook hands. Carnahan left, and Wynn shuffled toward his office sanctuary. A minute or so later he returned bearing a slip of paper.

"What's that?" Jeffrey asked, unable to hide the disappointment in his voice.

"What were you expecting?"

Jeffrey shrugged. "Hell, I dunno. A new car maybe?"

Wynn laughed. "I'd never presume to pick out the right vehicle for you. But, speaking of cars, can you drive me to the nearest convenience store? I need to make a quick purchase."

"Sure," said Jeffrey, still puzzled by the lack of a present. *Is he gonna buy me something from a stupid mom and pop store? Won't Beatrix be thrilled by that!*

That evening, Braden sat in his apartment staring at the screen of his laptop. His plan to sell some of his stock to pay Gupta for the new information didn't look promising. His best stocks had taken a beating during a week-long market retreat. He assumed those shares would rebound, but it would take far more time than Gupta had given him. The two were scheduled to meet at noon the next day.

Selling his shares now meant taking a huge loss. Braden's portfolio would shrink even further.

He couldn't afford it. A quick look at his bank

account revealed pathetically little in savings and even less in checking. Even if he'd just been paid, it wouldn't be enough to cover his living expenses if he had to use it to buy Gupta's flash drive.

That asshole McComb would be happy to buy it. And if he gets what he needs from the phony Irishman, he won't need me.

Braden got up and paced; his nerves demanded activity, no matter how pointless. He had to figure out what to do. And damned quick.

Plead for more time? That brought a snort of derisive laughter.

Promise him double if the info pays off?

He shook off the thought without a sound.

He felt small and used. Helpless. And then he thought of Danica, the redhead who totally beat the snot out of someone twice her size. Braden didn't have anything remotely like her skillset. What little of value he'd acquired in life had come his way via something he considered odd—honesty. He could talk a good game when the stakes were low, but when it mattered, he shed his bluster and played whatever role his team demanded. Being up front worked more often than not. He hoped like hell Gupta would go for it. Braden had one trump card; he knew where the man with the machine lived. Gupta didn't.

The machine was likely just a computer. What made it special would have to be the program it ran that generated the data Gupta mentioned. But what kind of data? What sort would be of interest to a stockbroker, especially one who was already rich?

Stock price predictions! Of course! And I sure as hell know what to do with that kind of info. I just need to convince Gupta that we can make far more money using the data than selling it.

Braden simply had to sell Gupta on teamwork. It was his only option.

~*~

Tim's pal in Libby's hallway shrank away under Danica's fierce scowl. He stopped moving when he hit the far wall, and what little of his remaining bravado crumbled. "Okay, now, back off. It's just... I'm... Look, Tim said—"

Danica's glare silenced him. "Tim said what, exactly? That you could have sex with my friend in there? Is that it?"

"He called it the 'Girlfriend Experience.'"

"The *what?*"

"He said she would be acting. She would roleplay the 'Break-up and Make-up game.'"

"And you *believed* that crap? You went along

with it?"

"Well, yeah. He charged me two hundred bucks. Said he had it all worked out. But now, I just want my money back."

Danica squinted at him. "Are you shitting me? If you want a refund, you're gonna have to beat it out of old Timmy here, once the cops are through with him."

"There's no way I'm sticking around," he said sliding sideways along the wall.

"The police will want to hear what you have to say."

"Screw that!" he yelled over his shoulder as he scrambled away. "I didn't see anything!"

Danica watched him go, then re-entered the apartment and joined Libby as she stared down at Tim. "Are you sure he's not dead?" the girl asked.

Danica checked his pulse a second time. "I'm sure."

"Good," said Libby as she squatted on the floor next to him and spread out the fingers of one hand. "This is the one he hit me with," she added. Using the ketchup bottle like a pile driver, she began pounding his fingers one-by-one.

Though tempted to stop her, Danica knew

Libby had earned some revenge. When Tim moaned and moved his head, Libby stopped. She stood up and moved away.

"Call 9-1-1," Danica said gently. "I'd like to have the cops here before he wakes up completely." While Libby made the call, Danica knelt next to Tim, removed the wallet from his back pocket, and looked at a wad of twenty-dollar bills inside. She removed ten of them, put his wallet back, and gave the money to Libby when she finished the call.

"What's this for?" the girl asked.

"That's how much your ex charged his friend to have sex with you. You may need it to pay for repairing the door."

Libby glared for a long moment at the man on the floor, then spat on him. Danica gave her a thumbs up.

April arrived before the police. She carefully stepped over Tim, hurried toward Libby, and hugged her.

"She's okay," Danica assured her. "Just a little shook up." She pointed at Tim. "He didn't fare so well."

Tim continued to moan until he tried to flex his fingers; then he screamed.

Danica promptly sat on him with her feet on

either side of his head. "Be still, asshole. I'll let you up when the cops get here. Or would you rather I smacked you again?" She tapped him on the forehead with the ketchup bottle.

"Who the fuck are you?" he groaned.

Danica chuckled. "Just a friend."

April added, "She's your worst nightmare."

"When I find out who the hell you are, I'll be back. You'll pay, I swear."

Danica shook her head, unfazed by his words. She pulled her cell phone out and dialed Ranger Rick's number. If anyone had the tools to rig a temporary lock on the damaged door, it would be him. Besides, it gave her an excellent excuse to see him again.

Jeffrey held the car door open while his father worked his way onto the passenger seat, a painfully slow process. Once Wynn was in the vehicle, Jeffrey slammed the door shut, lumbered around to the driver's side, and got in.

"Do you want to visit any particular convenience store?" He'd been thinking of little other than the Danica video since Wynn asked him for the ride.

Wynn shook his head. "I don't care. You choose."

Jeffrey shuddered. Bea would have answered exactly the same way. *Only she'd have added something stupid like, "But don't go to the one on Highland. The guy who runs the place smells funny."*

Jeffrey drove to the nearest one he could think of and eased into a handicapped spot.

"You can't park here," Wynn said, gesturing at a blue sign bearing the ubiquitous white wheelchair symbol.

"Why not? You're handicapped," Jeffrey said. "It's no big deal."

Wynn grunted as he got out of the car. "Fine. If you get a ticket, don't expect me to pay for it."

"Want me to go with you?" Jeffrey asked.

"Nah. Stay in the car. Think of a good excuse to use when the cops show up."

Wynn wasn't gone long, and when he returned, Jeffrey had the car door open and the heater on. The old man got in slowly while Jeffrey shivered in the cold, impatiently waiting.

Once back behind the wheel, Jeffrey glanced at his father, expecting to see what he'd purchased. Wynn held nothing in his lap, no bag, no bottles, nothing.

Sensing his son's curiosity, Wynn tucked a folded slip of paper into Jeffrey's breast pocket.

"What's that?" he asked. "A receipt?"

"It's the solution to your problem about a birthday present for Beatrix," Wynn said. "And your employment problem as well."

"What the hell are you talking about?"

Wynn smiled. "I bought you a lottery ticket. A guaranteed winner."

"Guaranteed?" Jeffrey clamped his jaws tight to keep from screaming, then repeated the question. *"Guaranteed?* Who the hell can guarantee something like a lottery?"

"I can," Wynn said. "Trust me. I double-checked. The big drawing is next Friday night. By Saturday morning you'll be a big winner. Unless, of course, you just give it to Beatrix."

"You're insane," Jeffrey said.

"Believe what you like," Wynn said. "I'm ready to go home now."

Neither man spoke during the short drive back to Wynn's house. Jeffrey helped him inside, then went looking for a bar.

Guaranteed, my ass.

It didn't take long for him to remember what Bea had said about the hidden machine in Wynn's home office.

But that was all about stocks. He'd studied the printout Bea gave him. It didn't contain a shred of information about anything other than what came from Wall Street, and even that was severely limited, covering a mere thirty listings out of thousands.

Jeffrey settled for a sports bar, though he would have preferred a strip club, but he knew if he went to one, he'd spend too much. Once seated in a booth, he took the receipt from his pocket and examined it. He'd bought lottery tickets in the past, before he accepted that his chances of winning were less than miniscule. The ticket he held was for Lotto Grande, the biggest one in the nation. The grand prize was in the hundreds of millions of dollars. Therefore, there were likely a bazillion tickets sold, and the odds of winning were even smaller. *Microscopic. Ridiculous. Insane!*

He refolded the receipt, put it back in his shirt pocket, and silently cursed his father. The old bastard had deceived him often in the past, claiming his cruelties were mere practical jokes. This felt like another one.

Jeffrey vowed not to fall for it and ordered a

Long Island Iced Tea. With any luck, he could put away two of them before heading home to another dreadful dinner with Beatrix.

Chapter Twenty-two

"Courage is knowing it might hurt and doing it anyway. Stupidity is the same. And that's why life is hard." —Jeremy Goldberg

Much later that evening, while waiting for Danica to return after dealing with her emergency, Wynn drummed a pencil on the table beside the couch. He had nothing to do since he and Jeffrey returned from the convenience store. Relaxing wasn't one of his strong suits, so when the phone rang, he answered it happily. It was Carnahan.

Though it had only been a few hours since the attorney had left, Wynn was impatient. "It's about time, Arch. Is everything set?"

"I'm fine, Wynn. And you?"

Wynn shook his head. "Sorry, man. I didn't mean to be rude. I've just been worried, that's all."

"Forget it. I thought you might want an update. I already had most of the details worked out and got all the necessary paperwork turned in. It'll take a while before we get our credentials."

"Great!" Wynn said. "And you set up the trust account with Encore? That was the outfit you recommended, wasn't it?"

"Indeed. I used the seed money you gave me. And having your permission to access your accounts for all these years will make transferring your holdings much, much easier. I'll email you with the account details in case you want to make additional deposits. And I'm glad you're okay with not liquidating all your holdings, as we once discussed. You've got shares in some great companies. We need to hang on to them."

"And the bonds, too?" Wynn asked.

"Of course. There's a good mix of commercial and municipal paper. I know we talked about focusing on stocks that pay good dividends, but the bonds do, too. We've got to have something that generates income, otherwise the foundation will eventually run out of cash. I know you don't want that to happen." He paused and took a breath. "And as I've mentioned in the past, I need to be aware of what you're doing, so I can help you avoid mistakes."

"Like what?"

"Like anything that would result in higher taxes."

Wynn exhaled, but the effort turned into a cough which he finally got under control. "C'mon, Arch! If I'm transferring damn near every penny I have to a charitable foundation, I would hope my tax bill would be negligible."

The accountant chuckled. "Don't forget, you're the head man of that foundation, and the feds will be well aware of it. But we'll work on it, okay? The IRS has a funny way of looking at things. It often seems like their rules and regs are meant to prove how much of their money you'll be allowed to keep."

"*Their money!*"

"I told you they have a funny way of looking at things."

"Whatever. I want to get it done."

"I've got a good start, but I'm not nearly finished," Arch said. "You've got more brokerage accounts than anyone I know."

"That's old news, Arch."

"Oh. I almost forgot. You have to start interviewing prospective members for the board of trustees. Unless, of course, you want me to pick my own people."

"Not as long as I'm still alive, but you already knew that. Didn't you? I don't want any freeloaders; I want people who care and want to do more than just enhance their social resumes."

I just hope I live long enough to get it all squared away.

~*~

Danica felt more than just simple relief when Rick arrived at Libby and April's apartment. Though she had been able to maintain the appearance of being calm and in control, the episode with Libby's perverse boyfriend had left her rattled. She hadn't put what she felt into her voice when she called Rick. That changed when he arrived.

He knocked once on the damaged door, and it immediately drifted open. Abandoning the grip she had on her emotions, Danica hurried over and hugged him. "I'm so glad to see you," she breathed. "I knew you'd come and help."

Rick hugged her in return and gently patted her back. "It's okay, Dani. I'm sure everything's gonna be fine."

She sniffed and palmed an errant tear from one eye. His smile helped calm her down and brought her back to reality.

"I saw two patrol cars in the parking lot," he

said, maintaining their hug a bit longer. "They were headed out. You didn't give me many details when you called, but..." he paused, let go of her, quickly surveyed the other two women in the room, and squinted at the front door. "...I'm beginning to get a hint."

He turned again and stared directly at Danica, his face as sober-looking as she'd ever seen it. "Please tell me you didn't kill whoever smashed their way in."

"She didn't kill 'im!" piped April.

"But I wouldn't have cried if she had," added Libby. "He deserved it."

Rick exhaled in an exaggerated fashion. "Do you have any idea how worried I am about you sometimes? I mean—" He shrugged. "I don't know what to say. I'm just... I don't know. I care about you, and I don't want to see you get hurt."

Danica managed a nod, her emotions not yet fully under control. "That's really sweet. And it means a lot to me."

Rick put his hands on her shoulders, his grip firm but gentle. "Dani. C'mon. Are you listening? I said *you* mean a lot to me."

"I— It's just..." She swallowed. "I feel the same way about you."

They stood looking at each other without

moving for what felt like a ridiculously long and awkward moment. A kiss would have been nice—better than nice—but she hesitated to make the first move.

Rick pulled her closer, they kissed, and she eased back. It had been a nice kiss, almost chaste, but it still had her heart beating faster, and sent crazy thoughts tearing through her head. *What am I doing? Why now?* She wouldn't have been surprised if Libby and April started singing, "Rick and Dani, sittin' in a tree, K-I-S-S-I-N-G."

Happily, neither girl made a sound.

Rick's smile faded, replaced by his previous look of concern.

Please don't give me a lecture.

His voice was calm, rational. "It's not just what might happen to you when you get involved in these fights that bothers me."

Danica gave him a slight head shake. "They haven't been fights, really. More like take-downs. I don't like bullies; you know that."

"I don't like 'em either. But the thing is, the creeps you've taken down aren't normal. They've all got a crazy streak—a mean, vicious, *criminal* streak. They don't give a damn about rules or laws. They operate like... I dunno... animals. Some of them are bound to want payback. You didn't just hurt them; you hurt their pride."

"And their nuts," Libby interjected from across the room.

Her comment didn't alter the tension in Rick's voice. "It's their need for revenge that worries me the most."

"I get it." Danica gestured toward April and Libby. "But I worry about those two. The moron who broke in knows where they live and where they work. They can't stay here, and I can't hang around to protect them."

"We have to move anyway," Libby said, her voice wrapped in sadness. "My job is going away, and April can't afford to stay here on her paycheck alone."

Grateful for a change of subject, Danica asked Libby where she worked.

"I teach riding and stuff at Sunrise Ranch." She pursed her lips. "Things were goin' great, and Mrs. Malloy, the lady who runs the place, was gonna make me assistant manager."

"So, what happened?" Rick asked. "Sunrise Ranch has been around a long time."

"It has," said Libby. "And it's a wonderful place. It's not just some kinda dude ranch where people with lots of money can go and play like they're cowboys. It's mainly for handicapped kids. The first time I saw the smile on the face of a little crippled boy who we got up on a saddled pony changed everything for me. I knew I had to work there; I had to be a part of that."

"They do a big fundraiser every year, don't they?" Rick asked. "Pony rides, petting zoo, photos. I've been to a couple of them."

"They used to, but they won't do one this year," Libby said. "Mrs. Malloy's husband always got his civic club to run it. But he had a stroke, and the club now says they won't do it; there's not enough interest. Mrs. Malloy can't do it because she spends all her time taking care of him. They aren't rich, and it costs a lot to keep the ranch running."

Rick and Danica shared a look. "Sounds like something your boss might be interested in," he said.

Danica agreed. "And I'll make sure he finds out all about it!"

"Um, guys," said April. "I hate to spoil this tender moment, but what about our door?" She turned her attention to Rick. "If we can't lock it, what're we gonna do?"

~*~

Lionel McComb arrived at his office at the usual time—10 AM. His coffee was ready and waiting for him, along with a hot, buttered croissant, some imported marmalade, and a short list of issues needing his attention. One item in particular stood out enough to make him ignore his food and shout for his secretary. "Constance!"

McComb's stunning clerk floated through his door as if she knew he would summon her the moment he saw the list. "Yes, sir?"

"Did you verify this notice?"

"If you're referring to the Albright account, yes, I did. The information is correct. Everything in the account has been transferred to another firm."

"Which one?"

"I believe it was Encore, but I'd have to—"

"Never mind," McComb grumbled. "I'm sure you're right, damn it." He waved her away.

Constance backed out of his office and closed the door. Ordinarily, McComb would have had a conversation with her while he ate. She was unquestionably the most attractive woman among the upper tier of GE&M staff. Her physical charms being almost irresistible, she had proven herself more than adept at wooing wealthy clients into the fold, and had been paid handsomely for her efforts. The desertion of Wynn Albright, however, tore his mind away from her delightful shape and talents as she returned to her desk.

He immediately picked up his phone and called Franklin Duffy, one of his many contacts in the brokerage industry. "Franky? It's Lionel."

Duffy preceded his response with a slight groan. "Lionel. How are you?"

"Pissed, if you must know."

"Glad to hear it. I hope it lasts through our match on Saturday. How's that new putter of yours?"

"I'm not calling about golf, God damn it," McComb groused. "I need to know if Wynn Albright still has an account with you."

"He did the last time you asked me. Why? Is he tired of dealing with you and your antique approach to investing?"

"Screw you, Franky. You know I wouldn't call unless it was important."

"To you, anyway," Duffy said. "But if you insist, I can check."

"I insist."

"Stand by."

McComb tapped his fingers relentlessly until Duffy came back on the line. "It's funny you should ask about the Albright account. He closed it out yesterday. Transferred everything to… uhm….”

“Encore? Was it Encore?”

“Yes. Encore. What’s got you so fired up?”

“I hate those people at Encore. They all act so damned superior. They never share information and never discuss clients. It’s frustrating.”

“I believe it’s referred to as being ethical,” Duffy said.

Rather than respond to the pious prick, McComb hung up on him and reached for the list of contacts and their phone numbers he kept in the top drawer of his massive desk. The list contained most of the movers and shakers in his industry. He called them one-by-one and got the same answer. Albright was consolidating, and he was doing it with a firm that wouldn’t share a shred of their knowledge about what he was buying and selling. Or when he was doing it.

McComb didn’t care about the loss of a client, even though that client represented a significant amount of capital. What bothered him was the fact that he would no longer be able to copy Albright’s market movements. The man had never lost money on an investment—ever! McComb had enriched himself by copying every trade Albright made.

Now that was gone.

And the only person he could think of to blame was Braden Daley. What had the idiot done to make Albright put all his eggs in one uncompromising basket?

Chapter Twenty-three

"Forty for you, sixty for me. And equal partners we will be."
—Joan Rivers

Wynn stayed awake until Danica got back the previous evening, but he was too tired to ask her for details about the emergency that required her attention. For that, he waited until the following morning.

Danica greeted him in the kitchen, clear-eyed and smiling.

"Guess it went well last night," he said.

She nodded. "Can I fix you something for breakfast?"

"All I need is coffee."

She poured them each a cup then took a seat across from him at the kitchen table.

273

"Care to enlighten me about your emergency yesterday?" he asked.

She gave him a brief recap then quickly changed the subject. "Have you ever heard of a place called the Sunrise Ranch?"

Her question took him by surprise. "Yes, sure, I've heard of it. Never been there though. Why?"

"Libby, the girl whose ex-boyfriend we had to deal with, works there. But her job is in jeopardy. The place is on the verge of closing."

"Too bad," Wynn said. "But I'm sure she'll be able to find work somewhere else. But let's slide back a little bit. Tell me more about this guy who broke into her apartment. You said you stopped him once he got in, and then the cops came and took him away."

Danica's head bobbed up and down. "Yep."

"What was he after? Why was there so much commotion?"

The smile on Danica's face faded. "He was going to force Libby to have sex with some random asshole. The creep paid Libby's ex two hundred bucks for the privilege."

Wynn pursed his lips. "Either of these guys have a name?"

"Tim's the ex," she said. "I don't know the

other guy's name, but I can think of several words that would fit him well. And they're mostly four-letter ones. Anyway, Tim is the cops' problem now." She squirmed a bit in her chair, then continued. "I want to talk to you some more about Sunrise Ranch."

Wynn felt sure he knew where she was headed but played along. "What about it?"

"I think we need to look into it and maybe help them out. Based on what Libby told me, they do some wonderful work for kids who deserve a break."

"I see," he said, avoiding anything that might sound like encouragement. He wanted to see how strongly she felt.

"Rick said he's heard great things about the place and what they do."

Wynn pursed his lips once again. "I thought you wanted to look into programs for kids who age out of foster care."

"I do! But that's a much bigger issue. This one…" She exhaled. "Honestly? This one tugs at my heart."

"Sometimes that can be a warning sign. There are so many scammers out there, and they love to get their filthy mitts on charitable money. It's not like they care about who gets hurt. They're only in it for themselves."

He took a sip of his coffee, carefully set the mug on the table, and then rubbed his chin as if mulling over her comments. "I think this ranch might be worthy of a contribution from the Knox Foundation. But we're not an official entity just yet. Archie says that's going to take some time."

"Oh," Danica said, downcast.

"But maybe that's a good thing. It would give you time to look into the place and determine if it's really and truly something we want to support."

Danica's attitude changed in an instant. She all but levitated out of her seat at the table. "Will you help me? I mean, I don't even know where to start."

He couldn't help but laugh. "You slay me. Last night you took down a creep, probably somebody with a criminal record, and this morning, you're a kid in a candy shop."

She sobered slightly. "Is that a bad thing?"

"Not at all." He chuckled. "It's part of your charm."

She shook her head. "Rick said something along those lines last night."

"Oh? Are you two... I mean, have you—"

"We're *dating*, okay? That's all. For now, anyway."

Wynn smiled. "I'm glad to hear it. Rick's a good guy. You could do an awful lot worse."

"We'll see," she said. "So, can you help me get started?"

"Of course. But you need to understand my time is limited."

"I know you need your rest."

"I'm not talking about that," he said, unable to disguise the sadness in his voice. "I don't think I have a great deal of time left on this planet."

~*~

Braden arrived at the fast-food restaurant where he had met Gupta/Shaughnessy previously. As before, the lunch hour crowd left few seats open, so he scrambled toward the first table available and sat down just ahead of an older woman carrying her lunch on a tray who had the same idea.

She stared down at him over her food as if she expected him to surrender the spot. "Well?"

He smiled up at her. "Well, what?"

"Have you no manners?"

He shrugged.

"If you're not going to leave, may I at least join you?"

"Ah, no. I'm waiting for someone."

"The table seats four," she said. "Surely you don't need all that space."

"But we do need privacy."

"We're in a *public* place," she said, her voice radiating irritation.

"Yeah, I guess." He spotted Gupta entering the store and waved to him. "Do you mind? My... uhm... friend is here."

A man much larger than Gupta bumped into him when Gupta stopped to look for Braden. The big man frowned at Gupta and said something to him Braden couldn't hear. Gupta appeared puzzled by the remark, but when he saw Braden, he walked straight toward him.

"My lunch is getting cold," said the woman standing beside Braden's table.

He shook his head. "Nothin' I can do about that."

When Gupta arrived, he eyed the woman with undisguised suspicion then looked at Braden. "Who's she?"

Braden responded innocently. "Beats me."

"Move yer ass, lady," Gupta said as he pushed past her and took a seat opposite Braden.

The woman's face reflected a combination of anger and disbelief. "You have some nerve!"

"So?"

"You don't even have any food. Either of you. You're just sitting in here taking up space. That's not right. That's not right at all!"

"Go tell that to someone who gives a shit," grumbled Gupta.

Thoroughly shocked, the woman's mouth opened and shut wordlessly for a moment before she stalked away.

"You're in a mood," observed Braden.

"Whatever." Gupta exhaled, settled back in his chair, and nodded toward the big man he'd encountered near the entrance. "See that guy?"

"Yeah."

"He called me something I hadn't heard before. Kinda pissed me off."

Curious, Braden asked. "What'd he say?"

"He told me to get outta the way and called me a peckerwood."

Braden chuckled.

"What's so goddam funny?" Gupta snarled. "I've never heard of a peckerwood."

"He was being nice. I suspect he'd normally have called you a pencil dick."

Gupta glared at him. "Okay, smartass. The price of your thumb drive just went up two grand."

"Just *two?*"

"Make that five grand now, shithead. You got fifteen K on you?"

Braden felt surprisingly relaxed. "Nope. Barely brought enough to cover my lunch."

"Then what the hell are we doing here? Don't you want to know what I recorded?"

"I already know," Braden said. "It wasn't hard to figure out, especially after you told me the dumb ass's wife discovered some printouts containing impossible data."

Gupta's eyebrows dipped in suspicion. "Go on."

"Albright must have a computer program that predicts stock prices, and based on the fact that the guy has never lost a cent in the market, those predictions have been spot on."

After a slow scan of those seated nearby, Gupta responded. "And you're not interested in that data?"

"Oh, hell yes I am. But getting my hands on it

won't be easy. That's why I came here to talk to you."

"I'm listening."

Braden drummed his fingers on the table for a moment then asked, "What do you know about the stock market?"

"Not much."

"Ever heard of stock options? Calls and Puts?"

Gupta looked uncomfortable. "Yes. No. Maybe. Shit, I dunno. I'm not into that stuff."

"You can sell stock options without owning the stock they're based on," Braden explained. "It's a promise to buy or sell shares for a set price on a future date. If you know what a stock will sell for down the road, you can make a fortune on the options."

"What's the catch?"

"To completely avoid risk, you have to know what the stock will sell for in the future. Albright's program makes that problem go away."

Gupta still looked uncertain.

"I want to make a deal with you. Hear me out." He leaned toward Gupta and lowered his voice. "If I had Albright's computer, I could generate a helluva lot more cash than you'll get by selling your thumb drive. I'm willing to share it. You interested?"

"Yeah. But I already told you, I don't know shit about stocks and bonds."

Braden lowered his voice to a whisper. "Maybe so, but you know how to sneak into houses and hide microphones. I 've been to the house where the machine is. I need you to break in and steal it."

"What's in it for me? I'll be taking all the risk." Gupta squinted at him. "You're just too chicken shit to do it yourself."

"I told you. I'll split the money I make selling options. But here's the thing," Braden paused while he pulled his cell phone from a jacket pocket. "There's a woman living there who's kinda like a bodyguard. And there's a good-sized dog that makes a racket whenever anyone comes to the house."

"A woman bodyguard?" Gupta snorted. "Whoopee. Scare me."

"Check this out." Braden played the video clip of Danica knocking out the guy trying to rob a convenience store. "You wanna mess with her?"

"She's hot," Gupta said. "Great ass."

"And she'd kick yours across the road if she had to." Braden chuckled at the video. "Look, I know her. In fact, I'm going to take her out to dinner pretty soon. The guy she's protecting is sick, and I mean seriously sick. I followed her when she took him to the hospital, and he looks like shit. I doubt he'll last much longer."

"So, why not just wait 'til he dies, then go in and steal his equipment?"

"'Cause who knows if it'll still be there? What if he gives it to her? What if he decides to delete the program? We have no control over that. Besides, the sooner we get our hands on it, the sooner we can start making money with it."

Gupta sat back and rubbed his chin. "What if I told you I was gonna sell the thumb drive to McComb anyway?"

"I'd say fine, as long as you do it *after* we get the computer. McComb won't be able to stand knowing the program exists if he doesn't have it. He'll go nuts because he won't know how to get it." He suddenly frowned. "You wouldn't tell him, would ya?"

Before Gupta could answer the old lady they dealt with earlier returned. "I noticed," she said, "that neither of you bought anything for lunch, so I got you something. I hope you like cherry soda."

She then dumped a medium-sized serving on each of them.

"What the fu—" Gupta began as he struggled to stand and wipe the red liquid from his clothing. The big man he'd run into when he entered the restaurant towered over him and shoved Gupta back down into his chair.

Braden looked from one to the other, speechless.

"Nobody messes with my momma," the big man said. "Especially not some needle dick like you. C'mon, Ma." With that, the mother and son walked away arm-in-arm, laughing.

Braden went to get paper towels while Gupta fumed. Upon his return, Braden asked Gupta the one question for which he truly needed an answer. "Are you in, or not?"

Chapter Twenty-four

"How come you never see a headline like 'Psychic Wins Lottery'?" —Jay Leno

Beatrix knew that brooding and badgering Jeffrey about her birthday wouldn't motivate him to actually do anything about it. A gift would have been nice, and anything she'd put on the list she'd given him would've been appreciated. At least a little.

Not surprisingly, he hadn't said a word about it in days. Instead, and as usual, Jeffrey did nothing but complain. He didn't like the TV shows she enjoyed, didn't like how she looked or where they went, and he especially didn't like the meals she prepared.

His food allergies made cooking hard, and he constantly reminded her of the one time she served him cashew chicken. It caused him to swell a little, and he whined about not being able to breathe. He demanded she have an ambulance take him to the hospital. It turned out to be no big deal; he hadn't eaten enough to be seriously hurt. But now they couldn't go anywhere without dragging along a couple EpiPens—injectable doses of epinephrin. It gave him a topic he'd been bitching about for years. And lately his grumbling had gotten worse. He preferred griping over gratitude.

As she stood in front of the washer and dryer they had to install in the garage for lack of space in the house, Beatrix began to weep. Her life totally sucked. Her dreams had all been dashed, and all because of her selfish, lazy husband. No, she thought, make that her selfish, lazy, *cruel* husband.

Jeffrey's actions over the last few months had demonstrated that he no longer loved her, assuming he ever had. She couldn't remember the last time they'd been intimate. He wouldn't even sit close to her on the sofa. In fact, she realized, he had neither kissed nor hugged her in recent memory.

Angered by the unfairness of it all, she ransacked his clothing to remove the junk he never bothered to remove from his pockets. In doing so, she came across a business card and a folded slip of colored paper in one of his dress shirts. She ignored the food stains on the front of it, content for them to become permanent, and looked instead at the business card which read:

Archibald J. Carnahan, Attorney at Law

The back of the card listed the services he offered. She ignored things like estate planning and tax preparation and focused instead on divorce.

What the hell is he up to?

She then unfolded the odd slip of colored paper and examined it.

A "Lotto Grande" receipt? My idiot husband, who never skips a chance to moan about being broke, wasted good money on a stupid, lottery *ticket? And not just any lottery ticket—oh, hell no—he bought one where the odds are a gazillion to one! What on Earth was he thinking?*

After getting the load of wash running, she returned to the house with both the business card and the lottery receipt in hand. She set them on a counter and checked a clock on the stove. It would be hours before Jeffrey returned from work.

That thought led to another: why had he been so close-mouthed about his job lately? He used to come home grumbling about all the idiots he had to deal with on the phone or responding to the emails they sent. But lately he hadn't talked about any of it. And that was just... odd.

She snatched up the two fragments of paper, wandered into the living room, and retrieved her cell phone. The results from her Internet search for "Lotto Grande" appeared quickly. She knew they offered extravagant jackpots, but she hadn't realized the current prize had grown to nearly a half-billion dollars. Even more surprising, a winner had been announced the night before, but no one had claimed the reward.

Boy, if that was me, I'd be standing there with my hand out two seconds after the numbers were drawn. The thought made her laugh.

And then she checked the numbers on the website against those on the lottery receipt. Her breath caught in her chest; her legs suddenly went wobbly, and she collapsed on the sofa in shock.

Danica glanced again at her buzzing cell phone and once again declined to answer it. Braden, the guy she'd met in the convenience store while checking in on her young friend April, had called several times over the past few days. Dealing with him just didn't seem important, especially now that her relationship with Rick had escalated into something... new. The past few evenings they'd spent together had been amazing.

She definitely had feelings for him and knew

Rick had feelings for her. But that sort of thing was all new to her. She'd never been involved in anything like a real romance. The few times she'd had sex were more convenience and/or curiosity than anything else, except for her drunken encounter with the bastard who stole her car and left her broke and homeless.

Rick wasn't anything like that. He cared. He came to her when she needed him, and he had pitched in and helped Libby and April when *they* needed him. He even installed a replacement door in their apartment. When Libby offered to pay him for it, he declined saying she needed the money more than he did.

When Danica made the same offer, he declined that one, too. "Not very long ago," he said, "you were living in the woods under a tarp. You had nothing. Nada. Zilch. Do you honestly think I'd take money from you now that you've got a life and a job?" He followed that with a laugh. "That's not what friendship is all about."

Friends? Was that what he thought they were? No. It wasn't possible. She still remembered when he arrived at Libby's apartment. She remembered the hugs, the look in his eyes, and their kiss. Especially the kiss. And she remembered how it all made her feel.

Loved.

Loved? Seriously?

She shook those thoughts aside. Relentlessly reviewing them only made it harder to focus on the task at hand—figuring out if Sunrise Ranch was in legitimate need. It certainly appeared that way to her. But her feelings didn't amount to anything. Feelings were meaningless. Wynn wanted facts, the colder and harder the better.

At his suggestion, she'd contacted Archie and asked him if he knew anyone in the service club which had previously hosted the Ranch's annual fundraiser. The ever-resourceful lawyer said he would check and called her back the very next day.

"This is a crazy kind of issue," he began. "And sadly, it's becoming less and less rare."

"I'm not following you," Danica said.

"My friend was, until recently, an officer in the club you asked about. He resigned his position and his membership over the group's decision to quit helping Sunrise Ranch. It turns out the club's new president is a wheeler-dealer at a firm that wants the land for a huge data warehouse."

"Libby didn't say anything about the ranch being for sale."

"It's not," Archie said. "At least, not now. But if

the place goes broke...."

"Ah." Danica sighed. "Then that big shot can buy it and stick a big, ugly, warehouse on it. So much for the kids who need the ranch! I can't believe one person can have that much power in a club that exists to help people."

"According to my friend, this guy is adept at making 'friends' and donating big sums to their favorite charities. He earned their trust and their votes. Evidently, that's how he got the president's job."

Danica's temper flared. "That's just not right!"

"Nope, it's not. It's called politics. Back-scratching."

She mused over the issue for several seconds then asked, "How do you think Wynn will react to that bit of news?"

Archie chuckled. "How 'bout you tell me after you deliver it to him?"

Wynn's desk chair hadn't felt right for months. But it had nothing to do with the chair. His body had changed. He'd lost weight. Clothing that fit him at Christmas hung on him now like window dressings.

He had little appetite and less energy. The

machine was killing him, and it wouldn't matter if it went away or not. The decline would continue. The date of his death remained the only thing still in question, which is why he ran the machine one more time using the obituary option, hoping for the answer.

As expected, two sheets of paper slid into the output tray. Wynn grabbed them, looked over the names and dates, and sucked in a breath when he spotted his own. It would occur sooner than he expected, much sooner than he'd planned.

He suddenly needed more time, but the machine never lied and never made a mistake. It never let him down. Until now.

Summoning what little strength he had left, Wynn set about neutralizing Annabelle Knox's creation. There was no one he could leave it to, and that included the two most trustworthy people he knew—Archie and Danica. He could not risk poisoning them as he'd allowed himself to be poisoned, a process that began long before CeeJay's bullet damaged the machine and sped up the process.

Annabelle's marvelous window on the future had to go, and Wynn had a plan that would not only eliminate the machine but also the contaminated building which housed it.

Heat had always been an issue when

operating the device. Two things kept it from getting dangerously hot: a container of liquid coolant that underlay the whole machine and a thermal cut-off switch. Wynn disconnected the switch and drained the coolant from the reservoir. Neither action required a great deal of time, although dumping a bucket full of coolant in a toilet proved taxing. But he managed.

He rested for a while, then shuffled into the living room where he collapsed on the sofa and waited for Danica's return from the grocery store, one of the many chores she'd taken it upon herself to perform. Roscoe curled up next to him.

When Danica entered the house, she put two grocery bags on the kitchen counter and immediately came to check on him. Roscoe raised his head but didn't make a sound. Wynn stroked the dog's chin as a thank you. No one needed the additional noise.

"How're you doing?" Danica asked.

"Fine," croaked Wynn, his throat parched and dry.

Danica's lips formed a brief pout before she responded. "What'll it be, boss? Water, coffee... Bourbon? You name it; I'll pour it."

He rewarded her with a smile. "Water, please."

"Comin' right up!"

He watched her glide into the kitchen, pull a bottle of water from the refrigerator, pour a serving, and deliver it to him.

"Have a seat," he said. "There's something we need to talk about."

"Does it have anything to do with Sunrise Ranch?"

When he shook his head, her cheery smile faded. "It's about the machine I told you about."

"The one you want me to bury?"

He nodded. "Turns out you won't have to."

"That sounds like good news."

"It is, sorta." He took as deep a breath as he could manage before going on. "Once I'm gone, either dead or in hospice—"

"Please stop." She put a hand on his shoulder. "I don't want to hear that."

"You have to. I— I can't make this optional. I need you to listen."

She sighed but said nothing and waited for him to continue.

"We all die at some point. My time's coming, it's just... a little sooner than expected. I've made some provisions, and it's important that you know about them. First off, I had Archie put my car in your name. He also—"

"You're giving *me* the car? Doesn't Jeffrey want it? Beatrix complains about theirs all the time."

Wynn coughed and waved off the objection. When able to breathe comfortably again he went on. "Jeffrey's going to be fine. As of a few days ago, he's worth more money than he knows what to do with."

Danica laughed. "What'd he do, win the lottery?"

Wynn stared at her. "How'd you know?"

"I didn't! I had no idea. No one's said anything about it. Are you serious?"

"Yes. And it bothers me more than a little bit that I haven't heard anything from either of those two. The lottery ticket was a gift from me."

"That's just... bizarre."

"I agree," he said. "But it's the primary reason I'm leaving the house to you."

Danica's face registered disbelief. "You're *what?*"

"Hear me out. This house is old and... well... crappy. It's also contaminated. The machine in my office has made that room unusable, and the contamination may spread."

"Gee, thanks. That's some gift. No wonder you didn't want to give it to Jeffrey."

He shook his head. "Let me finish, please. The insurance is paid up, so when the place burns down—"

Danica's eyebrows shot up as if nuclear powered. *"Burns down?"*

Wynn's energy had all but disappeared. "Will you ever let me finish?"

"Yes," she said. "Of course. It's just... You startled me. A lot!"

"I'm tired," he said. "Really, really tired."

"I'm sorry. Please, go on."

"Once I'm gone, I want you to clear anything you want to keep out of the house. Your stuff, my stuff, I don't care. Grab whatever you don't want destroyed. Then I need you to go into my office and turn on the machine. I'll make sure you'll see it the moment you walk in the room. Just hit the start button. It's red. You can't miss it. Then punch any of the other buttons. Doesn't matter which one, then grab Roscoe and get the hell out of the house. Drive away. Far away."

"But... I'm not sure...."

He patted her hand. "It'll be okay. Either the

place will burn to the ground, which is my preference, or the fire department will put it out. Either way, the place will be a ruin. I want you to have the remains hauled away. You can use the insurance money to build a new house on this spot or sell the lot and use the money for something else. Whatever you want, whatever you need."

"Wynn," she said, still blinking in surprise. "I don't know what to say."

"Just say you'll do it. Please?"

She nodded. "Okay. If you insist."

"And take care of my sweet boy." He patted Roscoe's head. "Okay?"

"Of course."

Chapter Twenty-five

"Having a bad boss isn't your fault. Staying with one is." —Nora Denzel

Braden Daly frowned at his cell phone for the third time that day. He couldn't believe the redhead was ghosting him. She never answered his calls and didn't respond to his texts. The same held true for the multiple voice messages he'd left for her.

What the hell did I do? I thought she was all set to go out with me. Now I've got to put Gupta off for the umpteenth time. There's no way he's getting into Albright's house if Danica and the damn dog are standing in the way.

He recalled that Gupta claimed the dog wouldn't be a problem. He'd simply give it a sausage loaded with what he called "special K." Braden assumed he meant ketamine. When he asked Gupta if that might be dangerous for the animal, his response was a squint and a "So what?"

A phone call from Mr. McComb came as a surprise, but he answered with as much calm as he could put into his voice. "At your service, sir," he said.

"What the hell did you do to our client?"

"You mean Mr. Al—"

"Yes, of course that's who I meant, you idiot. He's pulled all his funds from the firm. My sources tell me we're not the only brokerage he's done this to."

"Geez," said Braden. "How many was he doing business with?"

"Does it matter?" McComb fired back. "Or do you work for more than one?"

"Just asking, sir. That's all."

"Tell me why he's done this."

How the hell should I know? "Do you think I had something to do with it?"

"Frankly? Yes."

Braden could hear the man breathing.

"And another thing, Daley. Why haven't you been making regular reports? I haven't heard from you in days."

"I left a message," Braden said. "You didn't

respond."

"You seem to have forgotten who you're talking to!" McComb's voice carried an edge Braden hadn't heard before. His anger seemed thoroughly misplaced.

"I don't understand why you're so—"

"Angry?"

"Yeah."

"Oh, gee. I don't know. Maybe it's because I think you screwed up our chances of finding out how the hell Alb... I mean our client—no, our *former* client—made so many trades without ever losing a fucking cent."

"All I can tell you," Braden said. *All I'm* willing *to tell you.* "Is that the man is sick. I don't know what's wrong with him, but he looks like shit, and he's been in the hospital more than once in the past couple weeks. His bodyguard is running errands for him."

"What's wrong with him?"

"I don't know. Cancer, maybe. My uncle had it, and he looked like shit near the end, too."

"Find out," McComb grumbled, "and get back to me as soon as you can. Don't screw this up; it's your last chance."

<Click>

"Screw you and the high fucking horse you rode in on," Braden shouted at the man who was no longer on the line.

Braden needed to consult Gupta again. Though he had an idea for getting the redheaded bodyguard out of Albright's house, it wouldn't do any good if Albright remained in it. They had to wait until he either died or went back into the hospital—options over which he had no control.

Tim Fannin would never get used to being locked in a jail cell. He couldn't begin to imagine what a lifer had to endure. Though he'd only been a county prisoner for a few days, it felt like a lifetime.

He'd concocted a story claiming his innocence for the jerk from the public defender's office who supposedly represented him. That is, if his case ever came to trial. The man did, however, arrange for bail which Tim's elderly aunt agreed to cover provided he helped her move into something called "assisted living."

His aunt could still get around okay. She wasn't mortally wounded or anything. He couldn't understand why she would need assistance just to stay alive. Old people. He never could understand them. And, he figured, the only way he would ever *be* able to understand them was if he became one, and that didn't seem likely. He enjoyed life, especially the *fast* life. He thrived on excitement, usually the expensive kind.

One thing he certainly *didn't* like, aside from captivity, was the shame of being beaten up by a broad. If only he had the bitch's name he might be able to track her down. Libby would know it, and she would know how to reach her. And, since Libby had earned one hell of a smackdown herself, he needed to arrange things to his advantage.

He had overheard one of the guards talking to another about some crazy chick who had taken down some punk during a robbery. The guard even shared a video of it on his cell phone. Tim asked to see it, too, but the guard told him to kiss off.

It didn't matter to Tim. Not really. He hadn't gotten that good a look at Libby's friend anyhow. Probably wouldn't have recognized her even if she was in the stupid video.

He did know one thing about her, however. She was sneaky. She took her shots before he was ready and hurt him quickly, then broke his nose and knocked him out. That had earned her a way bigger smackdown than what Libby would get. He'd see to it the bitch died, but not until he'd had some fun with her and made her scream.

His rage made it possible to survive his

incarceration; he used the time to think of different ways to hurt, humiliate, and ultimately kill her. All while Libby watched.

All he had to do was keep his bandaged nose clean until they processed his bail money and let him out. He wished he knew what was taking his stupid aunt so long. She should've paid the cops the same day she agreed to cover his bail.

Maybe, he thought, he needed to pay her a visit, too.

~*~

"You really need to eat something," Danica said. Wynn looked even more awful than usual. "When was the last time you took more than a bite?"

"Yesterday." His voice had become little more than a gruff whisper. Sometimes she had to strain to hear him. She recalled her disappointment at seeing the untouched serving of the casserole she'd prepared for him the night before.

"Let me fix you some eggs, okay? Scrambled, right? With cheese?"

"Yeah, sure. Whatever."

"Why not eat 'em in the living room? You wouldn't have to move."

He managed a nod, and Danica assembled the

ingredients for his meal. The doorbell and the dog went off at the same moment, though Roscoe made the most noise. His anxious dance back and forth through the house and into the foyer continued until she calmed him and reached the door. She took a quick glance through the peephole and stepped back in surprise.

What the hell is he doing here? How does he even know where I live?

Roscoe had grown impatient and let the world know with another barked outburst.

"Oh, hush," she commanded as she opened the door and shoved her leg into the opening to keep Roscoe from squirming through.

"Good morning," Braden said. "I hope I'm not disturbing anything."

She tried not to look annoyed and pushed Roscoe further back. "No. It's fine. I just— How'd you know where to find me?"

He laughed. "I bribed your friend, April, at the convenience store. When you didn't answer my calls or texts I figured the only way I could connect with you would be face-to-face."

"I'm sorry about that," Danica said. "I meant no disrespect. It's just that I'm kind of in a relationship now, and I didn't want to... you know... take a chance on messing that up."

Braden appeared momentarily crestfallen, then he brightened. "I get it. And you're probably doing the smart thing. But listen, if it doesn't work out... I mean, if something happens... You can always call me. Okay?"

She smiled. "Yes, sure. I'll keep that in mind."

Braden shook his head. "It's funny, but I remembered something you mentioned about being a country music fan. Zac Brown Band, right?"

"Yes." *Where's he going with this?*

"Well, I got two tickets to an upcoming show they're doing in Atlanta. I thought if you didn't want to go to dinner with me, maybe you'd want to see the band instead."

"I'd love to go and see them, but like I just told you—"

"I know; I know. But here's the thing; I don't know squat about country music. I've never listened to it. The only reason I got the tickets—"

"Was to get me interested in you?"

"Well, yeah. I wouldn't have put it that way but... Pretty dumb, huh?"

She shrugged. "No. It just tells me you don't give up easily." She thought for a moment, knowing

Rick shared her taste in music. "How much did you pay for them? I might be willing to take them off your hands."

Before he could answer, Roscoe once again became frantic. He barked and danced anxiously between Danica and Wynn, whom she could no longer see on the couch.

"Hang on," she told Braden. "I'll be right back."

Leaving the door slightly ajar, she hurried into the living room to check on Wynn. He had slumped completely off the sofa and lay on the floor. Roscoe acted just as he had the very first time she encountered him in the park. When she knelt beside Wynn, Roscoe curled up next to him.

She checked his pulse which felt dangerously weak. Frantically trying to remember where she left her cell phone, she stood up to begin the search and bumped into Braden who had come inside after her.

He quickly backed away and apologized.

"I've gotta call 9—" Danica began.

"I already have 'em on the line," Braden said, handing her his phone.

Danica quickly relayed the situation to the dispatcher who assured her that EMTs would arrive soon. She thanked Braden and returned his phone.

"Glad to help," he said. "What's wrong with him? He looks terrible."

"He's dying." She sighed, put her hands on Wynn's cheeks, and stared down at him. "C'mon, boss. Come back to me."

It startled her when he blinked. His gaze whipped from side to side, then came to rest on her. "Call Jeffrey, please," he whispered. I want to see him one last time."

As the ambulance pulled away, Braden stepped closer to Danica on the front porch intending to comfort her, but she stepped aside.

"You all right?" he asked.

"Yeah. But I've got stuff to do; gotta make some calls. I'll go to the hospital later. I don't want to spend my time sitting in the stupid waiting room at the ER." She faced him squarely. "Can we talk later? This is obviously a bad time. I just need to think straight, and that'll take a while."

"Of course. No problem. That is, assuming you'll answer the phone the next time I call."

She gave him a weary smile, said, "Okay," and then went back inside the house.

Braden returned to his car, climbed in, and

called Gupta. When the phony Irishman answered, Braden said, "It's time. Albright's on his way to the hospital, and his bodyguard is leaving pretty soon."

"Any idea how long he'll be in the hospital?"

Braden issued a snort of humorless laughter. "I seriously doubt he'll be coming back."

"Holy shit! You didn't shoot him, did ya?"

"Nah. He's just an old guy whose time is up. Now get your ass over here and grab the machine."

"You're not sticking around?"

"Hell no. I've got to report to McComb. I can't wait to see the expression on that bastard's face when I tell him Albright's on his last leg, and his secrets are gonna die with him."

"Yeah," said Gupta. "You do that."

"Bring the equipment to my place. You've got the address. We can work from there."

"Sure thing," Gupta said.

Braden had but one thing on his mind: how best to lower the informational boom on McComb.

Chapter Twenty-six

*"It's the very awfulness of [murder] that makes reading
about it feel so cozy."* —Louise Doughty

Beatrix assured herself that she had given
Jeffrey the benefit of the doubt. He'd had several days
to come clean about the lottery ticket, if not about his
plans to divorce her and leave her with nothing. Quite
a birthday present *that* would have been.

But she'd decided his plans would never
materialize. Ever. Not to her, and certainly not by
Jeffrey Albright, son of the master tightwad Wynn
Albright. She was done with Jeffrey and all of his crap.

It's why she had taken such great care to mask
the almond milk she'd used to make him the most
delicious smoothie he'd ever have. And, if she could
get him to drink enough of it, the last one.

When Jeffrey entered the kitchen that

morning she greeted him with a shy smile. She felt it important to set him at ease, make him comfortable, and not give him any reason to be suspicious. She poured him a cup of coffee and settled it near the cream and sugar as she always did. Then she took a sip of her portion of the almond milk infused smoothie.

"Oh. My. God," she groaned as if she'd just had an orgasm. "This stuff is fan-damn-tastic!"

"What are you talking about?" he asked, staring at the thick liquid in her glass. "Are you having a milkshake for breakfast?"

She shook her head, no. "This is way better."

"Is it a smoothie?"

Trying not to smirk, she said, "Yes. But not just any smoothie. I got the recipe from a Cordon Bleu chef."

"Where?"

"On the Internet, of course. I've been meaning to try one forever but just never got around to it."

"What's in it?"

She smiled. "Lots of stuff, but the magic ingredient is... Are you ready?"

"Yeah, yeah."

"Ice cream."

"So, it *is* a milkshake. Geez Bea, what's the matter with you? Why does everything have to be such a big deal?"

After another sip she groaned again. "Hey, if you don't want yours, I'll be happy to drink it."

He didn't look convinced.

"It's chock full of vitamins and stuff," she said. "Healthy stuff. Way better than a stupid sweet roll or a bowl of sugar cereal. That's all you ever eat for breakfast. It's no wonder you're in such lousy shape."

He laughed. "That's rich, coming from you."

"Are you saying I'm fat?"

"Fatter than me, that's for damn sure."

She glowered at him but let the insult slide knowing she'd have the last word. "At least I'm willing to do something about it." She hefted her glass, took another big gulp, licked her lips, and batted her eyes at him.

"Oh, for cryin' out loud," he said. "Lemme have some."

She emptied the blender into a tall glass. While standing well beyond his reach, she waved it back and forth in front of him. "Wanna come get it?"

"Not particularly. Just hand it to me. Why the big production?"

"I thought I'd make it a little more fun," she said, adding a bit of a frown.

"Just gimme the damned thing. I've gotta get outta here and go to work."

She set the beverage in front of him. "So early?"

"Somebody screwed up the schedules. I don't have any control over it."

She watched as he took a small sip and then smiled. "You're right," he said. "It tastes pretty good."

Her nod toward the big clock on the wall got his attention. "If you're behind schedule, you might as well polish that thing off so I can wash the glass."

"Yeah, yeah," he said and guzzled the rest without taking a breath. "I— Uhm... Oh, shit!"

Beatrix smiled at him. "What's the matter hon?"

"What the hell did you put in that thing?"

She watched his face begin to swell. "I'm pretty sure it's the almond milk you're feeling right now."

His eyes seemed to double in size. "You *put*

that shit in my drink? On purpose? Jesus, Bea! You know I can't— Where are my Epi... EpiPens?"

"These?" she asked as she pulled a pair from the pocket of her apron.

He looked relieved until she dropped them on the floor and stomped on them. She missed one but crushed it on her second attempt. By then, Jeffrey's breathing had become labored.

"What the fuck?" he gasped. "Are you trying to kill me?"

"Actually, yes," she said. "I am." She then extracted the lottery receipt and the attorney's business card from the other pocket of her apron. "Care to explain these? I mean, while you can still talk? You won a goddam lottery, and you didn't bother to tell me?"

Jeffrey shifted in his seat trying to reach for his wallet and cell phone which he normally left on the kitchen counter. Of course, she'd gotten to them long before he entered the room. She held up his phone. "Looking for this?"

"Call 9-1-1," he said. "Please! For the love of God!"

"Uhm, no. I don't think so." She put his phone back in her apron pocket and walked to the refrigerator. From there she removed a bowl of grapes and blueberries.

Jeffrey looked both terrified and confused. "What the... What are you *doing?*"

"Hush now." She slid her chair back but remained squarely in front of him. It was important that he realize how entertaining his death would be to her. "I'm just going to sit here and watch you get what you deserve for trying to cheat me out of a fortune, and for planning to desert me, you weak, selfish, sniveling little bastard."

He shook his head, quite vigorously she thought, for someone struggling to breathe. The swelling had continued; his hands and arms were expanding along with his face and neck.

"I— I didn't. I never...."

Beatrix ignored his protests, reached into the bowl, and grabbed a modest helping of fruit. She started tossing grapes and berries into her mouth one after another. Chewing and smiling, ever so smugly, felt good. "Any last words, Jeffy baby?"

His face shifted from fear to anger. "Why?"

"Because you ruined my life, you cheap shit. You had a chance to—"

Suddenly *she* couldn't breathe. Somehow she'd managed to inhale a large, red grape, and the damned thing had clogged her windpipe.

Ignoring Jeffrey, she tried to cough it up, but it wouldn't come. Beating on her chest didn't help either.

She stared at her now puffy husband who had managed to work a smile into his swollen cheeks. *The bastard can hardly breathe, and yet he looks as if he's laughing at me!*

The difference between them, she knew, was that while he got very little air, she was getting none. Panicky, she moved toward him, gesturing toward her throat, hoping he might do something. She pantomimed punching her chest.

Jeffrey only shook his head. His efforts at breathing generated a slight wheeze.

Damn you! For once in your sorry life, help me!

She dropped to her knees on the kitchen floor, still trying to dislodge the grape. And as everything around her began fading to black, she felt her head smack onto the linoleum. After that, she neither saw, smelled, nor felt anything.

Danica's first call went to Rick, her anchor when things got crazy. She told him about Wynn.

"Have you called his son?"

"Not yet," she said. "I wanted to talk to you

first."

"I can meet you at the hospital. There's nothing pressing going on today at the park."

"Oh, crap! I'm sorry. I didn't even think about you being at work."

He chuckled. "I'm sitting in my Jeep drinking coffee before going into the park office. It's not like I'm directing traffic for a speech by the Governor."

She felt a little silly. "Thank you. How 'bout I call you later? When things calm down."

"Great idea," he said. "Talk to you soon."

Danica then dialed Wynn's son. After several rings and just before she was about to end the call, he answered.

"Jeffrey, it's Danica I've got—"

"Help me." He sounded as if he was being strangled.

"What's wrong? What's going on? Where's your wife? How—"

"Can't... breathe."

"I'll call 9-1-1," she said. "And I'll be there as soon as I can."

Wasting no time, she dialed the emergency number and gave them Jeffrey's address.

"What's his condition?" the operator asked.

"He can't breathe! That's all I know. I'm headed there now."

"If you beat the EMTs, call back and report. Got that?"

"Yeah. Will do," she said then clicked off, silently praying she could call them back with good news.

She grabbed the car keys and headed for the garage. Roscoe wanted to come, too, but she left him behind. "Sorry, buddy. I'll be back later, and we'll go for a long walk. I promise."

The car started without a hitch. She backed out of the garage and into the street without closing the garage door or bothering to look for oncoming traffic either way. Fortunately, there was none.

With her focus on Wynn and his son, she failed to fulfill a primary objective of a Marine in an emergency—situational awareness. She didn't notice Braden sitting in a car parked two doors down the street. She blew past him without a glance.

Jeffrey's house wasn't far away. It looked dark, sad, and quiet when she arrived. There were no ambulances or rescue vehicles. She pulled into the drive and hustled to the front door which was locked. She pounded on it and shouted Jeffrey's name, but no one came to open it.

Shifting quickly to one side of the building, she gazed through a window hoping to see what was going on. All she could make out was a dim, cluttered living room. She moved on, working her way to the back of the house, peering into every window she found. At last, she found one that gave her a view of the kitchen and the two bodies inside.

Using her elbow, she smashed the pane in the lower half of the window. She wadded up her jacket to protect herself from broken glass still in the frame, then climbed through the window and landed inside.

She checked on Jeffrey first, though neither he nor Beatrix were moving. He managed to blink as she hovered over him. He lay on the floor beside his wife, clutching a cell phone in one hand and a bit of paper in the other. He shook it at her.

"Take it," he whispered.

"The EMTs are on their way," she said, ignoring his weak gesture.

"I won," he said, his voice barely audible, his face bloated but pleading. She relieved him of the paper scrap and shoved it in her pocket just as someone, presumably the EMTs, banged on the front door.

Danica raced to let them in and led them to the

kitchen. They pushed past her and went to work on the two prostrate forms.

"Do you know what happened?" asked the female EMT examining Jeffrey.

Danica shook her head. "I called him to deliver a message. He told me he couldn't breathe. I called y'all, and here we are."

"This one's gone," said the other tech leaving Beatrix where she lay.

"This one ain't far behind," said the tech dealing with Jeffrey. "I'm guessing it's a food allergy." She pulled a syringe from her kit and gave him an injection then looked up at Danica. "It's epinephrine, but it may be too late. In any case, we've got it from here. Police are on the way, and you need to stick around. They're going to want to talk to you."

As promised, the police showed up as the EMTs loaded Jeffrey in the ambulance. They took off with their siren blaring.

Danica called Rick for the second time that morning. When he answered, she couldn't help but blurt out, "Everyone's dying around me!"

Rick calmed her down enough to ask what happened. She told him what little she knew and would have said more, but one of the cops made it clear he needed to speak with her. "Just a sec," she told him then returned to her conversation with Rick.

"Meet me at the hospital in an hour or so, okay?"

"I'll be there," he said.

"Thanks." She wiped away an annoying tear. "You have no idea how much I need you right now."

Chapter Twenty-seven

"When karma lands, it lands hard." —Tom Fitton

Braden hadn't driven more than a half block away from Wynn Albright's house when he realized he'd made an idiotic mistake. He immediately stopped the car, turned around, drove back, and parked two doors down from the house he'd just left. He chalked his error up to distraction, that being Danica, the alluring redhead in yoga pants with whom he'd just spent a bit of quality time.

He watched her zip past him in Albright's car, accelerating all the way down the residential street. Once she'd driven out of sight he pulled forward and noticed she had left the garage door open. He couldn't believe his luck. Both Danica and Albright were gone, and the dog had made his acquaintance only a short while ago. Hopefully, he wouldn't bark too much when Braden went back inside.

After all the stress he'd endured while talking Gupta into helping him, it turned out he didn't need him after all.

The dog met him as he went in through a door from the garage to a hallway. Braden used a soothing voice and moved slowly, hoping the dog would assume he meant no harm. Eventually he wandered away.

Braden walked down the hall looking into each of the rooms he found. The first one he assumed to be Danica's; the furnishings looked new, and the room was neat and tidy. The second one had to be Albright's bedroom, so he ignored it. Two rooms remained, one of which housed a bathtub and toilet. Braden headed for the last one.

He entered Albright's office wearing a smile. The computer he sought occupied one side of the desk. A printer sat on a small table nearby. Piles of various stuff littered the floor, but he was only interested in stacks of paper. There were plenty of those, but none of them had the data he desired.

The desk drawers proved equally unrewarding, but he finally located a folder buried under some bills on top of the desk. Several sheets of paper listed stock prices, just as he had hoped. There were winners *and* losers, data with which he could readily generate cash.

As he focused on the dates featured in the headers of each page, his excitement ebbed. Only a few of the dates were in the future, and those didn't leave a great deal of time for big swings in the option prices.

"But," he told himself, "I've got the guy's computer. I can run the program anytime I want."

He checked his watch. It wouldn't do to have Gupta show up just as he left with the prize. And, now that he had the ability to generate data from the future, he no longer needed the phony Irishman. Gupta could go screw himself. He might be able to sell his stupid little thumb drive to McComb, but Braden had the egg-laying goose, and those eggs would be 24-karat. He had no intention of sharing them with anyone.

The dog didn't make a sound as he hauled the computer out to his car.

Rick Johanson recalled the first time he'd been at County General Hospital with Danica. They'd been little more than strangers back then, though it hadn't been that long ago. Now they were... What? He wondered, lovers?

Not exactly. Not nearly as close as I'd like,

though I'll readily admit I've had countless thoughts about making love to her. If that day ever comes, I'll be eternally grateful. For now, though, she just needs a friend.

I can be that friend.

He hadn't expected to see anyone other than Danica in Wynn's room and came to an abrupt stop when he spotted a man roughly Wynn's age standing at the foot of the bed.

Danica introduced him as Archie Carnahan, Wynn's lawyer.

"The hospital called me," Carnahan said. "I didn't know I was on Wynn's emergency call list."

The two shook hands, after which Danica ushered them out of the room, down the hall, and into a waiting area where they could all sit down.

"One of his doctors has already been in to see him," Carnahan said, sadly shaking his head. "It doesn't look good."

Rick turned to Danica. "Have you heard anything about his son?"

Danica teared up. "He's gone. I checked as soon as I reached the ER. His wife is dead, too." She told him about her visit to Jeffrey's house.

"Aw, criminy," Rick said. "Does Wynn know?"

"He's been asleep since I got here," she said, "but even if he'd been awake, I don't have the heart to tell him."

Rick gazed at Carnahan. "What do we do now?"

"Wait, I suppose. Pray for a miracle. But just between us, Wynn's been saying he didn't have much time left."

They took turns; one sat beside Wynn's bed while the other two sat in the waiting room. Rick went last, and when he returned, Danica shifted on the sofa to make room for him beside her. "He's still out," he said.

Danica leaned against him, and he put his arm around her.

Carnahan smiled at him. "Miss Winters here just nominated you for a position on the board of trustees of Wynn's newly created foundation."

Rick looked at him in surprise. "She nominated *me?*" He gave her chin a slight nudge. "Why on Earth would you do that?"

"'Cause you're an honest, decent guy. You've got a good heart, and you're... I dunno, real. You care about people; you—"

"I care about *you*," he said.

"And others, too!" Danica reached out to the attorney. "Explain it, please?"

"Miss Winters hoped that Wynn's creation, the Annabell Knox Foundation, could make a donation to an organization she's involved with."

"Sunrise Ranch?" Rick asked.

"Yes. But there are two problems. First, the foundation is brand new, and we're waiting for the government to recognize us as being legitimate. The other issue is that Wynn didn't have time to fill all the positions on the board."

Rick squinted at him. "How many are there?"

"Five, total."

"How many have been filled?"

"One," said Carnahan. "That's me. You'd be number two."

Rick hugged Danica. "Why not both of us?"

"Miss Winters is the foundation's sole employee. Board positions aren't paid, except for expenses, and those will be minimal based on Wynn's wishes. Besides, she said she didn't want to be a trustee. At least, not right away."

Danica reached for the box of tissues on a side table and found it empty. She then searched her pocket for one and extracted a slip of paper. "Shoot. I thought I had a Kleenex in there. Can't blow my nose on this, whatever it is. Jeffrey gave it to me."

"May I see it?" Rick asked.

She handed it to him.

"It's a lottery receipt," he said. "Jeffrey *gave* it to you?"

"Yes." Danica's face then registered surprise. "So, *that's* what he meant!"

"What are you talking about?" asked Carnahan.

"Jeffrey gave me that receipt and said he won."

"Hold on," Rick said. "It's easy enough to check." He withdrew his cell phone and accessed the Internet. Within moments he was shaking his head in wonder. "It's true. I checked the numbers. There was only one ticket sold for Lotto Grande that got all the numbers right. The store that sold it gets a prize, too. The grand prize hasn't been collected." He turned slowly towards Danica. "That's yours, darlin'."

"But I didn't buy the ticket! It belongs to Jeffrey."

"If he had any family, it would rightfully go to them, but he was Wynn's only heir. There's no one else." Carnahan smiled at Danica. "Since he gave it to you, there's no reason why you shouldn't have the prize."

Danica appeared completely flustered. Rick had never seen her that way, and it struck him as charming.

"Y'know," added Carnahan, "Georgia is one of the few states where lottery winners are not required to identify themselves publicly. No one other than the three of us and the folks who run the lottery need to know."

Rick grinned like a mad man. "So, Miss Moneybags, it looks like you no longer need Wynn Albright's foundation to bail out Sunrise Ranch."

"Oh, my God," she breathed. "You're right."

Gupta reached the address Braden had given him, ready to steal the device the homeowner had used to make his fortune. Thanks to the conversation he'd recorded, he knew exactly where the secret machine was hidden. He pulled his car into the garage and went directly into the house.

He remembered the guard dog Braden had warned him about and came prepared to deal with it—a sausage containing a dose of "Special K," enough to kill a canine of any size.

While creeping through the house looking for an untidy office, he kept the deadly, unwrapped snack in his hand. When he found the room he'd been looking for, the dog still hadn't shown up. That's when he glanced out the window and saw it outside trotting toward the house. Gupta then noticed a doggy door in the wall of the office. The animal would arrive in seconds!

Gupta quickly blocked the entryway with a chair and grinned as the suddenly befuddled dog tried and failed to get in.

After tossing the poisoned sausage in a tall trash can, Gupta went in search of the paddle switch that controlled the bookcase behind the desk.

Still grinning about the dog, he smiled even wider when the bookcase slid aside revealing the mysterious machine Braden told him to retrieve.

He couldn't wait to deliver it to McComb, claim his reward, and be done with Braden and his pitiful plans for sudden wealth. *What an idiot he is!*

Lionel McComb sat at home contemplating a third martini when he heard the chime of his front door. If everything had gone right, his man "Shaughnessy" would be making a much-anticipated delivery. A quick check of his doorbell camera confirmed the visitor's identity.

Since his staff only worked on the weekends

when McComb held a semi-annual soiree for his VIP clients, he had to go to the door and open it himself. But considering what he would soon have his hands on, that represented no challenge at all.

"Come in; come in," he said to the little man standing under the portico on his front porch. McComb made no effort to assist his visitor with his burden. "Follow me. We'll put it in my office. I have the perfect spot."

While Gupta bore the weight of the machine, McComb gestured toward the top of his desk, an even larger version of the one in his office. He'd had it custom made from lumber removed from his parents' home after they mysteriously died. The insurance proceeds from their deaths, plus the money he made when he sold their home, had bankrolled his education as well as his rise in the world of high finance.

Gupta set his burden down on the shiny, wooden surface then held out his palm. He made it clear he wanted a payment rather than a handshake.

"All in good time," McComb said. "Have you already spent what I paid you for the thumb drive?"

"I have expenses," the smaller man said. "And with inflation the way it is—"

"Yes, yes. That's a pain for all of us, isn't it?"

Without waiting for an answer, McComb walked across the room to a small but elegant bar decorated with a pair of golf trophies, some framed photos, and other similarly themed memorabilia. After gathering ingredients, he poured himself another martini.

"Want one?" he asked Gupta. "I've got the best gin money can buy." He thought for a moment then added, "It ought to be, considering the cost."

Gupta ignored the offer. "You said you'd pay me in cash, on delivery." He pointed at the machine. "Well, there it is."

"Indeed. But does it work?" McComb rubbed his chin. "As I recall, that was part of the deal. Not that I thought you might try to screw me with some collection of shiny mechanical crap." He recrossed the room and focused on the device. "It looks homemade." Bending closer, he poked a finger at the four buttons on top and their single-letter labels.

"S-L-O-W?" He straightened. "That's not very encouraging."

"I don't know anything about this thing," Gupta said, "except where it came from."

"And," said McComb, "what it can supposedly do. I need to test it before I pay you anything." He nodded at a wall behind his desk. "There's an outlet over there. Plug it in, and we'll give it a test run."

Gupta complied and stood, waiting, across the wide desktop while McComb contemplated the limited choices provided by the four buttons. The stock broker spoke over the annoying hum of the machine. "I'm guessing the 'S' button means stocks."

Gupta shrugged and continued to look impatient.

McComb took a sip of his drink then pressed the 'S' button. The machine immediately went into a higher gear and started vibrating, although the noise level curiously went down. After only a few seconds, McComb felt some heat. He touched the surface and noted how warm it was. He touched the side, too, and quickly pulled his hand away. "The damn thing runs hot!"

Moments later, it spit out a sheet of paper, and then another, after which the noise level increased. He heard Gupta's voice urging him to shut it off, which he did.

The level of heat from the machine was startling, but the data on the two sheets of paper startled McComb even more.

"What's on there?" asked Gupta.

McComb glanced at the numbers then looked up. "They're sports scores."

"*What?*"

"Scores. For games that haven't been played yet. Basketball mostly, but... hold on... There's a horse race in here, too."

"No shit? We could bet on 'em," Gupta said, suddenly excited. "Online, y'know?"

McComb frowned. "Screw that. I want stock prices." He looked again at the SLOW buttons. "I'll bet the 'L' means low to high."

"And the 'O'?" asked Gupta.

"Options, maybe? Let's find out." McComb promptly restarted the machine and punched the "O" button.

As before, the apparatus rattled and whirred, then a new noise came from near the output tray. "Shut it off," Gupta said. "I think it's outta paper."

Thoroughly annoyed, McComb turned off the power, withdrew a handful of paper from a desk drawer, and thrust it at Gupta. He grabbed it, maneuvered closer to the machine, and attempted to load the paper. It took three tries before he succeeded and announced, "That son of a bitch is hotter'n hell!"

"Whatever," McComb said. He restarted the machine and hit the "O" button. He loved options.

The machine emitted more noise, more heat, four sheets of paper, and some smoke before McComb shut it down.

"We got another page of sports scores and three pages of...."

Gupta couldn't contain his curiosity. "Three pages of what?"

"Obituaries!" McComb tossed the sheets across the desk. "What kind of bullshit is this? Did you know this would happen?"

"Of course not! Don't blame me. Besides, you've got two buttons left to try."

McComb eyed Albright's device with deep suspicion. Even standing a few feet away, he could feel the heat emanating from it.

"We should let it cool down," Gupta said. "Besides, we know it works, so how 'bout you go ahead and pay me now?"

"I haven't seen *any* stock prices," complained McComb. "You know that's what I want. God knows I've waited long enough." He restarted the machine and hit the "W" button. "I can't imagine what that'll produce. Based on what I've seen so far, it's most likely going to be wedding announcements."

The noise increased dramatically along with the heat, more smoke, and additional noise.

"I told you we should've let it cool down!" Gupta shouted.

The equipment coughed out a partial sheet of paper that abruptly burst into flame. McComb reached for the power button, but backed off due to the extreme heat. Gupta was already running toward the door.

"Wait for me!" McComb yelled as he scrambled after him.

Neither of them made it out before the machine exploded and turned McComb's office into a massive firepit.

Chapter Twenty-eight

*"Surprises are foolish things. The pleasure is not
enhanced, and the inconvenience is often
considerable."* —Jane Austin

Braden had no idea why Gupta didn't try to
bargain with him since Braden had grabbed the prize
before Gupta got to Albright's house. Though tempted
to call and ask the phony Irishman what was going on,
he realized that would be stupid. Sleeping dogs, he
figured. Let 'em lie.

Instead of worrying about Gupta, Braden
zeroed in on his prize—Wynn Albright's desktop
computer. Braden considered any PC over two years
old to be out of date, and the one he'd grabbed was
much older. The ugly thing actually had a slot for 3.5-
inch disks. He'd seen them in a display of obsolete
computer stuff in a campus museum years earlier,
but he'd never actually touched one.

The old bastard may as well have been using a stylus and tablet!

Ignoring the machine's technological cobwebs, Braden cranked it up in order to access the program he was certain would turn his life around. A screen popped up that had none of the digitally prehistoric earmarks he'd anticipated. Instead, it displayed a full-screen image featuring a couple at their wedding and a place to enter a password.

He stared at the screen, dumbfounded. Eventually, he put his hands on the keyboard and entered the numbers 123456. That generated a disturbing response:

PASSWORD INCORRECT. TWO TRIES REMAINING.

Shit! He pounded his fist on the table beside the antique computer. *This machine is a damned Civil War relic; how can it have modern security?*

I need a hacker.

Gupta! I bet he'd know how to get in. But then....

Returning to Gupta's good graces would be difficult and utterly impossible without a huge pile of cash—cash he didn't have, and wouldn't ever have if he couldn't run Albright's program. He told himself he should have known Albright was too smart to leave it unprotected.

That makes me *the idiot, not him.*

Rather than risk another failed sign-in, Braden let the machine sit while he contemplated other options. With Albright dead, or nearly so, there was no rush. He had time.

If nothing else, I could take it to McComb and let his techno-zombies have at it. I ought to be able to charge him a pretty penny for that!

He spent the rest of that day and the next, a Sunday, relaxing, confident in the knowledge that things would soon be looking up. They just had to.

A Monday morning newscast, however, provided a different scenario. According to a reporter on the "Wake Up, Hot-Lanta!" broadcast, wealthy brokerage firm executive Lionel McComb had burned to death in his upscale, Buckhead mansion. The body of another man, as yet unidentified, had been found near him. The cause of the fire was still under investigation.

Swell. Just goddam swell. I'll bet the other guy is Gupta. Now what?

No longer having anyone to catch up with or report to, Braden opted to just stay home. Maybe he'd gotten it all wrong.

~*~

It had been a week since Wynn's death. His passing had struck Danica like a mortar round. She struggled to take in the epic changes he'd made in her life, and his absence from it left a hole she knew might never be filled. Roscoe helped, immensely. And Rick, of course.

What would she have ever done without him?

It caused her to gently pat his leg as he drove them to Sunrise Ranch where Danica intended to check on her investment.

"You could've just donated some money to the place," Rick said. "You didn't have to buy it."

"I thought about that, and I talked it over with Archie. We decided a donation wouldn't work. The Malloys ran it for years, but they can't go on. Mr. Malloy's stroke changed everything for them. Libby's pitched in, and she's done a super job, but it's too much for one person."

"Isn't her friend April there now, too?"

"Yes, and as far as I can tell, that's working out fine. They'll move into the house as soon as the Malloys move out and get settled in an assisted living place in town."

Rick shook his head. "So now you own a ranch, complete with a barn, a stable, and a house, and you're not going to live there?"

"It's for Libby and April. It's part of their... What did Archie call it? Remuneration." She wanted to lean against him, but the gap between the front seats was too wide. Instead, she rubbed his thigh, a little higher than before. "Anyway, I thought you were happy that Roscoe and I moved back in with you."

"Oh, I am, deliriously so!" he said. "*Beyond* that, even."

"Because, y'know, I have another house."

"Yeah, but Carnahan said it's gotta be torn down."

"He didn't say when." She gave him an ever-so-innocent smile and drummed her fingers on his leg.

They drove down a long, gravel drive and pulled into a parking area beside the stable. A small, pre-fab building on concrete blocks bore a western-style sign that read: **Office**.

Libby came outside and waved at them as they exited Rick's Jeep.

"C'mon in!" she said and greeted them with hugs. "Didn't you bring your dog? I wanted to meet him."

"Roscoe's been acting depressed. I think he misses Wynn." Danica shook her head. "I couldn't get him out of his doggie bed."

"That's too bad. I thought he might enjoy hanging around with the horses." Libby ushered them into the office and closed the door. As she turned toward her desk she looked out the window and suddenly stopped. "Oh, hell," she whispered. "It's Tim. I'd know his crappy car anywhere, even if it didn't sound like a garbage truck."

The sound of the rumbling vehicle increased as it came closer.

Rick shot a look at Danica. "That's the guy from the apartment, isn't it? What does he want?"

"Trouble," said Libby before Danica could respond. She pointed at him as he got out of his car. "He's got a gun!"

Danica stared at the man coming toward them. His face had some bruising, most of which she assumed had drifted downward from his broken nose. It surrounded his mouth with a purplish halo. The hand Libby smashed with the ketchup bottle that fateful night was in a cast.

"Lib," Danica said, "go get in the bathroom, now. And lock the door."

"Hang on," Rick said. "Can't we just pretend not to be here?"

"We can try, and I hope that works." Danica looked around the cramped office until she saw a large stapler on the desk. She snatched it up and held it by her side, hidden by her leg. "But if it doesn't...."

Tim soon banged on the office door. It sounded as if he'd hit it with a hammer or the butt of his gun.

"Easy," whispered Rick. "We've gotta stay quiet."

"Open up, Libby," Tim growled. "I know you're in there. We've gotta talk."

"Talk, my ass," Danica muttered quietly.

"Okay then, if you insist. I'm coming in my way." With a loud crash, the door swung open, and Tim stepped in with his gun leveled.

Rick raised his hands to shoulder height. "Hang on, now. No need for violence."

Tim stared at Danica. "You're here, too? Hot damn—a twofer! Where's Libby?"

"Take it easy," Rick said. "We can work out whatever's—"

"Shut up, asshole!" Tim shouted. "I wasn't talkin' to you." Then he fired his gun.

The bullet struck Rick and spun him away from Danica and toward the wall. Danica's training kicked in, and she instantly counterattacked. The stapler proved extremely effective when she rammed it full tilt into the underside of Tim's jaw.

His head flew back, and he fired another round

that went into the floor. The instant he rocked his head forward, Danica backhanded him in the temple with the opposite end of the stapler. The blow sent him crashing into the side of the open door.

Disoriented and barely able to remain upright, Tim seemed to be waiting for the *coup de gras*. Danica was only too happy to deliver it. She aimed a kick to the center of his chest. The heel of her dress boot hit his sternum and propelled him out of the building and onto the gravel outside.

She leaped after him, ready to strike again, but he wasn't moving. The gun lay by his side. She grabbed it in case he woke up. "C'mon out, Libby," she yelled as she hurried back inside to check on Rick. "Call the cops, and tell 'em to bring an ambulance. Rick's been shot."

"What about Tim?" the girl asked as Danica examined the hole in Rick's upper arm. It bled intensely.

"He's out. Hopefully for good. Have you got a first aid kit?"

Libby grabbed one from a nearby shelf, set it on the floor beside Danica, and pulled out her cell phone. "I'm calling 9-1-1 now. Is there anything else I can do? I want to help!"

"Where's April?" Danica asked as she tore

open Rick's sleeve to get a better look at the wound.

"I'm right here," April said, peeking around the edge of the door. "I was in the stable."

Danica handed her the gun. "Keep that asshole outside company. If he wakes up—"

"Shoot him?" Libby asked, looking hopeful.

Danica stifled a laugh. "It's tempting, I know. But just keep him covered until help arrives. Both of you, go!"

"Darn it all, Dani," Rick said looking at his torn sleeve, "you've ruined one of my best shirts!"

She leaned into him, put her hand behind his head and gently guided his lips to hers. When the kiss finally ended, she pulled a short distance away, smiling. "I'm pretty sure I can afford to get you a new one."

~*~

Archie Carnahan welcomed Danica and Rick into his spacious office, waved them into comfy seats on his sofa, and settled himself in an easy chair facing them. "I'm glad you came," he said. "I could have delivered my news over the phone, but it just didn't feel right." He gestured at the sling supporting Rick's injured arm. "Healing okay?"

"Yeah," Rick said, putting his good arm around

Danica. "I've got a live-in nurse."

"You're a lucky man." He eased back in his chair. "So, to bring you up to date, I have a contact in the Medical Examiner's office who got me copies of the autopsies for Wynn's son and daughter-in-law. The results are rather surprising."

He leaned forward, closer to them. "The ME believes Jeffrey's death was most likely a homicide."

Danica appeared shocked. "You're kidding!"

The attorney shook his head. "His death was due to a food allergy, which his wife surely must have known about. Apparently he ate something containing tree nuts and suffered a fatal reaction."

"That sounds awful," Rick said.

"And what about Beatrix, his wife?" asked Danica.

"According to the autopsy, Beatrix suffered from a tracheal stenosis."

"Come again," Rick said as he and Danica shared quizzical looks.

"I looked it up," Archie explained. "It means she had a blocked windpipe. Apparently she choked on a grape."

Danica sighed. "She struck me as someone who was always unhappy, kinda angry."

Rick chuckled. "Sounds like she encountered the grape of wrath."

Danica swatted his good arm. "I can't believe you said that!"

"Maybe it's true," Archie said. "Anyway, that's what I wanted to share." He eased back in his chair. "Oh, and by the way, we need to get back to work rounding up three more bodies to serve on the board of Wynn's foundation."

"I'm afraid that'll have to wait a little while," Danica said. She reached into her pocket and retrieved a sheet of paper which she handed to Rick.

"What's this?"

"It's a confirmation from the airline. I bought two, first class, round-trip tickets to Miami."

"Miami? As in Florida?"

"That's the one. When you told me you were taking some time off work, I thought this would be a great way to help you relax and heal."

Rick looked puzzled. "Being in Miami will help me heal?"

"No, silly," she said. "That's where we're going to board a cruise ship."

"Seriously?"

"Seriously." She grinned at him. "I hope you won't mind sharing a cabin. They call it a suite, but I'm not sure what the difference is."

Archie laughed. "You'll find out. Be sure to give me a holler when you get home."

"And what about Roscoe?" Rick asked.

"He and I go back a long way," Archie said. "He can stay with me while you're gone. I could use the company."

~The End~

Josh Langston

About the Author

Josh Langston writes books that amuse, anger, enlighten, and entertain, qualities you'll find in *Only Sure Things*, his sixteenth solo novel. His short fiction has been published in a variety of magazines and anthologies, and two of his short story collections have placed in the Amazon Top 20 for genre fiction.

In addition to writing, Josh loves to teach, especially to students aged 50 and over. His classes on novel writing, memoir, and independent publishing feature a humorous approach to learning and are quite popular. A great sense of pride for him is the number of his students who have gone on to write and publish books of their own.

If you are a member of a book club and would like to arrange a chat with Josh for your group, you may contact him at: **DruidJosh@gmail.com**. And be sure visit his website, too: **JoshLangston.com**. His blog is called "Sage of the South" for a reason!

And now for an added bonus: Chapter One of *Raising Rosie*, the sequel to *Only Sure Things*. Just when she thinks she's got it all together, someone new shows up in her life—a relative she never knew existed. If you're ready for more of Danica, here's your chance. Get ready for another wild ride!

Josh Langston

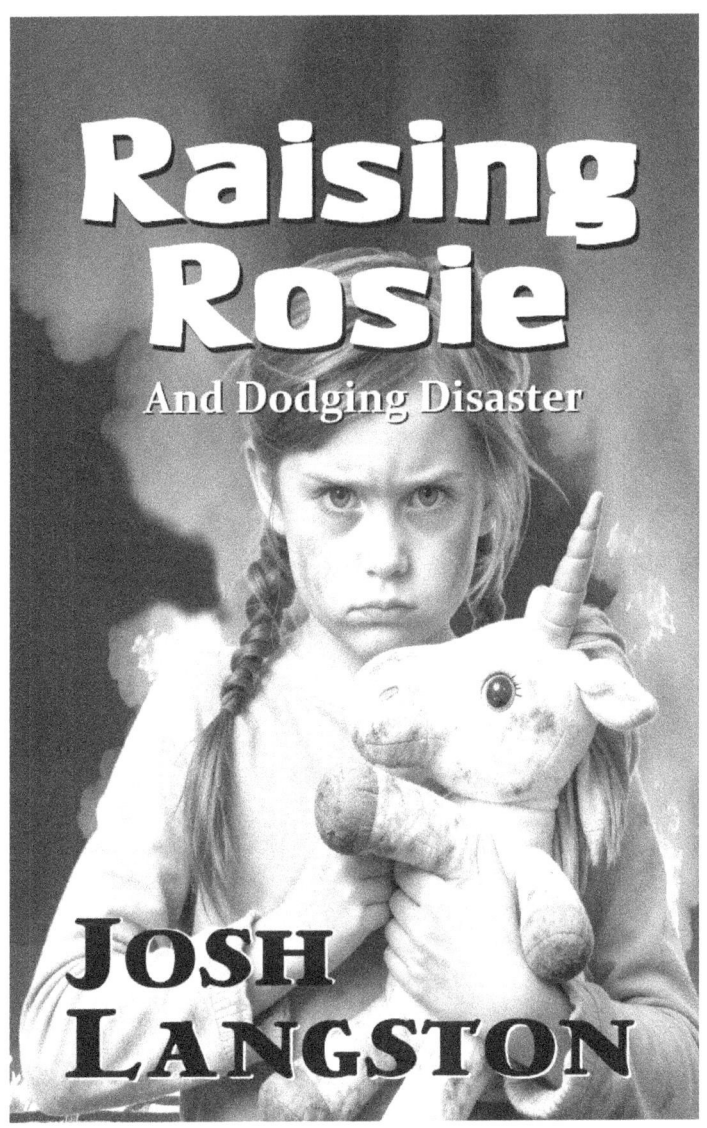

Raising
Rosie
And Dodging Disaster

JOSH
LANGSTON

Raising Rosie

Chapter One

"All that I am, or hope to be, I owe to my mother." —Abraham Lincoln

By the time she turned six, Rosie figured she knew what some of the colors meant. The important ones anyway. That task had been the primary goal in her young life. No one had ordered her to solve the puzzle, but it had taken quite a while for her to realize why no one could. It was simple, really; they couldn't see the colors.

While gripping the neck of Sparkles, her stuffed unicorn, Rosie fumbled with a zipper that ran the length of the toy animal's underside. Once she had it open, she slipped her hand inside and felt for the treasures within.

The crayons took priority, of course. She could name most of them merely by feel; each color had a slightly different temperature, and those she used the most were shorter. Then there was the money. Rosie didn't care about it, but Caitlyn insisted she keep it there. It was a secret. No one else could ever know, and Caitlyn made sure Rosie knew the consequences should she ever betray that secret.

"That dumb little toy is my safe," Caitlyn had told her many times.

Though not sure what a safe might be, Rosie accepted the terms. She had no desire to suffer another cigarette burn if she could avoid it. If that meant Sparkles served as Caitlyn's purse, then so be it.

The last thing she touched was a plastic bag stuffed with pills. Despite having a variety of colors, to Rosie, they were dumb. Boring. They also smelled. Rosie couldn't understand why no one else seemed to be able to tell the pills were hidden inside Sparkles; the stink was unmistakable, at least to her.

When the cops came, they ignored Rosie and focused on Caitlyn. Of the five men who broke down the door and burst into the room, only two wore uniforms. The others wore work clothing just like the people she saw on the street, the same kind who came to see Caitlyn, gave her money, and left with some of her pills.

Rosie didn't know where Caitlyn got the pills or how the people who bought them knew she had them for sale. Hamish probably told them, and he probably gave Caitlyn the drugs, too. His color was blotchy and mostly dark, and if he said something nice to Rosie, she knew he didn't mean it. The blotchy and dark never told the truth.

Caitlyn was blotchy, too, but in a lighter shade of gray.

Rosie watched as the men in street clothes marched Caitlyn out of their apartment. One of the two in a uniform knelt in front of Rosie and smiled at her. "There's nothing to worry about, little lady. We'll take good care of your momma. And we'll find a nice place for you to stay until she can come back and get you."

It wasn't the first time Caitlyn had been arrested. Rosie had seen it happen twice before, and Caitlyn returned the next day both times. The only difference this time was that Rosie hadn't been hiding.

The policeman's colors revealed little except that he didn't believe what he just told her.

~*~

Danica Winters sat at the counter in Rick Johanson's kitchen and gazed down at the travel brochures she'd spread out in front of her. Having recently enjoyed a Caribbean cruise with Rick, she yearned to continue traveling. Rick had been instrumental in Danica's astonishing turn-around.

Now that she had the means to do anything she wanted, anywhere, and at any time, she was eager to explore the world. Dog sledding in Alaska sounded wonderful, as did swimming with dolphins, or exploring castles and caves, or maybe learning how to surf or even skydive. As far as she knew, none of that was available locally. Woodstock, Georgia, hardly qualified as a major draw for world travelers.

She also knew she didn't want to travel alone. She wanted Rick by her side. Her relationship with the national park ranger had blossomed over the early spring and through the summer. She'd lived alone before, and more or less happily. Now, however, she couldn't stand the thought of living alone.

She had Roscoe, the big white dog Wynn Albright had left her, along with a car and a house no one could live in. Now that she'd arranged for the house to be demolished, all she wanted to do was find a destination that fit Rick's vacation calendar. He'd already told her he'd go with her anywhere she wanted to go.

Lying beside the travel brochures were the

blueprints for the project she had started the day they returned from their cruise. Her plan was to convert a failed motel into an apartment complex for kids aging out of foster care. She'd befriended two such teens, April and Libby, and they'd proven themselves by managing a ranch used primarily by kids with disabilities. Danica had purchased the Sunrise Ranch out from under the clutches of a company that wanted to raze the facility and build a data center on the property.

The construction work on the apartment complex was nearing completion, but Danica had plenty of decisions left to make about the interior and staffing, jobs she felt woefully unqualified to tackle. She pushed the blueprints, legal notices, and other paperwork aside. The travel brochures were far more interesting.

New Zealand looks awesome. What did they call that amazing warrior dance of theirs? She scratched her head in thought. *The haka! That's it. I've gotta do it. And I'm gonna get Rick to do it with me!* The photo in the brochure revealed heavily tattooed dancers in brief but colorful gear stomping, making horrible faces, and shaking spears. They looked as if their goal was to terrify the photographer.

When her cell phone rang, she merely stared at it. She didn't recognize the caller's number, but then, she rarely did. The phone, like virtually everything else she owned, was new. Yet, it had only been a matter of months since her "home" consisted of a cheap plastic tarp, an ancient sleeping bag, and a motley collection of clothing, mostly in need of a deep wash or disposal.

"Hello," she said, preparing herself for the caller's sales pitch. *Extended warranty, most likely.*

"Good morning. I'm Olivia Rankin with the Department of Family and Children's Services. I'm trying to locate Danica Winters."

Family and Children's Services? Danica shook her head. "That's me."

The woman on the line exhaled in relief. "Mrs. Winters, I—"

"It's *Miss* Winters," Danica said. "I'm not married. At least, not yet."

"Of course. I knew that. I just… Sometimes I get a little ahead of myself, y'know? We stay so busy here that—"

"How can I help you?" Danica asked, trying not to sound as impatient as she felt. She tapped a photo of a Māori warrior on the cover of the New Zealand brochure and wondered if she could make a face that looked that fierce.

"Right. Sorry," said the woman. "I'm calling because of your niece."

Danica felt her eyebrows spring upward. "I have a *niece?*"

"Yes," the woman said. "And I was afraid you might not know about her."

"My sister and I haven't spoken in... I dunno, years," Danica said. "I had no idea she had a child. What kind of trouble is the girl in?"

"It's not the child who's in trouble. It's your sister. Caitlyn Winters is currently in jail awaiting trial."

"For what?"

"Dealing drugs, I think," said the woman.

"Aw, geez." *What the hell, Cait? And you have a kid?* "What about the child's father?"

"We believe his name is Hamish Campbell, but that has yet to be confirmed. His whereabouts are unknown. I'm not privy to much information about your sister's case, but I do know the police are looking for him. Most likely on the same or similar charges. I understand he didn't have much interest in or involvement with the child. Your sister thinks he may have left the country."

Danica stood but suddenly felt weary. She

wandered into the living room and plunked down on a sofa. She had a sick feeling about what was coming. "So," she said, "what did you want to tell me about my sister's child?"

"To be blunt, I was hoping you'd be willing to take her in. Otherwise, she'll be placed in foster care, and that's not always a great option."

Danica's two young friends, April and Libby had both grown up in foster care, and they'd shared plenty of stories about what they went through. Danica couldn't imagine growing up that way. Despite the problems she'd had in school, and the treatment she'd received from her sister, Danica had parents who cared about her. She still missed them, years after their untimely deaths.

"What can you tell me about her?"

"Her name is Rose, Rose Winters, but she prefers Rosie. You know how kids are."

"Actually," Danica said, "I don't. I don't know anything about them, how to raise 'em or take care of them. All I know is they're expensive and need a lot of attention. And—"

"Would you at least be willing to meet her? She *is*, after all, your blood relative."

"I—"

"Rosie's a really sweet child. She's so young and so—"

"How young?"

"Six and a half."

Six and a half? Oh, dear Lord. "Listen," Danica said, "I really don't think—"

"Hold on a minute, before you close your mind to this. Think for a second. Has anyone ever given you a chance? I mean an honest-to-God chance at a decent life? 'Cause that's what this child needs, and she needs it desperately."

Danica closed her eyes and swallowed. Tears stung her eyes. Tears that didn't give a damn about destroying her façade of... *What? Strength? Or indifference?*

"Is she okay? I mean, health-wise?"

"Physically, she's fine. A little skinny I'd say, but otherwise perfectly healthy, only—"

"Only what?"

"She sometimes displays a bit of an attitude." The woman hurried on before Danica could probe deeper. "That's not unusual when you think about it. Kids on their own often adopt self-defense mechanisms that influence their behavior."

"I'm not following you," Danica said. "What's

wrong with her?"

"Nothing, honestly. I'm just asking you to give her a chance. Just take the time to meet her, then you can form your own opinions. I don't want mine to influence you in any way."

A six-year-old with an attitude? "I'm just...."

"C'mon. What could it hurt? I promise; a meeting would only require a few minutes of your time. A half-hour at most."

Danica shook her head but went ahead and agreed to meet her niece the following afternoon.

What the hell is wrong with me? I've got an entire apartment building to furnish and staff. I don't have time for this. I don't... Damn. I guess I need to make time for it.

Curtis Mathers had lived next door to Wynn Albright for nearly a decade, though they'd never developed anything remotely close to a friendship. For many of those years, Mathers, the long-time president of the neighborhood Homeowner's Association, had been after Albright to do something about the wretched condition of his house. All to no avail. Albright clearly didn't care.

Mathers had tried being nice. He'd tried using

sarcasm. He'd even managed to have the organization's bylaws changed so he could threaten Albright with cash penalties if he didn't improve his property. That didn't work either, due to a grandfather clause some idiot insisted on including. Only owners who'd bought into the area *after* the bylaws had been adopted were subject to the new rule.

As a result, he almost rejoiced when he heard Albright had died. It happened only a matter of weeks—according to some of the neighbors—after he'd taken in a homeless woman. That sounded beyond fishy to Mathers, and he'd shared his views on the subject with anyone who would listen to him, mostly other members of the HOA board.

Nevertheless, whoever ended up with Albright's house would have to live up to the new HOA bylaws. If they didn't upgrade the place, there'd be hell to pay. Or at least healthy fines. Mathers would see to that. Had anyone asked, he'd have told them he looked forward to collecting those fines; the HOA's treasury had historically run short of cash.

With any luck he thought, the new occupants might be neighborly, something Albright had never been.

His hopes improved when a crew of workers arrived and appeared to be doing something with the interior of the house. Despite Mather's desire to find out exactly what they were up to, a man claiming to be the job foreman who worked for the county turned him away.

"You mean this isn't a *private* restoration? *Taxpayers* are funding it?"

While adjusting his hardhat, the foreman assured him the authorities had been granted sufficient funds for the job, especially considering the need for extreme care due to contamination of the site.

That comment had set Mather's teeth on edge. *Contamination? Holy shit!*

The following day, Mathers stared in wonder when the next batch of county workers arrived, most wearing hazmat gear. When their bulldozer showed up, Mathers nearly went into shock.

He couldn't help but wonder if his sudden shortness of breath was due to whatever contaminated the site.

Or maybe I'm having a heart attack!

Damn you, Albright. You're dead, and you're still *trying to drive me insane!*

Only Sure Things